WOLF BOUND

A LUPI DI NOTTE NOVEL

CHRISTINE LEE

This book contains graphic violence, language and sexual situations. It includes physical/sexual abuse. Please be aware of possible triggers.

I dedicate this book to my miracle; my hero; my Rock: my son, Thomas. Without whom, I wouldn't be here to see a 35 year old dream come to fruition.

PROLOGUE

The Last War started ten years ago in the Middle East, with dirty nuclear weapons and biological warfare, but the Americans had to finish it, which may have been what caused the end of world. Fortunately, one day later, the Fae interceded, and cast a spell that remade the world. It almost destroyed the Fae. Instead, they've been locked into their dimension, and Faedresse was born, with a fraction of its former human population. The Other population, however, nearly exceeds the human population. But don't tell them that. It would scare the mundanes to know how many scary predators lived right next door.

CHAPTER 1

*B*ella smelled man. Well a man anyway. And wolf. Which made no sense. There hadn't been a man in her house since...well, that didn't bear thinking about. Neither the length of time nor the incident itself. What had she been thinking? And there had definitely never been a wolf, male or otherwise in her home.

I'm just overtired. Not to mention hungry. It was that last push to get the book done. Bella thought. *It's always like that at the end, barely pausing to eat or sleep, when the words are flowing. Kayla's always threatening to hire a live-in. Now that would be disastrous. About that smell...*

Jack had been in the house long enough to determine there was a female in human form in what smelled like a bedroom suite to his left and three—two males and one female—in wolf form down a hallway to his right. He appeared to be standing in a large family or living room, and was facing the front door, with archways to the right and left of that door that appeared to lead to formal dining and living rooms. That made this a family room then. To his left were the kitchen and an informal eating area, between him and what he'd bet from the smells were a master bedroom suite complete with bathroom, belonging primarily to a woman. He assumed the hall to his right led to more bedrooms.

He looked around himself at the family room. It was done in neutral creams, with large solid but comfortable pieces, with splashes of surprising color here and there to break it up. The micro-fiber suede-feel L-shape sectional sofa faced a large brick fireplace and equally large flat screen television, with accompanying audio-visual equipment.

Jack turned as he heard the female coming out of the room he'd determined by smell was a bedroom, and stopped. Just stopped. She was wearing a tight white ribbed tank without a bra and blue short-shorts. She seemed tiny to him, maybe 5'6' or so. Probably weighed about 120. No, given her generous curves, probably closer to 130. Chestnut red hair fell just a few inches below her shoulders, curling softly around her heart shaped face. Her eyes. Good lord, her eyes. True green, like emeralds, they almost shined. Given how spectacular he found her curves, he was amazed by her eyes, that they could hold his attention when that shirt did not hide her curves very well. He only hoped he wasn't drooling.

"WHO THE FUCK ARE YOU?" Bella asked, dropping into a defensive crouch, "and what the Hell are you doing in my house?"

"Language." Jack smiled, quite enjoying the view. "Jack Kincaid."

"Jack Kincaid? Swell, that doesn't tell me why you and your friends broke into my house." Ooh-boy. I'm in trouble. Bella thought, looking over the werewolf in front of her. He was big. Really, really big. Maybe 6'4". Brown hair. Light eyes. She'd have to get closer to tell for sure the color, and she was not getting any closer. No sir. Bad idea. Dangerous. His jeans hugged his—okay, eyes up. His t-shirt was snug over a very well developed chest and a set of arms that could definitely curl her—ooh, not much better, she'd always been a chest and arms girl. Face. Look him in the face. He's looking at my boobs.

"I'm the Primo of the Lupi Di Notte Pack." Jack smiled.

"Well, Mr. Primo bigshot. I've lived in this town for over 12 years, this house for over 4. There's never been a Were pack here. So what do you want?" Because a defensive stance is hard to hold for long periods of time, and because his continued leering at her boobs was bothering her, she straightened, and assumed a loose comfortable stance that would allow her to move easily. "And you didn't answer my question, why did you break into my house, you and your wolf friends? You could have knocked."

"I didn't break in, the door was wide open, and I've come alone. Miss-you didn't give me your name? I don't know what to call you. Anyway. I'm your new neighbor, bailed out the guy who spent all that money and then couldn't afford to live there. Just what are you anyway? You aren't a wolf, but I can't get a read."

"I'm a writer. Now what do you want?" Bella let her impatience come through in her voice.

"Well, ma'am, my wolves are nervous with another predator right next door. I've come over to buy you out."

"If you've just moved in, well, too bad, I was here first. You'll have to adapt. I have a great deal of property here. When I feel the need to run, which isn't often, I stay on my property, which is fully fenced. I sincerely doubt I will get into your way. And I'm not selling. Sorry. And if you didn't break in, how'd my door get busted? And I smell at least two more wolves, maybe three, back there in the guest rooms, AND IF THEY ARE IN MY OFFICE TOUCHING ANYTHING, I WILL KILL THEM." Bella yelled the last bit to get their attention. She hadn't e-mailed the book yet, damnit. She couldn't afford for it to be lost.

"I'm sorry, I didn't notice it was broken—wait, those wolves aren't yours?"

"Of course they aren't mine. I don't have wolves. They have to be yours. I told you, there haven't been wolves in Angel's Falls for the twelve years I've lived here." A curious look came over the strangers face, and Bella watched his eyes go amber about the time they both heard growling start from the hallway on the other side of the family room that led to Bella's office, as well as the three other bedrooms, and two bathrooms.

"They aren't of my pack. When I scented them, I assumed they were of yours. You say you don't have a pack." Bella had moved up to stand next to him and he looked down at her, eyebrow cocked. Bella looked up at him, and shook her head, no, no pack. "Then they are rogue, and are likely who broke into your home. You have no protection?" Again the head tilt in her direction, eyebrow cocked.

"My fangs and claws." Bella snarled, and smiled, showing her lengthening fangs.

"Then I will stand with you, if you will allow, as I am scenting three, and there is only one of you." Jack started stripping off his clothes, toeing out of his shoes.

"I appreciate the assistance. Temporary truce, but stay back from my attacks. Do not underestimate me." And from one second to the next her body shimmered into a huge red tiger, with barely perceptible white stripes. Her body, previously only approximately 130 pounds, somehow through the magic that is shape shifting, became 350 pounds. Bella didn't understand it, it just happened.

JACK WAS STILL TRYING to get out of his jeans when she did it and then the three wolves came into the family room, and he was out of time. Jack watched the tiger streak through the still open sliding door in the family room into the back yard as he started his shift, having barely gotten the rest of his clothing off. Apparently she wanted to take the fight outside. Couldn't blame her. Two of the rogues followed her, the third growling at Jack before following them. Jack couldn't believe the ease and speed of her shift, and she hadn't removed her clothes, and it hadn't torn either. It took almost five minutes for him to shift usually. This time, he made it just shy of three.

Jack raced through the doorway and saw the fight just ahead. Jack leapt on one wolf, a light grey with white markings, and sank his teeth into his left flank before leaping away to turn and check on the tiger. She seemed to be doing fine, as one of the wolves that followed her outside already seemed to be out of the fight, whimpering in the grass a few feet away.

The tiger was circling her opponent, a black female with white feet. Jack turned back to his opponent in time to dodge an attack. These wolves were all smaller than Jack, who was about 250 pounds, on the large side for the average Werewolf, but not by more than fifty pounds or so. But these wolves didn't even come close to 200 pounds, so he wondered about them. Not having a pack might mean they didn't have resources; homes, food, etc. Jack wished he hadn't had to go on the attack immediately with them. If they hadn't invaded her home, he might have tried to talk to them, see if they needed help. But he needed to get his head back in the game.

BELLA REALLY DIDN'T LIKE this. She'd never fought sentient creatures before. She'd never had to. When she decided to have a "hunt" she stocked her five acres with lots of Tiger bait, mostly rabbits and similar small game, and that was it. The first wolf was cocky, and got too close to her fangs early on. He was still twitching, but not for long.

This one was smarter, but wouldn't last much longer. Tigers are wolf's only real threat in nature, other than man, and this wolf was only a bit more than a third of Bella's size.

JACK FINISHED the grey wolf and turned to help his tiger, but pulled up as he realized she was moving in for the kill. The big cat was graceful, poetry in motion. The fight couldn't have lasted even five minutes, but the black wolf was tiring already as the tiger stalked calmly around her.

Jack could almost see when his tiger decided to end it. On her next turn, the wolf was slower to follow, and the tiger sprang, jaws snapping on the wolves' neck as her front claws ripped through the wolves torso, and it was over.

~

BELLA SPAT THE BITS OUT, and shook herself and then looked up to find the wolf, Jack's, eyes, on her. She huffed at him and then gestured him to lead the way back into her house. She could see him hesitate, obviously a gentleman who had issue with preceding a lady through a doorway, how sweet, but decided to show some trust to her, as the larger gentlemanly gesture, and complied.

Bella stopped just inside the door once he'd reached his clothes and was again facing her. She shifted seamlessly back to herself, once again dressed. She loved the magic of her shifting, that she could shift to something as large as her tiger, or as small as a mouse, and every time, her clothes disappeared and reappeared, and again it's all magic.

She watched him shift, which took longer than her shifts, and he was standing before her, in all his—gulp—glory. She thought he looked good the first time she'd seen him, but nude, fresh from the fight, he was magnificent. He filled her family room, where they stood, and the room wasn't small. She'd looked at him before, but only superficially. This time, she looked her fill, and after picking up his pants, he let her. Had she called his hair brown before? Brown was a bland word for what is hair was. Too long to be strictly military, he had locks curling over his forehead that made her itch to brush it back, and was a rich melding of browns and gold. His eyes, was it just her, or were they having trouble shifting back from amber to—there they are-- a very light green, like a sea green and his lips were quirked up in a grin as he watched her assessing him. Oh, those lips. She wanted to nibble those kissable lips. Bella licked her own and looked on.

His skin tone was the all-over deep tan of Mediterranean ancestry, maybe Italian or Greek, though given the name of his wolf-pack, she'd bet the former. His broad shoulders and sculpted chest made her heart pound, as did his deeply muscled arms. She was a sucker for well muscled arms and chests. His chest tapered to a narrow waist and washboard abs, with a full six-pack, oh-Lord.

Bella had to take a deep breath before looking further, and then her breath stopped. If she'd thought he was big elsewhere, it was nothing compared to what was between his legs, and as she watched, it continued to grow. Good Lord, how could it get any larger?— double gulp—ooh baby, I want some, please.

Bella had to move on before she fell to her knees and began begging. His legs were long and well muscled as well, and when he cleared his throat, Bella finally raised her eyes back to his. Bella looked down and smiled.

JACK WATCHED her as she took his measure, and scented her arousal, which raised his. Jack gazed at the girl—woman, she's a grown woman, damnit—before him and was stunned. Her wild red hair flowed about her face in tangled waves, and her green eyes shined from the recent shifts. She had high cheekbones and a well defined bow shaped upper lip, and a full kissable lower lip framed by an almost too sharp chin in that heart shaped face. God, he wanted to bite—kiss, kiss—those lips.

During his fight, his wolf started claiming her tiger as his own, and now he was finding himself drawn to her human form as well. This changed things significantly.

CHAPTER 2

"So, Tiger?" Jack had to clear his throat to speak.

"Yes, she's my preferred form, but I have others."

"Really? Before, you said, 'when you feel the need to run, which isn't often,' but at least every full moon, right? Because every were is forced to shift at the full moon."

"Yes, every were is forced to shift at the full moon. I'm not. I shift when I want. Whenever I want. To whatever I want. Well, whatever land mammal I want, that is." Bella twitched and crossed her arms self-consciously.

Jack took 3 giant strides and was suddenly gripping Bella's arms, lifting her a foot in the air to bring her eye level with him. "Hey!"

"What the hell are you?" Jack all but growled, sniffing her gasping breath, her hair, behind her ear. Oh, God. Behind her ear. Bella was a sucker for behind her ear. Bella whimpered and squirmed, her palms flattened against the big Weres chest.

"You're hurting me." Bella said quietly, because she didn't want to cry it.

Jack sniffed again, scenting arousal, anger and fear. The fear disgusted him. It was his job to run her out of town, but he wasn't going to hurt a woman. Unfortunately, he'd been feeling his own arousal since she'd entered the room, since she'd stood there looking him up and down, and scenting hers ramped his up. He put her down and backed away from her, running his hands through his hair. "Sorry." He growled.

"S'okay." Bella whispered, straightening her clothes.

"No. It's not. I don't hurt women."

"Don't you? I mean, don't all Weres? It's your thing. At least, the few I've met anyway." Bella turned away, probably a huge mistake, turning her back on an unknown were, but she was shaking, and needed something to do with her hands. She walked into the kitchen to the refrigerator and got out bottled water, holding it up in silent offer.

"Have anything stronger?" At Bella's negative, Jack nodded, and she placed the bottle in her hand on the island between them. The kitchen and breakfast area is between the family room and her bedroom. They now stood with the island between them, Bella trapped with the garage door at her back, and the stranger between her and the rest of her house. Way to go Bella! Bella took several swallows of her own bottle in an attempt to calm her.

"You haven't met any decent Weres then." Jack said, responding to her earlier statement.

"I think that was my point." Bella raised the water bottle, almost empty, and her eyebrow, at the Primo.

"Look, can we sit down. And can you tell me your name, please? And can you tell me what you are, if you aren't Were?" Jack was intrigued. He wasn't sure if he wanted to fuck her or kill her, or both, but knew things were not going to work out well for him at all.

Bella blinked at him a few times, finished her bottle, took another out of the fridge, grabbed the carton of ice cream from the freezer, a spoon from the drawer in the island, and gestured him to precede her out of the kitchen. Ooh-baby, look at that butt. No. Bad Bella. No butts for you. Up. Look up. Ooh. Look at those shoulders. No! Bad. Oy. I'm going to hell. Bella thought as she followed the gorgeous man to her family room, and settled on the couch in the corner furthest from him.

Jack raised his eyebrow at the ice cream in Bella's hands as she settled very carefully in the corner of the couch, and then he groaned as she moaned with the first bite.

Bella opened her eyes to a rather bemused expression on the Primo's face.

"Sorry. Haven't eaten in about 30 hours. As you know, not a good idea for us. Not as bad for me as for one of you, I don't have the same —mmm—urges? A were has, but I do have a much higher metabolism than a mere human.

"My name is Arabella Mia Blake. Bella. I'm a writer. And a shapeshifter. My shifts are not tied to the moon. At all. And not tied to any one shape." And Bella stuffed her mouth with ice cream so he could chew on those words a bit.

"Mmmm" Bella said. "Want some?" Bella asked, offering the spoon to Jack.

"N-no." Jack choked. Cleared his throat. And said again, "No" Jack closed his eyes. "How many of you are there?"

"How many of me? There's only one me. What the hell kind of question is that? How many of me? How many of you are there?" Bella laughed and then frowned as she realized she'd finished the ice cream and then rose to go find something else to eat.

"There are twenty-two of us." Jack said quietly. "Thirteen males, nine females. Ten of them are mated. That leaves me four females to take care of." Jack sounded tired. Bella turned on her way to the kitchen. Take care of? She'd file that away for later.

"Oh. You meant how many shapeshifters. I don't know. I was abandoned. Twice." Bella continued on to the kitchen.

SOMETHING IN HER TONE, if not the words themselves, set Jack's teeth to aching. "Bella? Abandoned? Twice?" His tone ordered her to respond. It was evident he was used to being obeyed. For some reason, Bella complied.

"I was adopted at birth, apparently. Abandonment number one. I don't know. I guess I'm supposed to feel special. My adopted family picked me special, and all that crap." Bella's voice was muffled as her head was buried in the refrigerator as she dug for something to eat. Jack found himself leaning over the island, trying to see the Promised Land. Just a little more...just a slight shift to the left...one more inch. Bad Jack! Stop it! I am going to hell. Jack thought to himself as he refocused on her words, and the pain buried in them. She was almost whispering by this point, and if his ears weren't so good, the better to hear you with, my dear, he might not catch...

"ALL WAS okay until right after—um—puberty. You know." Bella straightened and turned abruptly, and caught Jack half over the island in his attempt to see her bottom. "Lose something?" Bella asked with a smile, juggling the sandwich ingredients she held, shooing him back so she could put the stuff down. "Want a sandwich?" She asked innocently.

"Sure. You were saying. Puberty?" Jack smiled back. Bella scowled.

"Yeah. So, one night, I was in my room, and I started feeling sick. I don't know how to explain it. I was sweating, and shaking. Then it felt like my bones were breaking and knitting. I should back up and let you know we'd just gotten a German Sheppard puppy a few weeks back. He wasn't very big. He was mine. We'd been taking him to obedience classes, and they'd been talking about how I had to estab-lish dominance over him-"

"Oh, no." Jack rubbed his hands down his face.

"Yeah. So there's this puppy on the end of my bed. And I'm sweating and shaking and my bones are breaking and knitting. And I start screaming. My parents—my adopted parents, I'd always known that, they told me the truth from the beginning—were suddenly in the doorway. And then there were two German Sheppard's on my bed. The puppy and a larger one. Of course. Because I have to show my dominance over him—be the Primo, if you will."

"I won't, but I understand what you mean. What happened?" The

13

sandwiches were ready, but neither of them suddenly had appetites. They took them over to the table and sat across from each other.

"Well. I barked. The puppy yelped, peed, and my mom screamed. My dad yelled. The puppy ran out of my room. I tried to follow, but my mom was still screaming about a monster, and my dad-" Bella sobbed, got up, and walked to the door in the breakfast room over-looking her backyard. Jack rose and stood just behind her, not touching her, but just barely. "My father. The only father I'd ever known KICKED ME!" Bella sobbed, and turned into Jack. His arms came around her, and Bella allowed herself a few moments of comfort, the only comfort she had experienced in 12 years. Bella shook her head. She didn't know this man. She knew she couldn't trust him. He wanted her house, after all. She shook her head again, and then stepped away from him.

"He kicked me back, away from the door, kicked me hard in the ribs. I think he broke a few. Then he closed the door. I don't know if I hit my head, or if it was the shock of the first time shift, or the shock of him kicking me, or just the—just the shock, but I lost consciousness. For several hours. I don't know how long. When I woke up, I was me again. When I walked out of my room, they were gone." Bella was whispering again by the end. And Jack nearly jumped a foot.

"WHAT?!?" Jack yelled. Bella squealed and jumped, spinning around.

"They were g-g-gone." Bella said. She could see Jack fairly vibrating with rage, his green eyes glowing. "The house was empty. Abandonment number two."

"They just left you?" Jack growled. His green eyes were going amber, and Bella could see fur starting on the backs of his hands, coming out of his collar.

"Uh, Jack. You need to calm down. Redirect or something. You're losing it." Bella pointed at his hands and Jack looked down, startled to see the fur starting. He ran his tongue over his teeth, surprised to feel the longer canines.

Jack took deep breaths. "Then what happened, Bella?"

"I think we should stop memory lane at this point, it doesn't get better."

He started stalking toward Bella, scenting her fear. "You said something about a redirect, La Mia Bella?" He backed her to the wall next to her bedroom door, his nose buried in her hair just above her ear. "Mmmmm. My Beautiful. La Mia Bella. You smell like prey, love. Perhaps you need to be the one to redirect, humm?" He ran his nose down behind her ear, and felt her shiver, and smelled her arousal.

Bella felt Jack run his hands up under her shirt, and her head fell back. Okay. Can't be food prey to the wolf. She'll be prey of a different sort. And survive the night. And most probably enjoy it. Bella helped Jack pull her shirt off.

Jack's hands slid onto her waist as his nose continued its path down her neck, causing her to shiver. Bella moaned, and put her hands on Jack's arms to steady her, as his hands moved up her waist to her breast.

"So beautiful." Jack whispered against her throat, his hands weighing her breasts, his thumbs brushing her nipples into tight buds. He stepped into her, bringing his right knee between her thighs, to rest tight against her. "Bella."

"Please." Bella whimpered. She shuddered into his arms, trying to press against him at every point he touched at once. "Please."

"Please what, La Mia Bella, my beautiful love, please what?" Jack ran kisses down her clavicle to the top of her right breast, and lower, until he pulled her nipple into her mouth. Bella whimpered again as he tugged harder and then released. "Tell me, my Bella, what do you want?" He raised eyes gone amber in passion this time to hers, and rubbed his nose against hers, waiting.

Bella shook her head and then breathed deeply, and pushed against his chest. "Please."

JACK STUMBLED BACK IN SHOCK. She just looked up at him for a minute, as though making a decision.

Jack got his first clear look at her gorgeous body, and could have wept. The breasts he'd just had his hands and mouth on were beautiful. His eyes roved over those breasts. High, full, begging to be touched. Then narrow waist, but not completely flat stomach, a gentle curve, flaring out to hips that well balanced her generous breasts. Long muscular legs.

Jack ran a shaking hand through his hair. His shirt was rumpled where she had pulled and tugged at it, and his jeans, already tight, pulled uncomfortably across the front. He hadn't been this out of control since he was a teenager—and a new wolf.

BELLA SLIPPED HER SHORTS OFF, reached for his hand, and led him into her room. With her right knee on her bed, she looked over her left shoulder and smiled at Jack's dazed expression. "Please, you're a little over dressed." Bella said, her left hand still extended back for him.

Hands shaking, Jack pulled the shirt over his head, toeing off the sneakers on his feet as he unbuttoned his jeans. He started smiling again as her scent increased with her pupil size, and her breathing. Bella watched that button pop, and the zipper go down over that magnificent bulge, and she gulped quite audibly, looking up quickly when she heard Jack chuckle.

"Worried, Bella?" Jack asked as he eased the jeans down, being careful to leave the boxers in place for just a few moments more, taking off the socks with the pants.

"Worr-ahem." Bella cleared her throat. "Worried? Why would I be worried?" By the end of the sentence Bella was purring, and kneeling on the bed with her bottom in the air, arms braced in front of her for balance, still looking over her shoulder at Jack. "I can't wait."

JACK STALKED FORWARD so he could stroke that glorious rump, sliding his fingers between her cheeks as she purred, and down into her wetness and heat. He wanted to take her so badly. But this would be bad. He shouldn't do it this way. But it would be so delicious. But he could hurt her and he didn't want to hurt her. Oh God, she's so hot and wet.

"My Bella, love. I'm a wolf. I shouldn't take you like this. I am so close to losing control as it is. I don't want to hurt you."

"Jack, you aren't going to hurt me. Please, please. You just don't know. After. Next time, however you want, but please, just take me. Just grab my hips and go. Hard and fast, as long as you can. Please Jack. I'm begging you. And I don't beg easy. Please." Bella came half up and did a half turn, beseeching with her eyes. "Please." Bella squirmed with the way Jacks hand and fingers were still working her, trying to ready her for him. She was wet, but tight. Bella gave a final squeal and gasp, and came apart in his hands. "Jack!"

"Oh God!" Jack ripped his boxers off and Bella gasped again and then smiled slowly, and raised her eyes to his.

"Damn, boy. For a wolf, you're hung like a horse, you know that?" Bella smiled again and then turned fully back to the bed, wagging her behind at Jack in invitation. "Oh, please, please, please, please."

Jack adjusted her position slightly for his height, backing her a little to him, positioned himself for entry and then did exactly as she asked. Grabbed her hips, and entered her. Hard and fast. "Oooohhhh."

"Yeeessssssssss. Yes yes yes yes yes. YES!" Bella gasped with every slap of thighs, every slam of him into her. "Don't stopdon'tstopdon't-stop. Oh please don't stop." Bella wiggled and strained to help with each slamming thrust.

Bella could feel him everywhere. He filled her totally, and every stroke hit her end, and it should have hurt, but instead was exquisite. She'd never felt so complete. Not even when she shifted to her Tiger form and hunted.

JACK THOUGHT he was going to explode with each thrust. She was so tight, she was surrounding him, and she was everywhere. Her scent was drowning him, intoxicating him. He was lost. He had to keep going, he couldn't let her down, and he couldn't stop. "La Mia Bella. My beautiful. Mine." With each thrust he kept thinking my beauty my love mine. Each word hitting each thrust. "Mine, do you hear me? Mine."

"Yes. Oh yes. Please. More. Don't stop. Yes, please. Yours. Just don't ever stop"

~

BELLA FELT a tingling start at her right shoulder blade, but ignored it, she felt her climax coming, a big one. She'd had maybe three small ones, including the one he'd given her before he'd even taken off his shorts.

"Ahhhhh." Bella started screaming her impending orgasm. She'd lost complete control, she was wiggling and squirming all over the bed, and only Jack's firm grasp of her hips was keeping her in place for his thrusts.

"Bella, I'm-"Jack was feeling an intense need to stake his claim. To mark her. Bella was screaming, and Jack was convulsing inside her as he leaned over her and took the nape of her neck between his teeth and bit down, drawing blood.

CHAPTER 3

*B*ella came up off the bed swinging.

"What the hell was that?" Bella yelled, smacking Jack in the chest as she also attempted to feel around her neck at the same time.

"Hold on, hold on La Mia Bella. Let me see, it isn't that bad. It's a love nip, that's all. Oh, holy hell." Jack succeeded in getting Bella under control, and in his lap, and turned so he could see the back of her neck, which also exposed her right shoulder to him.

"What? What? What the fuck did you do to me?" Bella was squirming around on his lap so much, there was a growing concern beginning to rise between them again. "I'm not going to need a rabies shot, am I?"

"Rabies? What do you take me for?" Jack was chuckling as he cradled her against him. "Ahhh, my Bella love. This is going to be so interesting."

"You're a damn wolf, that's what I take you for! And stop calling me that, damnit! I am not your love, or your anything. What's wrong with my back? It itches. It's my neck you bit, but that just tingles." Bella was wiggling again.

"That's where you are wrong, my love. That's where you are

19

wrong. I should never have taken you that way. Should have stuck to the human ways, but no, your scent intoxicated me. And then I had to say the claiming words. And you answered them. Would you stop that infernal wiggling? Can't you feel what you are doing to me?"

Bella looked down at the returned evidence of Jack's desire, and sharply back up at Jack's face. "Sorry. Claiming words. What do you mean? And I answered them? No I didn't. I don't know what you mean. And human ways. I don't know what you're talking about. Maybe you should put me down."

"Oh no. I want you right where I can attempt to control your reactions to what I'm about to tell you. This is where it's going to get interesting. Just try to be still. And try to listen without interrupting. Please?" Jack waited for Bella's nod. She crossed her arms at the "control your reactions" but attempted to settle in for his explanation.

"Wolves are very territorial. It's all what's mine is mine, what's yours is mine, you get it? Anyway. We have to work very hard on our control, or we can't survive as humans. When I became angered by your story—well, that should have been my first clue that we, well, actually, it was really when my wolf was trying to claim your tiger—anyway—you were right that I needed to redirect my energies, or I'd shift, and possibly lose control. And we didn't want to kill each other, did we?

"Well, to still have to give some control over to transfer that anger from blood lust to sexual lust. I might have been able to handle it had we kept to a more—shall we say traditional?—position. But we didn't. We picked—"

"Doggy style?" Bella said, tongue in cheek.

"Wolf style." Jack said firmly. "And it doesn't help that your name is 'My Beauty'—"

"You are not blaming this on my name! I will allow as I—"

"Begged"

"—begged. Yes, I was going to say it. I begged you to—but my name has nothing—"

"No. I'm not blaming you or your name. I'm trying to explain to you what I don't fully understand for myself. I mean, I understand the mechanics—" Bella snorted, "—stop that—but I don't understand what or why it was triggered for us. We don't have an emotional tie. We don't know each other. Anyway. Stop interrupting. To continue. All I could think was 'my beauty, La Mia Bella, my Bella, my love, and that evolved to MINE. And then I was saying it out loud. Mine. And then I asked you to acknowledge it. And you did."

"Oh no!! Oh hell no!" Bella started shaking her head violently, until she became dizzy. Then she gave up and leaned her head against his shoulder. And his chin came down on her hair. "Oh Jack. What's on my back?"

"The same thing that's on mine. The pack tattoo. I'm sorry, babe. We're mated. And you know—"

"Wolves mate for life. I know. What are we going to do, Jack? You broke in here to scare me away. And somehow I end up telling you half my life story, we end up fucking-"

"Language. I made love to my mate. Thank you very much. When I'm forced to service the four unmated females, that is fucking, and means noth-"

"WHAT?" Bella scrambled away from him. "What the hell do you mean 'service'? 'Fucking'? I thought you just said we are mated for life? Make up your mind, dude. Either we are, or we aren't, but if we are, you will not be—"

"As Primo, I take care of the unmated females. I told you that when I described the members of the pack to you. I have to house them, cloth them, feed them, and service them, if they require it, until they are mated. They don't share my room, so don't worry, when you move in, it will just be you and me. I'll go to their room when I have to."

"Oh, bullshit, buddy-boy!!! Unless you are going to pick out 4 unmated males for me to 'service'—and I get veto power on what they look like—you don't get to do any 'servicing'. This is an equal-oppor-tunity-mating here, buddy." Bella stood before Jack in all her naked glory, arms waving, feet spread, eyes flinty, and chest heaving. Jacks eyes rose and fell with that heaving. Bella suddenly stopped. "You know what? Doesn't matter. I absolve you of—" she waved her hands around, "—this. I'm not a Werewolf. I'm a—whatever I am, and I'm happy just the way I am. And I'm not moving in with you. Who said I was moving in with you? But know this. I don't share. As long as you share the bed of others, you won't share mine."

"Sorry, sweetie, but it doesn't work that way. I have to take care of the bitches—and I'm not trying to be cute here, they really are bitches —I would gladly get rid of them if I could. And we've established that a wolf mates for life. Pack magic has already been invoked, as evidenced by the tattoo. The Primo's mate has definite roles to play in the Pack."

"Okay, you know what? I can't deal with this right now. I don't even know you, Jack. How the hell did this happen?"

"Well, like I said, my wolf seemed to be trying to claim your tiger. I think my wolf recognized a mate in you. We were obviously drawn to each other in this form, and then, when we—" Jack rose and walked slowly to her, placing his hands on her shoulders, "—made love," Jack emphasized the words, "my wolf took the opportunity to claim his mate."

"Well, isn't that just swell?" Bella bounced her forehead off his chest a few times, earning herself a headache for her troubles. "I need a shower. And food. And sleep. I'm not sure what order I need that in." Bella sniffed. "Mmm. Definitely the shower first. I wonder what those sandwiches look like." Jack tried to keep hold of her and sniffed.

"You smell wonderful love. Come back to bed." Jack smiled at Bella as she stood next to the bed, looking down at him.

"I smell like you, wolf. I've been up for hours. And I heard the phone ringing. Kayla's probably going crazy. I really don't need her showing up, so I need to go into the office and e-mail the book already, before I pass out for a day or so." Bella ran her hands through her tangled hair. "Ugghhh. I didn't comb out my hair after washing it. It's a mess." Bella turned toward the bathroom.

CHAPTER 4

*J*ack was suddenly up and next to her, taking her hand. "You mentioned before about being up for hours, and what is this about e-mailing? And who is Kayla?"

Bella laughed. "What's with the sudden twenty questions? Okay, wait here, I have to use the restroom. Give me a minute." Bella shook her head with a smile as she squeezed his hand before releasing it to walk into the bathroom. She was just finishing when she looked up and realized Jack had followed her anyway.

"I want to know everything about you. You fascinate me. I think its part of the mating, possibly." Jack walked to the "his" portion of the bathroom, where the oversized shower was, and the second toilet and sink were, and very unselfconsciously began using it.

"Hey! I asked you to wait outside." Bella protested, turning her back, embarrassed. She'd flushed, and was now washing her hands at the sink on the "hers" side of the bathroom, near the double sized Jacuzzi tub. Bella heard the other toilet flush and turned back to the shower to turn it on.

"I've made love to you, La Mia Bella."

"Yes, lover-wolf. I was there. Doesn't mean I want to pee in front of you, or watch you pee in front of me. Okay?" Bella finished adjusting the water temperature to her liking and turned to Jack, who was standing directly behind her smiling. "We don't know each other, remember? Now would you go away so I can take my shower?"

"I love how you just called me lover-wolf. You almost purred." Jack ran his hand up her arm to her shoulder and then cupped her cheek. "The way you purr when I-"

"Jack! Shower! I'm taking a shower now, okay?" Bella pushed against his chest, and he didn't budge; only chuckled.

"I'll join you. I'm sure I smell like—kitty cat." Jack ran his nose behind her ear and smiled when he felt her shiver. Jack stepped in behind Bella and adjusted the water temperature.

"Hey, I had that the way I wanted. And who invited you? Watch your hands!" Bella slapped at his hands as they roved over her behind, and Jack backed her into the wall of the shower. "Jack." Bella whispered in exasperation.

"Bella." Jack whispered into her hair, smiling. He couldn't seem to stop smiling.

Bella felt Jack pressed thick against her stomach—did the man ever rest? Bella thought—as his hands roamed up her sides to her breasts. He never seemed to tire of touching her breasts. And he was right, she did constantly purr while he did. But she was starting to feel seriously tender. "Jack, please." Bella squirmed against him. "Jack, I told you, I don't share. Unless you tell me now you will never again be with those other females--." Bella looked into his eyes.

"I'm sorry, La Mia Bella love. I just can't stop touching you. Craving you." Jack took a deep breath and then stepped back. "I cannot. I am the Primo. I have responsibilities. Okay. Shower. You stick to your side of the shower and I'll stick to mine. I'll make mine quick. Okay?" Jack took another deep breath, filling his lungs with her scent. He loved her scent. Flowers and musk, fruit and spices. Exotic.

"Poor lover-wolf. If it makes you feel better," Bella took a deep breath, filling her lungs with Jack's wolf-musk and man-scent, and leaned her head on his back, "I'm having difficulty saying no. I don't understand this." Bella pushed off Jack's back and turned to her side of the shower.

The shower was a true two-person; large enough to accommodate comfortably even a couple of people of Jack's size, it had shower heads at both ends.

"Distract me, Bella. Answer my questions, love kitten." Jack made a face at her fruit scented shampoo before closing his eyes to apply it, missing her enjoying the view of his arms raised above his head, scrubbing through his hair, and what the movement did—below.

"Umm, I've forgotten the questions." Bella gulped as she took the shampoo herself and turned away. Jack squinted an eye at her and then smiled.

"Why up so long—how many hours now?"

"Umm, maybe 46-48 now? I was writing. Finishing. I always do that at the end, you know? Go into a big push while the ideas are flowing. I forget to eat, sleep. I was hitting deadline, and then, it was all just there." Bella rinsed the shampoo and added the conditioner. She rinsed her eyes and opened them to find Jack looking at her, rubbing soap absentmindedly over his chest.

"Writing?"

"I told you I was a writer. When I introduced myself. I write novels." Bella reached for her shower pouf and body wash, and began scrubbing.

"Okay. I missed that. More on that later. Who's Kayla?" Jack was distracted by the movement of the pouf across Bella's stomach and lower body. Bella cleared her throat.

"Kayla is my editor. And my best friend." Bella turned and pulled the hand-held showerhead down to rinse off.

"Editor?" Jack gulped, thinking he'd like to go where that shower-head was going...

"Yes, she edits my manuscripts before they go to the publisher."

"Oh, right. Editor." Jack growled. Cleared his throat, and watched Bella finally rinse the conditioner out of her hair.

"E-mail. You said something about e-mailing?" Jack sounded almost desperate by the time Bella turned the water off and stepped out of the shower, grabbing a clean towel from the stack on the shelf and handing him one.

"Yes, my finished book. I still need to e-mail it to Kayla. I told her in an email a few hours ago I was finished but that I was going to grab a shower and some food before I e-mailed it and then pass out for about a week. I've heard the phone ring a few times, she must be frantic by now." Bella walked through the pocket doors into the attached closet, again a "his and hers" affair, the "his" side empty. "I have some sweats and oversized T-shirts I usually sleep in, if you want something clean to put on?" Bella turned to Jack, stumbling to a halt as she watched him rubbing the towel across his thighs—and between.

"I'll take the T-shirt, but I'll keep my jeans, thanks. What are you doing with men's clothing?" Jack growled the last, stalking toward Bella.

"Down, big boy. I prefer men's sweats, the women's versions aren't really well made. They're too—I don't know—froufrou, or something. And the T-shirts are very generic." Bella tossed a navy blue shirt at Jack as she pulled a pair of jeans, a bra, panties, and tank top out for herself.

"Froufrou?" Jack asked, pulling the T-shirt on without looking at it, and following her back into her bedroom through the rest of the closet. "And why is your place set up for two when there's just you?"

"Bought it that way." Bella shrugged, slipping into her bra and panties and then her jeans and top. She sat on the side of her bed and sighed, reaching for one of her combs to try to deal with the tangles. "I loved the acreage, and the rest of the house. What did I care if the bathroom had two toilets? I am so tired." Bella's hands fell at her sides, her hair only half combed out.

"Let me see that." Jack took the comb from Bella, and slid around behind her, settling her in the Vee of his legs. He slowly combed through her hair, gently untangling every strand. Bella sighed and then purred in pleasure. Jack chuckled. "You're purring again."

"I can't help it, you bring it out in me. How are you doing that? How can we go from adversaries to lovers, craving each other so intensely, in such a short time? It's—it's scary Jack. This is scaring me Jack. I don't even know who you are, but I'm terrified you are going to go away and take my every happiness away. And if you knew my past, you'd know—I don't rely on anyone for my happiness, and I don't trust anyone. So what the hell is going on?" Bella turned to face Jack, staring into his eyes.

"Maybe you need to tell me more of that past, La Mia Bella." Jack said, staring intently into Bella's eyes.

"I-" Bella shook her head. "No. No, I don't think that's a good idea right now. I need to know more. More about you, and about this, and I have things I need to get done, and I need sleep, damnit." Bella took the comb out of Jacks hands and rose, stepping away from the bed.

"Bella," Jack called, but Bella just shook her head, waving her hand back at him.

Bella walked out of the room, leaving the comb on the bedside table, and Jack followed.

"What do you think? Are they safe?" Bella indicated the sand-wiches they'd made a couple of hours earlier.

"I wouldn't risk it. Go do what you need to with your book. Call your friend. I'll put something together to eat, call a friend to fix the door. I need to call my Secundo, and a couple of wolves to come take care of the mess we left in the back anyway." Jack pulled Bella into him, his hand on her cheek, and kissed her forehead.

"Okay. Thanks Jack. I just need—I don't know. A few minutes where I'm not drowning in your scent I think." Jack's hand clenched, and stopped just before he would have hurt her. "I'm sorry Jack, I don't mean—"

"I know what you mean. It's okay. Go on. Its okay, La Mia Bella." He looked down into her eyes, and Bella looked up into his.

Bella turned and crossed the family room, almost afraid to walk away, absolutely terrified to see the damage the strange wolves had wreaked on her office and the other rooms on this side of the house. She turned just before she reached the hall, and found him looking back at her.

Jack grinned and then turned to clear the table of the mess they had left before finding something to feed his woman.

27

CHAPTER 5

*B*ella walked into her office and breathed a sigh of relief and then grimaced. She could smell the wolves. She went and opened the windows before grabbing her phone and dialing Kayla. At least they had done no damage. Bella checked the other rooms and opened the windows as she soothed Kayla, assuring her she was about to e-mail the book right then.

"I know, I'm sorry. I fell asleep. I took a shower and then I made the mistake of lying on my bed, just for a second I told myself, and that was hours ago."

"I've been so worried!! A few more minutes, and I was heading over there!" Kayla mumbled around the ever-present wad of gum. Kayla always had a huge wad of gum in her mouth, ever since she gave up smoking. Except when she took up drinking instead. But then she gave that up too and back to the chewing. Lovely habit, but better than the smoking or the drinking, Bella supposed.

"Sorry, again. Look, I'll leave you and your gum to it. I'll get it sent, and then I'm going to eat, and probably get more sleep. This one really wrung me out." Bella was headed back toward the first bedroom, the one she'd made her office, shaking her head. Bella sat at her computer and moved the mouse to wake it.

"Hey, leave my gum alone." Kayla said, much more clearly, having apparently taken the gum out of her mouth at Bella's reminder. Kayla knew Bella hated talking to her with a mouthful of gum, so Kayla usually took it out. "I'll wait and confirm receipt. How are you feeling about this one, you said it wrung you out. Why?"

"No reason, just a longer push than usual. But Kayla? It's good. Real good." Bella had set up the email by this point, and hit sent. "Prepare to be amazed." Bella finished the save to her USB drive and pulled it out, shutting down the computer, and walking out of the room.

"I can't wait. I'll call you to schedule dinner." Bella walked into the family room and smelled wolf and meat.

"Kayla, I gotta go." Bella hit the disconnect button before she started growling. There were two strange wolves at her broken door. The men looked up at her at the sound.

"Uh, Jack." The tall blond called nervously.

"Yeah, Sean. Give me a minute. I want this steak ready when Bella comes out." Jack called from the kitchen. About that point, a petite blond woman walked up to the back door and walked into Bella's house, causing Bella to break into a near roar.

"No, Jack, you need to come out here now. I think Miss Bella is out here now, and Brigit is here, and I don't think Miss Bella is happy. I think she's—vibrating." The blond male wolf tried to move between Bella and the female wolf, but the female was having none of it.

"Where's my Jackie?" The blond Brigit called, and Bella unsheathed her claws, literally.

"That's my Jackie, bitch." Bella snarled, flashing fangs.

"Oh shit." The blond wolf said, and there was a crash from the kitchen.

"Bella!" Jack called, racing in, shoving Brigit at the blond and pulling Bella to him but Bella didn't care, she was busy straining toward the competitor in her home. "Sean, get Brigit out of here. Bella, baby, its okay. The pack is assembling out back so I can introduce you. I haven't told them yet. Bella, sweetie. Please." Jack finally succeeded in turning her to him, and then heard a gasp behind them.

"You mated with the bitch?" Brigit screeched. Jack looked up to see Sean and Declan struggling to pull Brigit out of the house. "Well, Bella sweetie, even as his mate, you have to share him with his unmated females. Or didn't he tell you?" Brigit sneered.

Bella shifted her hands back to human, and ran her tongue over her teeth to confirm they were fully returned to normal before smiling at Jack. Bella straightened away from Jack and turned. "But he's my mate, Brigit dear, and never yours."

Brigit screeched and lunged at Bella. Jack leapt in front of her, knocking Brigit back. "She is now your Prima. You will show her respect, or face me." Jack growled.

Sean and Declan backed out of the house, allowing Brigit room to decide. Jack advanced on Brigit, who backed away. Bella followed, and looking up, found herself facing nineteen other strange wolves.

Bella turned to Jack, "I'm hungry. I haven't eaten in 48 plus hours. I'm going to eat. I'll be back." And walked into her kitchen.

Okay, Bella, breathe. Just Breathe. Bella took several deep breaths, leaning on the island in her kitchen and then looked around. Jack had a salad tossed on the island for her, and a steak in the oven. From the smell, almost overdone. She turned it off, and pulled it out. It looked like Jack had everything ready for her. She transferred it to the waiting plate, pulled the bar stool out, and settled in to eat and listen to Jack deal with his—well, apparently, their—pack.

"Thank you all for coming so quickly. As Bella said, she hasn't eaten in about two days, so bear with her while she eats. I'll try to answer some questions while we wait." Jack looked out over his wolves. The females of his mated pairs looked very happy for him, as did the males, the others just looked confused.

"Uh, Primo?" Turner Warren called.

"Yeah, Turner. What's up?" Jack responded.

"I thought you came over to run her out. Now you've killed three of her wolves, and have mated with her?" Turner scratched his head.

He was an expert at looking like he didn't have two thoughts to rub together.

"These three aren't her wolves. Bella doesn't have a pack, she isn't a Were. These were rogues who'd broken in before I got here, and looks like they meant her no good." He heard Sasha giggle. He turned in her direction. "What's going on over there, Sasha?" Sasha was one of the unmated females, and his favorite. She was never interested in his body, just wanted to work for what she got. Currently, she kept his house, and did most of his cooking. Hopefully Bella would let him keep her.

"Where'd you get the shirt, Jack?" Sasha asked, pointing.

"Bella, why?" Jack looked down and then groaned. Everyone laughed. There, in white script on the navy shirt 'Cats do it on all fours'. "Oh, lord."

"So, cats, huh?" Sasha asked.

"Cats, Sasha, as in Tiger. That's Bella's favorite animal to shift to." Jack smelled his Bella coming up behind him and smiled.

"Telling all my secrets now, Jack?" Bella asked, eating a candy bar she'd found in the cupboard. Jack turned to her.

"Did I not find you enough to eat?" Jack asked.

"Two days is a long time for a shifter to go without eating. I'll likely be eating most every moment I'm not sleeping for a while to rebuild." Bella smiled, not wanting to point out what all they'd done in the last couple of hours to eat up a great deal of her energy. But Jack got it, he smiled back knowingly. Sasha stepped forward and then knelt at Bella's feet.

"Prima-"

"Bella" Bella interrupted.

"Prima Bella-"

"Just Bella, please."

"Thank you, Prima. Bella. My name is Sasha. I am an unmated female, under the Primo's protection. Currently, I cook and clean for him. I want to formally pledge my oath to you as my Prima, and request the opportunity to continue to work for both of you. I do not seek the services of the Primo's—body—my Prima. I only wish to work and serve please." And Sasha knelt fully supine in front of Bella. Bella looked up at Jack for help.

"Oh get up, doormat. Don't bow to the whore bitch! She's not my Prima." Brigit stalked forward and kicked Sasha out of the way. Bella heard a distinctive crack as Sasha yelped and curled in on herself, hugging her clearly broken ribs.

Bella roared and leaped at Brigit, and with one swing flung her ten feet away. "No one kicks someone who is down. Not in my presence. Ever. Do you hear me? Ever!" Bella screamed, stalking at Brigit, who lay stunned for a moment and then sprang up.

"I claim right of challenge." Brigit called, looking triumphant.

"What?" Jack cried.

"What?" Bella called.

The assembled wolves began muttering amongst themselves as Sean and Declan grabbed Brigit again and pulled her away from Bella. Bella moved back to Jack where he knelt over Sasha.

"What the hell is going on?" Bella asked Jack under her breath, figuring it was a doomed undertaking among all these Weres and their super hearing. "Sasha, dear. Are you okay?" Sasha moaned.

"Brigit claimed challenge against you. She hopes if she can take you out, she takes your place as my mate."

"The hell!" Bella fairly yelled.

"Ssh." Jack looked up at Bella and then back down to Sasha, his hands never leaving her as he checked for injuries. "Take you out, and she's my mate. Sasha love. A couple of broken ribs. We need to get you shifted so you can heal them."

"Hey, I've issued challenge over here!" Brigit called.

"And we will deal with that when we've taken care of Sasha, now be quiet, Brigit." Jack ordered in a low growl, heard clearly across the yard as he sat down on the ground and carefully pulled Sasha into his lap.

"So what's happening here?" Bella asked.

"Sasha is not a dominant or strong wolf. She can only shift at the full moon. As her Primo, I can force her. it is not pleasant for her, it's in fact very painful, but it's better than the pain she's in, as once she's shifted, she will heal quite quickly, and once she's healed, I can help her shift back." Jack tried to patiently explain as he carefully pulled Sasha's clothes off.

"Okay. I need some quick background here. I take it Brigit is one of the unmated females, like Sasha, and she liked to enforce the whole, uh, Primo servicing thing, right? But Sasha didn't? Am I getting it right?"

"Yes." Jack almost had all of Sasha's clothes off. Sasha was a very pretty woman, black hair and brown eyes. Bella thought she was tiny, maybe five feet even, 100 pounds soaking wet And Bella was getting very uncomfortable having another woman naked in her man's lap. Except he wasn't her man, right? Jeez, she was getting so confused. This mate thing was messing with her head. She'd really overreacted when that Brigit came into her house. It helped that she could tell Jack was not the least aroused by the situation, or the woman he was holding.

"Okay. I think I like Sasha. And I definitely don't like Brigit. I'll be kicking her ass just as soon as we fix up Sasha. No one hurts one of my friends." Bella smiled at Sasha, and ran her hand through her hair. "And if Madam Sasha wants to clean up after me, and cook for me—wait, she can cook, right Jack?" Jack smiled and nodded, "good and then if she wants to and then who am I to stop her?"

"Thank you my Prima." Sasha gasped out, and gripped Bella's hand.

"Now you stop that Prima business. I told you, it's Bella. And no more talking. What do you need from me, Jack?" Bella looked up at him, worry clear in her eyes.

"Give me some room, I don't know how this will affect you. It could take half the wolves, but I will try to keep it directed, that's why I'm holding her. She'll be okay. She's not a little girl, La Mia Bella." Jack reached for Bella, but she backed up.

"I know, Jack. Take care of our wolf. I'm looking forward to being spoiled when she's recovered, okay? I'll look after everyone else." Bella backed several steps away, and met the original blond wolf she'd seen at her door, the one Jack called Sean.

"Hi, I'm Sean Michael Kilpatrick, Jack's Secundo." Sean slumped awkwardly next to Bella.

"Hi Sean. Bella Blake. What are you doing?"

"You outrank me. To show respect and my subservience to you, I need to make sure I'm lower than you. Your people don't do this?" Sean seemed surprised.

"Straighten up Sean that looks really uncomfortable. And ridiculous. And I don't have 'people.'" Bella looked around for a chair or something to stand on, to ease his discomfort, since it was apparent he wasn't going to straighten. "Maybe if I had something high I could sit on, and something low you could sit on, would that work?"

"Let me look around, Pri—" Bella snarled. "Bella."

JACK WATCHED Sean and Bella interact for a moment. He wondered if she'd noticed she had claimed his pack as her own, his people as her own. He knew Sasha had noticed, her eyes were watching their interactions closely while they were together. And the other wolves closest to them had surely noticed, and spread the word. He felt they were accepting her, and she'd barely opened her mouth to them. All but Brigit. Well, she was always a problem. No one wanted her. Except Declan. Poor Declan. He hoped he wasn't hurt too badly when Bella ripped Brigit apart. And he had no doubt she would. She was a fierce fighter. He would not lose her! Jack looked down at Sasha.

"Ready, Sasha?" He smiled. Sasha nodded. "Okay, my dear. I need you to relax and breathe deeply. As deeply as those ribs will let you. Can you do that for me, love?"

"Careful, Jack. I don't want our Prima coming after me." Sasha gasped out.

"You let me worry about her. You stop that talking right now; remember what your Prima said. And what I said. Relax. Breathe deeply. Feel my wolf moving through you." Jack opened his wolf, and breathed it into Sasha. Sasha whimpered, shivered, and then convulsed. Jack felt his wolf rising, and forced it into her. Sasha gave another convulsion and then stiffened, and screamed as Jack finally shoved all his power into her, forcing her shift. Sasha's scream became a howl as she erupted in fur, fangs and claws and leapt out of Jacks arms, shaking herself all over.

~

BELLA WAS SITTING on the tabletop of the picnic table she'd forgotten she owned, and Sean on the seat, when she heard the scream and leapt up.

"Easy, Bella." Sean was next to her. "Almost done." And it was, within a few minutes Sasha was howling, and then, she just was. The wolf, a beautiful white wolf with those same brown eyes Bella remembered.

"Why did it hurt so much?" Bella asked, refusing to look away as Jack rose slowly, stiffly.

"Because she was hurt, and because it was forced on her. Some Primo's use the force shift as a punishment." Turner Warren had walked up on her other side, doing that awkward scrunch thing. Bella whipped around to stare at him.

"Oh, not Jack. He'd never do anything like that. Jack is a great Primo." Sean was quick to say. Bella looked over at Sean, and smiled and then looked back at Turner when he made a sound.

"Prima Bella, my lady." He was now kneeling. "I wish to offer my oath and fealty." He dropped to a fully supine position. At that point, Sasha stalked up and wuffed, joining him in the position. Seven other females, and ten other males then came up behind them, and assumed the same position.

"Umm." Bella said, looking around for help. Sean smiled at her and then assumed the same position in the front row next to Sasha. When Bella looked up, she realized that was all of the wolves except Jack, Brigit, and the male wolf with Brigit. At that point the male finished what was apparently an argument with Brigit, and joined the rest of the pack supine before her, while Jack joined her, taking her hand in front of the pack. "Jack?"

"Wolves of the Lupi Di Notte pack; do you swear your loyalty to my mate, Arabella Mia Blake?" Jack called clearly, looking out over his pack. He ignored a snort from Brigit. There was a chorus of "I do"'s from the assembled wolves, and a single "wuff". "Do you swear to obey her as you obey your Primo?" Again the chorus, and the "wuff". "Then rise and greet your new Prima."

"Wait, what?" Bella asked in confusion as the group rose and started to assemble them into a line. There was much shuffling, but it seemed organized until Brigit approached, and tried to insert herself into the line.

"As my mate, you are Prima with me. If I am unavailable, they will come to you for direction." Jack was watching closely the disagreement at the back of the line.

"What the hell is going on back there? And don't think I'm not going to be returning to that later, buddy-boy." Bella was stretched onto her toes to see the altercation in the back.

"You know, I think I like it better when you call me lover-wolf" Jack whispered into her ear before turning to the group. "Enough!" Jack called. "Brigit!" Jack growled.

"Yes, lover? You wanted me?" Brigit scampered up to Jack quickly, playing her hands across his chest. Bella growled, but held her ground. She knew what was hers.

"No, never did, Brigit. Back up, and kneel before your Primo and Prima" Jack's voice changed with the second half of his statement. Only the first few wolves in line heard the first statement, but no one mistook the command in the second statement, not even Brigit.

"But lover-" Brigit started.

"Stop it!" Jack commanded. "You are embarrassing yourself. You have issued challenge to my mate. You have refused to swear loyalty and fealty to her. You are outside pack. You do not belong in this line. You will stand aside until we are ready to address your unprovoked attack on not only my mate, but Sasha, your sorella lupi, your sister wolf. Not to mention the challenge. Stand. Aside." Jack then turned his back on her and began introducing his wolves to Bella. There were so many, she soon lost track of their names. She realized their place in line established their dominance and ranking in the pack. The wolf that was standing with Brigit was Declan Mackenzie, Jack's Terzo. And it looked like she wasn't the only mate to "inherit" her mates ranking. The next five wolves were all mated, and so their mates shared ranking.

Bella was impressed by the fact that in a few instances, it appeared, at least to her, that a few of the males in the pairs came up in rank due to their females being more dominant. What really rankled was that all of the remaining unmated females fell to the back of the line, regardless of dominance. Sasha brought up the rear.

CHAPTER 6

hey settled with Jack and Bella sitting on the tabletop, and the pack sitting on the ground, ranged around them. Sean and Declan sat on the seats of the picnic table below them. It took some shuffling to arrange. It seemed that Bella's new rank did bump them down just a bit. So Bella now took Sean's usual position on Jack's right, with Sean on Jack's left, and Declan on Bella's right. Bella felt a little bad. When she tried to tell Sean sorry, he grinned at her and said he wasn't. She wasn't sure how to take that. Brigit was sulking off in a corner of the yard, still within sight.

"Okay. We may have a problem. It's unknown if the three rogues Bella and I took out were the only ones in town." Jack looked out at his wolves worriedly.

"Wait, Bella helped with that? I thought you said she isn't a Were?" Sean looked up at Jack.

"She's not, but she took out two of the three." Jack patted the shirt, and at the wuff of the Sasha-wolf, looked down at that shirt and pointed at the word "Cat". "Remember the tiger?"

"Two of them?" One of the wolves, she thought it was Turner, spoke up.

"A tiger?" One of the females, she thought her name was Kathy, sitting next to Sasha spoke up. Sasha wuffed.

"I'm a shapeshifter." Bella spoke up, looking at Jack to make sure he was okay with it. "I can shift to any land mammal, at any time, regardless of moon-phase."

"Can we see?" Kathy again.

"I'll demonstrate when I address The Bitches challenge. Until then, I'm saving my energy for kicking her ass for kicking my friend Sasha." Bella smiled over at Sasha and Kathy smiled back, stroking Sasha sensuously. Mmmm will have to think about that one. Bella thought. She heard a snort from the Brigit corner. Bella saw Declans shoulders slump. Uh-oh. Bella looked up at Jack. Yep, Jack noticed too.

"About that, my mate was attacked in her own home. By rogues. And by one of my own wolves. And then Sasha, a wolf under my personal protection, in the act of swearing loyalty and fealty to my mate, was attacked. How will we answer this?" Jack looked out at his people. Bella looked at him and then at the people he cared for. There was so much she still didn't know about him or his pack.

"Banishment." One of the wolves called out, Bella couldn't remember her name, or her mates.

"Hey!" Brigit yelled, running forward. "What about my challenge?"

"Perhaps her punishment should be addressed after the challenge. After all, the challenge may resolve the issue of punishment?" Sean spoke up from Jacks left. There were nods from the assembled wolves.

"That seems to make sense to me. Bella?" Jack turned to her.

"I just want to get this done so I can go to bed." Bella yawned like she was bored, but really, she was very tired, and they needed to get this show on the road, or she was going to go into her house, lock them all out, and go to bed. "As long as she understands, I'm not a Werewolf, and will not be shifting into a wolf-form, but to my fighting Tiger form. She may wish to withdraw her challenge." Brigit snorted.

"You need to pay attention to her, Brigit. She took two wolves in her Tiger form." Brigit just stared back defiantly. "Well then, unless there are objections?" Jack waited a moment, and hearing none, he turned to his Secundo. "Sean, you and John need to get the area ready. I'll prep Bella. Declan, I assume you'll be assisting Brigit?" At Declan's nod, he turned to the assembled wolves. "Because I have a stake in the outcome of this challenge, I will stand down, and allow Sean to take control of the ring."

Jack stepped down and took Bella's arm, leading her closer to her house, and further from the wolves. Jack put his hands on her face and just stared in her eyes for a moment and then bumped her nose with his. "Don't you go getting killed out there, La Mia Bella. I will not be mated to that bitch. Don't you do that to me, you hear?"

"Oh ye of little faith." Bella reached her arms up around his neck and snuggled in. "I can take her." She gave him a deep kiss. "I mean, in my only fight I took two wolves by myself, right?"

Sean had been working quickly, with the help of John and a few others, to organize everyone in a square in Bella's yard delineating the fight area.

"Okay, I guess I'm ready when everyone else is." Bella took a deep breath. "Wait, is this—I mean, how far do we go? When do we know who's won?"

"A challenge fight is to the death, unless one of the fighter's yields and the opponent accepts." Jack was very quiet, and Bella suddenly understood why he was so worried. "What do you mean you've only fought once. You mean earlier? That was it?"

"Yes. Usually, when I want to hunt, I go out and get a bunch of rabbits or other small game, let them loose back here, shift, and go hunting. That's the extent of my fighting. Earlier today was the first time I had to fight a sentient creature. I did not like it. I'm not looking forward to this. I mean, I'm more than ready to teach her a lesson, but kill her? I will because I won't let her kill me, but I don't like this Jack." Bella leaned her head against his chest.

"Still ready to go?" Jack rubbed her shoulders.

"No reason to put it off." Bella ran her hands up his chest. "Besides, I take her out, and that's one less I have to worry about wanting your bed." Jack clutched her close to him, kissing her deeply.

CHAPTER 7

They rejoined everyone else, and Bella stood loosely, calmly across the makeshift ring from her opponent. Jack stood on Bella's left, and Sasha moved to her right, and it seemed to Bella that it made Sasha happy to be there. Sean stood in the middle of the open area. Everyone else was ranged around the area, and if there was an order to it, Bella could not discern it; however, it did seem to her that they seemed to be closer to her end than Brigit's.

"Alright everyone. We are here because Brigit claimed right of challenge against Bella. We've chalked lines to designate the boundaries, DO NOT cross those boundaries. As soon as you have both shifted, I will howl the release, and the challenge will begin. You may enter the ring and begin your shift." Sean stepped aside as Brigit stepped into the ring. Brigit started stripping, and Bella just stood there. Everyone stared at her, waiting for her to strip, but she just stood calmly, smiling serenely. When Brigit had finished stripping, and had begun her shift, Bella finally stepped forward.

From one step, she was upright, fully dressed Arabella Mia Blake, human, and the next she was a 350 pound red Tiger with white stripes. She roared once, and sat placidly to wait for Brigit to complete her shift.

CHRISTINE LEE

The Pack started buzzing, but Bella didn't allow them to distract her, her eyes were on Brigit as she finished.

"La Mia Bella, don't you play with her like you did that other wolf. You take her fast and hard so we can go to bed. You hear me?" Jack called quietly, though most of the Pack was close enough to have heard. Bella swiveled her expressive ears to let him know she'd heard, but kept her focus in place.

Brigit was finally finished, after about seven minutes, and after a look at Bella to ensure she was ready, Sean howled, and the fight commenced. Brigit lost no time in streaking toward Bella, and Bella launched herself at Brigit.

Brigit went for Bella's throat, and Bella soared over her cleanly and landed with a sliding turn, and sank her fangs deep into Brigit's right rear flank. Brigit ripped free and limped as Bella spat fur, meat and blood as she spun to be ready for the next attack.

Bella didn't wait for Brigit to regain her bearings, but dove in low, aiming for the same flank but missed, instead getting a large chunk of her underbelly. Brigit howled in pain and Declan was screaming suddenly for her to yield.

Bella didn't know what to do. She was frozen in place, with a huge mouthful of—she didn't want to think too hard about it—and all she wanted to do was spit it out and back away, but she didn't know if she was supposed to at this point or not. She raised her eyes and found Sean and Jack close in front of her, and sensed Declan near her, but couldn't see him. She could hear Brigit whimpering. Bella started growling, and moved so she could see Declan as well. She looked at Jack for direction.

"Brigit, yield, please." Declan was yelling in Brigit's ear, and Brigit was snapping at him between whimpers.

"Sean, you need to call it, Bella doesn't know what to do at this point." Jack growled.

"Brigit, do you yield?" Sean asked. Brigit growled, a universally accepted response for 'NO'. "Bella, she will linger with this wound. You must finish it. Take her throat." Sean and Jack backed up and Declan howled. He had to be pulled away by two other wolves.

Bella blinked at Jack then looked at Brigit who snarled at her. That was all it took. Bella released her belly, and whatever she'd had in her mouth, and lunged for her throat. Brigit could not move quickly enough to protect it, and Bella had her. One strike, and she'd ripped Brigit's throat out. Bella backed away, spitting out the fur and meat while she heard the last gasps and rattles, and then it was quiet.

Bella shook herself as she heard the wolves cheering her, all but one. Declan was howling, holding Brigit's lifeless body in his arms. She backed away from all of it as she rubbed her muzzle on the grass. When she thought she had as much of the blood as she was getting off, she moved to the middle of the ring and turned a circle until she faced Jack, who went to his knees before her.

"You okay, Mate?" Jack choked. Bella wuffed. She heard gasps when she stalked up to Jack, still in his human form, and butted his head with her massive tiger head. Jack laughed. Bella backed up and shifted once more into her fully dressed human form and Jack grabbed her, still laughing and kneeling before her, with his head now resting against her stomach. "Oh, Mate. Life will not be dull, will it?"

"Doubtful, Jack. Very Doubtful. Can I get some sleep now?" Bella laughed too when Jack tickled her belly before standing and bringing her up so he could kiss her deep and long.

"Soon, La Mia Bella. I need to help Sasha shift back, and direct this cleanup, and make sure Declan is okay. I think he's going to take this very hard." Bella turned to look at him as Jack spoke. She'd been avoiding looking at what she'd done, but she couldn't be a coward forever. "Looks like Leroy is taking him in hand. That's good." Jack told her.

"I didn't like that Jack. I don't want to live like this. Don't make me live like this." Bella turned away as she saw Sean and John and a few others begin the cleanup even without direction from Jack. Sasha padded up to them and butted her head against Bella's hip. "Hi, sweetie. Ready to be human again?" Sasha gave a huff of affirmative.

"Let's move away from everyone else then for some privacy. Bella, will you be okay for a bit?" Jack seemed reluctant to release her.

"Yeah, take care of our Sasha, but hurry back." Bella smiled tiredly, and turned to a couple of wolves who were waiting to talk to her.

"Prima, I know you've met so many of us today, let us introduce ourselves again. I'm Tony Warren, and this is my wife, Ashley. We are so happy the Primo has taken a Mate finally. I don't know if you've noticed, but our Pack has no children. A Pack without a Prima is usually barren, because it is the Prima that helps the females to keep from shifting during the full moon, so they don't lose the babies." Tony had been speaking all in a rush, and paused at this point to take a breath. Bella glanced at Ashley, and noted the tears in her eyes. "My Ashley really wants babies, Prima."

"Tony, Ashley, it's wonderful to meet you both again, truly my honor, and please, call me Bella." Bella moved over to Ashley and took both of her hands. "I don't know how that is done, but whatever I can do to help, I will, okay?" Bella looked at Ashley, and made sure she knew she meant it. Boy, Jack had some explaining to do.

"Oh, Pri—I mean Bella. Thank you so much!" Ashley squeezed her hands, and turned to her husband and hugged him fiercely. At that point, Bella saw Jack gesture at the back door, and she nodded gratefully. Bella moved in that direction, nodding and smiling, and stopping to talk only when absolutely forced to.

CHAPTER 8

*B*ella finally closed her newly fixed door and sighed deeply, closing her eyes, her head bouncing back on the glass door behind her for a moments peace. Her eyes flashed open when the arms came around her.

"Hey there, La Mia Bella." Jack lifted her into his arms, slipping his leg between hers, one hand beneath her firm round bottom and the other in her hair while he buried his nose behind her ear. Bella shivered and wiggled against him, sliding her arms up his.

"Hey there, lover-wolf." Bella purred, rubbing her nose on Jack's throat. "I'm really tired, baby." Bella's stomach growled and she giggled. "And still hungry." She slid her hands further up his arms to his shoulders, pulling herself further up his body and wrapping her legs around his waist. She laid her head on his shoulder. "Do I have any food left?" Jack chuckled. "And I'm not supposed to be doing this. I told you. I don't share, damnit. What is wrong with me?" Jack chuckled.

"I asked Sasha to bring something over. She'll be over any minute. Then you can eat, and I'll get you right into bed." Jack almost growled the last. He had both hands under her at this point, holding her tightly against the evidence of his desire for her. Bella rubbed and squirmed.

"About the sharing—" Bella snarled, "perhaps we need to discuss some changes to Pack ritual?"

"Mmmm. You think of everything." Her doorbell rang. "That must be her?" Bella expected Jack to put her down, but he didn't, simply walking to the front door with her in his arms. He freed one arm to unlock and open the door to Sasha and one of his wolves.

"Sasha, John. Thanks so much." Jack gestured them in. Bella smiled at Sasha and then looked in surprise at John, who was bringing several bags in.

"Jack, what's all that?" Bella asked in confusion.

"Well, La Mia Bella. You said you weren't moving out of your house. So I'm moving in. So is Sasha. You told her she could cook and clean for you. John, my things go in the room off the kitchen, Sasha will be picking one of the rooms off the hall on the other side of the house. Just not the first room, that's Bella's office." Jack followed Bella's sniffing nose, and Sasha, in the direction of the kitchen.

"Hey, who said you guys could move in?" Bella said absentmindedly as she leaned away from him, reaching for the food greedily. Sasha mock-slapped her hands away, shooing her in the direction of the table.

"You don't expect me to live away from my mate, do you?" Jack looked down at Bella worriedly. Bella looked up at Jack. "We can all go to my house…"

"Oh, no, I'm not leaving my house. I love my house."

"You might like my house you know." Jack teased.

"Nope. I live in my house. But Jack, sorry, you go home. Sasha can move in, you'll likely want the room on the end back there, it has a private bathroom, and a private entrance to the backyard. Are you sure you want to put up with me? You don't even know me, but I should warn you, I'm a real pain to deal with, especially when I'm on deadline." Jack finally put Bella down and looked at her.

"What do you mean I go home?" Jack sounded so upset.

"Jack, we just met today. I don't know you. You don't know me. We are not moving in together. You can't just move into my house. You have to slow down here." Bella looked at Jack intently. Jack took a deep breath.

"You aren't saying no to us forever?" Bella could see his wolf trying to rise in his eyes, in the green trying to go to amber.

"No, I'm just saying we just met." Bella emphasized.

"Okay. I can live with that." Jack looked up and found John and Sasha had been frozen during the discussion. "John, my stuff goes back. Sasha, you still want to stay?"

"Oh, yes, please." Sasha seemed very happy.

"Then it's settled." Jack ordered and then looked down at Bella. "For now."

"Okay." Bella smiled.

Bella turned to the kitchen and then sat down in the chair at the head of the table and Bella almost bounced in place waiting for the plate to be placed in front of her. It smelled so good

Sasha placed the plate in front of Bella and stepped back nervously. "Now this isn't much, just leftover lasagna. I hope you like it." Sasha folded her hands under her chin and waited, breath held.

"I'm sure it's wonderful, Sasha. I love lasagna. Most any Italian food, actually." Bella smiled at her and then took a bite. And moaned. It was sooo good. Sasha clapped happily and then went back in and got a plate for Jack. Bella kept eating, but peripherally at least noticed the wolf, John, calling Sasha away briefly. After several bites, she felt she could finally come up for air.

"Oh my word! That is wonderful." Bella looked up at Jack and saw him grinning at her. "Sorry, it's just really good, and I'm just-"

"Really hungry?"

"Yeah."

"It's okay, baby. Eat your food. It's late, and I need to get you to bed." Jack wiggled his brows at her, and Bella laughed, shaking her head at him. Bella went back to eating. Jack chuckled, and started eating.

"Jack?" The wolf, John, called. Jack looked up, still chewing, but motioning for John to have a seat. Bella waved her fork at him, but kept eating. "I got Sasha's bags put in her room—" he looked at Bella,

"—she did pick that room you mentioned to her, Prima. Boy, that girl can pack fast." Bella started making noises, and raised her fork at him to indicate to wait a minute.

"Please stop calling me 'Prima' like some—I don't know. I'm Bella. Please? I would appreciate it. Thanks so much, John." Bella smiled beautifully at John, not noticing the effect her smile had on him, and went rapidly back to the last of her food, scooping up vegetables with the bread Sasha had brought. She didn't even realize she was making yummy 'mmhmm hmmmhmm' noises.

John raised an eyebrow at Jack and he just smiled. "Thanks, John. You'll expand the perimeter to include this place like we talked about?"

"Yes sir. This place completes the big square, so it's easy enough. It would be nice if we could move between the properties though." John looked between Jack and Bella.

"Perimeter?" Bella questioned, looking up from her clean plate with a frown. It was unclear to Jack if the frown was for the topic of conversation, or the fact that her plate was clean. Before he could wonder, Sasha was bustling back into the kitchen, whipping Bella's plate away, and replacing it with a plate with a large slice of lemon meringue pie. Bella smiled and hummed some more, rocking in her seat while she dug in. She didn't even notice Sasha's quiet offer of a slice to John.

"John handles security for the pack. Because we just moved to town, we all live next door. John and several of the wolves work a security detail around our property. I wanted to make sure they expanded it to include yours, now that your part of the pack, and Sasha has moved in." Bella nodded.

"Gotcha. And you want access through my fences between properties." John nodded while Bella looked at Jack looking at her. "Let me sleep on that, okay? Speaking of sleep, I need desperately to catch some, or I'll be passing out soon. John, it's been great." Bella popped the last bite of pie into her mouth, and patted John on the shoulder on her way past as Jack growled. Bella looked back with a frown to see John on the floor and Jack on his feet, hands in his hair, his back to the table. Before she could say anything, Sasha grabbed the plate from her and gestured her to follow her into the kitchen.

"Mated females do not touch unmated males. Ever. Or the other way around. Jack reacted automatically, as did John, but Jack realized before he connected that John didn't solicit your touch, nor did you know what you were doing, so he's cooling his temper. If we ignore them a few minutes, John will be able to pick himself up, and Jack will calm down." Sasha was practically breathing the words into Bella's ear in an attempt at privacy, but shouldn't have bothered, as they were basically still in the same room, with werewolves for that matter, and their hearing was supersonic, almost. Bella nodded.

"Thank you so much Sasha for bringing over the food. It was delicious. Whenever I wake up, which could be tomorrow, or next week —believe me, after I finish a book, it's hard to tell—we'll go over what I like to eat. Only one hard and fast rule: stay out of my office. I mean it. No one touches my office. Just close the door. I'll clean up the last book in a day or two, okay?"

"No problem. I'll put off making the shopping list until we talk, in the meantime, I'll clean around the office, and of course your bedroom while you sleep." Sasha smiled at Bella and then glanced over to where the men had finally seemed to relax a bit again, both on their feet and facing each other, talking quietly. She nodded at Bella.

"Okay, great. 'Night, Sasha." Bella waved in the direction of Jack and John, and went into her room. Closing the door with a sigh and then went through her closet into her bathroom, grabbing a nightshirt on the way.

Bella was just walking back out of the bathroom when Jack walked in.

"Hey." Bella said quietly.

"Hey." Jack replied. "Sorry-"

"Sorry-" Bella interrupted. "No, I'm sorry. I shouldn't have touched him. Sasha explained. "I didn't realize. I didn't—"

"I know baby." Jack walked forward and took her in his arms. "It's okay. I caught myself." Jack squeezed and then released her. "If I

49

promise to just hold you, can I sleep over, or are you going to kick me out tonight?" Jack smiled down at her.

"Jack." Bella searched her feelings, and realized she really didn't want him to go. She just hadn't wanted him to move himself into her house without even asking. She had to put her foot down sometime. But for tonight, whether it was really her own feelings, or the mating magics, or whatever, she wanted him with her. "Stay."

CHAPTER 9

*B*ella started to stretch luxuriously, but stopped when she felt her legs hit something. Or someone. She froze. And then remembered, and smiled, as Jack's hand slid from her breast down her side to her hip, and slip inward. Bella slid her own hand back to Jack's hip, where it rested tight against her, his cock thick and hard against her ass.

Bella felt Jack run his nose behind her ear, making her shiver as she began to purr, and bucking against him as he rubbed against her. Bella lifted her leg, shifted to allow better access for his roving hand, as she moved her own over his hip and down between them.

Suddenly Bella found herself on her back with Jack over her on all fours, gazing down at her, his eyes the amber of his wolf in rage or passion. Bella grinned up at him and reached both hands for his gorgeous cock, that thick, long glorious appendage she could spend hours worshiping. She reached up and bit his bottom lip playfully before starting down his body, but Jack stopped her, grabbing her arms.

"Oh, no, La Mia Bella." Jack took her hands from him, and raised them over her head, and reached down for a nip of his own at her lips.

"I'm hungry." Jack growled. "And you, my love, my Beauty, are on the menu this morning."

∾

JACK STARTED DOWN HER BODY, kissing and nipping his way, and running his hands down her arms until he reached her breasts. Jack loved her breasts. He could spend hours worshipping her breasts. He caressed them lightly with his hands—he'd found early on she did not care for squeezing ("Jack, they are not squeeze balls, okay?")—and licking and teasing around one nipple while Bella writhed beneath him purring and moaning.

Jack finally pulled the nipple into his mouth and worked it with his teeth, tugging and nipping until Bella started grunting. "Jack please" Bella called out. Jack felt her hands in his hair, tugging and pulling, not to make him stop, but to keep him in place.

"What baby. Tell me what you want. Tell me baby." Jack breathed on her breast before pulling the nipple back into his mouth.

"More. Please, Jack. Harder. BITE!" Bella cried out, bucking against him clenching her hands in his hair and scissoring her legs under him.

Jack thought she was a wonderful contradiction. Don't squeeze her breasts, but bite her nipples just short of drawing blood, please, and she went crazy. Jack laved her nipple with attention and then turned to the other and repeated, working the first with his fingers. Bella was nearly wild by this point, bucking and squirming and making those noises that made him crazy.

Jack started kissing, licking and nipping his way down her stomach. Bella obligingly spread her legs wide, lifting her knees and letting them fall back and rocking her hips forward. Jack smiled into her red curls and rubbed his nose just there, where the scent of her arousal was strongest. Bella's hands left his hair and fisted in the sheets beneath her as he parted her lips and licked once, making her hips lift completely from the bed. Bella roared and the sheets ripped. Jack chuckled, and licked again and then settled in. He just learned something else about his kitty cat, his La Mia Bella. She really liked him from behind, like the first time, but she really liked attention to her clit too. And he was going to pay a lot of attention to it now.

Jack flicked, and licked, and sucked at her clit, and then Bella was coming apart in his hands. Her juices flooded his mouth, and her scent flooded his nose, and Jack lapped it up. Bella was wiggling and bucking, roaring and grunting and squealing. Lord, he loved the noises he could make her make.

Then he slipped a finger inside her, and she exploded again, her hips bucked off the bed, her head rolling on the pillow. "JACK!" He worked her with his finger as he flicked her with his tongue. "Jack, please, Jack." Bella pleaded.

Jack reached his left hand up to Bella and took hers, holding it tightly as he slid another finger inside her, increasing the pressure and speed of his flicking tongue. Bella's hips rose and fell with his rhythm, and her whimpers increased, punctuated with a breathy "Jack" with each pump.

When Jack counted the third orgasm, he licked her thoroughly, and smiled up at her as he slid his fingers out of her and licked those too. "Okay baby?"

"Jack, please." Bella breathed, panting, reaching for him. He could see her eyes were glazed. He loved it.

"Please what, La Mia Bella? Tell me what you want baby?" He asked as he slowly stalked back up her body.

"I want you, Jack, now, deep inside me. Please Jack." Jack had reached her mouth and took her in a deep kiss. He knew she would taste herself on him. Jack shuddered. He wanted inside her too. He wanted to face her, watch her eyes as he slid deep, but he was too tall for true missionary with someone her size.

Jack sat up and pulled Bella with him, onto his lap. "Bella?" Jack held her poised over him with a question. Bella put her hands on his shoulders and wrapped her legs around his waist, and smiled. Jack grinned, and plunged her down on him.

BELLA THREW her head back and roared. God, what a feeling. He filled her so completely. Jack shuddered around her and she felt his hands tightened on her waist. Bella raised her head and met his eyes. Then she smiled and just rode him.

"Oh God." Jack said resting is forehead on hers. "You are so tight. I'm not hurting you?"

"Oh, no baby. You feel incredible. Don't stop. Don't you dare stop." Bella ground out as she raised her knees higher against his waist, taking him deeper, bracing her hands on his shoulders as she met him thrust for thrust.

Bella felt every inch of him stretching her. This position was wonderful, almost as good as her favorite "wolf style" as he called it. It pushed all her buttons, and they could look into each others eyes, which was wonderful in missionary, but doesn't work when your height difference is so great, like theirs. She couldn't figure out how he was thrusting so strongly from a seated position like that. The man had some muscles! And then Bella stopped thinking, and could only feel.

JACK COULD TELL when Bella started to lose it, she became almost as slippery as an eel, wiggling and squirming in his arms, it was all he could do to keep his hands on her. The noises he loved were back, and it was a good thing, because he couldn't hold it for much longer. A few more thrusts and he'd be gone himself.

"Jack!" Bella called, thrashing in his arms.

"Go, baby, I'm right behind you." Jack told her, holding her close. And then he was there, two thrusts, and he did follow her, Bella roared and he howled, and they both collapsed on the bed.

BELLA GIGGLED. "Well, hell, I thought I said I wasn't going to do that." She rubbed a lazy hand along his flank and Jack chuckled. "At least we know we work well together in bed. We need to find time to get to know each other so we can figure out if we work elsewhere, you think?"

"Oh, kitty cat love, we definitely work here. And we'll make everything else fit together too, you'll see." Bella looked up at him as he curled over her, his hand curled around her waist. "But I suppose we better get cleaned up for the day."

"Yep. We got things to do, lover-wolf." Bella reached up and kissed his nose.

CHAPTER 10

*B*ella walked out after her bath dressed in another pair of jeans and tank top. Jack's shower had gone much faster, and boy, had she enjoyed watching that.

"Prima Bella! I have breakfast ready for you." Sasha called from her left, indicating she should have a seat at the table to her right. Jack was already seated there, eating his breakfast.

"Mmm. Okay, thanks Sasha. I don't usually eat breakfast." Bella sniffed, and followed the plate to the table and sat next to Jack—who was seated at the head of the table. What the?—and picked up the fork. Sean was across from her, not eating, but talking to Jack.

"Good Morning, Prima Bella." Sean said.

"Mmm mmning." Bella responded, enjoying her eggs and bacon and potatoes. Bella finished chewing. "Sorry Sean. Good morning. Sasha, now I know I didn't have any of this in the fridge. This is wonderful."

"Thank you Prima Bella. I got it from Jack's house so I'd have something to make for your breakfast." Bella paused with a forkful halfway to her mouth, looking from Sasha to Sean.

"Okay folks. Why does he get to be just 'Jack' but I'm stuck with

56

'Prima' Bella? Huh? Can we please drop the titles? I'm just Bella, I'm just me. Okay?" Bella ignored Jack's grin at her as she stuffed the forkful in her mouth defiantly.

"Yes ma'am." Sean said, avoiding her eyes, doing his usual slump when around her, which meant he was practically lying on the table because Bella was leaned over the table enjoying her breakfast.

"And stop that slump thingie." Bella waved her fork at Sean between bites.

Sasha smiled and turned her back on them while she did mysterious kitcheny things. Bella shook her head. She looked at Jack, who was trying to hide his grin behind his coffee cup. Wait, coffee cup? She didn't own any coffee cups, or coffee, or coffee makers.

"They aren't going to obey me, are they?" She asked him.

"As soon as you give an order that makes sense, they will, La Mia Bella. I promise." Jack smiled at her.

"Oy. Ya'll are makin' me crazy!" Bella pushed back her chair and picked up her plate, and Jack's, taking them into the kitchen to Sasha.

"Oh, Pri—I mean, Bella, I could have gotten those." Sasha said, taking the plates from Bella.

"I can clear a table, Sash. I may not like cooking or cleaning, but I can at the very least clear a table. Hey, I can tell you about the foods I like now, if you have a moment?"

"HOW ARE things going over there, Sean?" Jack asked, watching Bella out of the corner of his eyes. He wondered if other mated men felt this way about their women. He couldn't stand to be away from her for even a moment. It almost killed him to leave her in her bath.

"Everything is very peaceful, Jack. As you can probably imagine, no one really misses Brigit. And everyone was very impressed with Pri—with Bella's actions yesterday." Sean looked over at the kitchen himself.

"And Declan?" Jack asked, bringing Sean's attention back to him.

"Ah, yes. Declan. I guess I should have said no one but Declan misses Brigit. But even Declan acknowledges she crossed the line yesterday. Several lines. He'll be okay. I think he'll be over shortly."

"Good. Any news of the rogues?" Jack looked back at the kitchen, watching Bella interacting with his weakest wolf. Sasha would never be dominant, but she was happiest serving. Jack was very happy Bella had agreed to having her work here.

"Nothing yet, but John is working with a couple of his boys, exploring the town to see what they can sniff out." Jack heard something in Sean's voice and looked over at him. Sean shrugged. "I'm happy for you, Jack. She's good for you."

Jack took a deep breath, sniffing the air. "But are we good for her?" He shook his head. "Tell them to be careful, we don't know what we are dealing with.

"You got it, Primo." Sean hesitated and then went on, "if it makes you feel better, she looks at you the same way."

BELLA LAUGHED. "Oh, Sasha, you are priceless. That is wonderful. You'll let me know if there's anything else you need?"

"Of course, Bella, thanks. The room is very comfortable. Declan is bringing me a television in a few minutes. Then I think the room will be perfect." Sasha was washing dishes as she spoke, and wiping down the counters.

"I'm so sorry there wasn't a television in the room, I never thought of that. Well, if you think of anything else, just let me know. I need to go clean up my office from the last book." Bella was turning toward the family room when she saw the wolf she remembered as Declan at the back door. Bella rushed to open it for him since his arms were full of TV. "Hello, Declan. Do you know where that's going?" Bella smiled at him. She thought he might not be too happy with her after what had happened with Brigit yesterday, but Declan smiled warmly back at her.

"Hello Prima Bella. It's for Sasha, but I don't know where her bedroom is." He had really clear blue eyes, pretty really, for a man, and black hair. He wasn't overly tall for a man, only a few inches taller than Bella.

The doorbell rang before Bella could respond, and Sasha was there, opening the door. "Ah, crap on toast." Bella said, slumping on the back of the sofa. "Kayla."

"Kayla." Declan breathed the name next to her, and Bella looked at him, surprised to see him scenting the air, almost going on point. "Who is Kayla?"

"Down, boy. She's human, she doesn't know about us, this, any of it." Bella straightened up and went to greet her best friend.

"Kayla! What are you doing here?" Bella called, meeting Kayla and Sasha in the entry hall, between the formal dining room on her left, the side of the house with the kitchen, garage, and her bedroom suite, and the formal living room on her right, the side of the house with the guest rooms and her office. The family room was directly behind her.

"Bella, since when do I need a reason to come see my best friend. Who are all these people?" Bella realized Jack was right behind her a moment before his hand landed on the back of her waist, and she sensed the other two wolves, Sean and Declan, behind them on their left and right, respectively. Bella bounced her head off Jack's arm once, and then stood straight. Nothing for it then. Time to face the music. Jack squeezed her waist, and leaned down, kissing her temple.

"Kayla. Of course, please come in. You've met Sasha, she's moved in to take care of the house, and me. You've always said I need a keeper. Well, now I have one." Bella smiled at Sasha, who beamed back, and then turned to Kayla, who looked a bit stunned.

"Hello, Kayla. A pleasure. Shall I get everyone some iced tea?" Sasha bobbed her head quickly at everyone, and then moved quickly to the kitchen.

When Bella turned, she saw Sean was frowning at her. Oops, she took the introductions out of order, and introduced the lowest ranking wolf first. Oh well, they could sue her. She's still trying to figure out what to say about Jack. She turned her eyes up to Jack's, and saw his eyes shifting from amber back to green, and a tick starting in his jaw. She mouthed sorry at him and then begged for help with her eyes. He just looked at her.

"Kayla, this is Jack. He's—he's my, um, he's my—" Bella stuttered.

"Her fiancé. Hello Kayla." Jack finally took pity on her.

"Fiancé? Since when? Bella?" Bella looked a little stunned herself, so she wasn't really answering.

"That's what I'd like to know. You might try asking, buddy." Bella stalked away from Jack, pulling Kayla to the couch. Jack looked stunned for a moment and then decided to skip over that for a moment.

"Well, Kayla," Jack steered everyone towards the sofa unit in the family room and gestured everyone to seats. "I'm tipping my hand a bit, but I'm desperately hopeful that when I ask, she'll consent." Jack settled with Bella in one corner of the oversized leather L-shaped sofa unit, pulling her close to him. Kayla settled at the opposite end of the same side, with Sean and Declan together on the shorter side.

"And these," Bella cleared her throat, "these are Jack's" Bella looked up at Jack, "friends. Sean and Declan. Everyone, this is my best friend and editor, Kayla Raymond." Bella settled back against Jack, feeling as though she'd run a mile. Bella nudged Jack and indicated Declan, making sure he noticed what she was, that he hadn't taken his eyes off Kayla since Sasha had opened the front door.

"Interesting" Jack breathed into Bella's hair where he was nuzzling her absentmindedly.

"Mmhmm." Bella responded. "So, Kayla. What can I do for you today? Problem with the book already?" Sasha walked in with a tray and a pitcher of iced tea and five glasses, with sugar and lemon slices. Everything looked so fancy. Where did all of that come from?

"No problems, Bells. Just the opposite. NYT three with a bullet! This one is going to the top, I guarantee it!" Kayla was perched on the edge of the seat in her earnestness. She had shoulder length blond hair and bright blue eyes set in a round face with a pert little nose that had always driven Bella crazy. She made Bella feel like an Amazon. A fat

Amazon with a beak nose. It always amazed Bella that they'd become such good friends anyway.

"You say that every time, Kayls." Bella decided that if Jack wanted to try to distract her with his nose everywhere, she'd play with his knee.

"What does that mean?" Jack asked, tugging on Bella's hair. Bella slapped at his hand and shifted a little away from him.

"Her last book is number three on the New York Times Bestsellers list, and rising. And this time it's going to happen, Bells, I know it! I also wanted to let you know I was up all night reading this latest, and it was great, as usual. You just keep getting better." Kayla seemed to remember the other two men in the room and turned to them. "Have you read any of Bella's books?"

Declan jumped up. "No, I should go get them?" He made as though to run off to find the books and Bella laughed.

"No, Declan. Relax, no need to run off. If you want to read them, I have copies in my office you can borrow." Bella waved him back into his seat.

"Now Bella that is no way to raise your sales. Royalties, you know." Kayla laughed.

"You would think you were my agent, Kayla. And really, if one person's sales are going to make or break me, I've got more problems to worry about."

At that point Kayla's phone rang in her cavernous bag, and she dug her ever present iPhone out. Bella thought she heard Jack mutter something like "Saved by the bell." Kayla spoke for a few minutes and then hung up, dialed again, spoke a minute or two more, and hung up again.

"Gotta go. And you are now at Number two Bells. Celebrate! I'll call you when they have your completion check ready, we'll have our party dinner, 'k? 'k. Love ya. 'Bye all!" And with that, Kayla was swooping out the door, already dialing her phone again.

Bella sat back and heaved a deep sigh. "She is so exhausting."

"She is so beautiful." Declan sighed. Everyone looked at him. "What?" He said.

"You hurt her, I kill you. Understand?" Bella had risen, and was leaning over him. Declan gulped, and nodded his head. "Good. I'm going to clean my office. Feel free to talk amongst yourselves, but don't say anything too exciting without me." Bella blew a kiss to Jack and walked away to her office.

CHAPTER 11

"So what's going on?" Bella asked as she came into the family room. She looked around. It was much more crowded than it was an hour before when she'd gone into her office. Jack, Sean and Declan had been joined by John, Turner and two other wolves. Bella heard voices and noticed Sasha had been joined by that female wolf Kathy she'd noticed stroking her so intimately while Sasha was in wolf form. Bella walked over to join Jack and his arm came around her automatically, making her smile. She pulled on his shirt to bring him down to her, he thought for a kiss, which she gave him briefly and then turned his head to breath in his ear, "check out Kathy over there with Sasha. I meant to talk to you about those two."

"Where is Kathy, La Mia Bella?" Jack looked around at the kitchen. "That's not Kathy, baby. That's Kelly. Kathy is married to Matt. What about Kelly and Sasha?" Jack looked down at Bella with a smile.

"Not now, I'll tell you later, this looks important. Catch me up." Jack kissed her on the nose.

"Bella, you remember John? Turner, Nate and Dean were helping him look into our rogue situation and they believe they've found something. They were just starting to tell me about it." Jack glanced

63

back at the kitchen with a frown before turning with Bella back to the waiting men in her family room.

"Hello, Prima Bella." John nodded. Bella decided it was really hard being dominate to every wolf in the room but Jack, when they were all so much taller than her. All of the men finally just decided to kneel on the floor until she and Jack settled on the short side of the sectional sofa. Sean, Declan and John sat on the long side, and Turner and the wolves that must be Nate and Dean remained where they were on the floor. The men on the sofa still had to slouch a bit uncomfortably, making Bella sigh. She looked at Jack.

"Really?" Bella shifted up on the arm of the sofa, which allowed the men to straighten, but then she was almost even with Jack, making him stretch his neck a bit. Bella giggled. "You realize this is insane, right?" Jack just shook his head and moved to stand behind her, solving the problem once and for all. Bella sighed and settled against him happily.

"Right." John looked away to hide a half-smile. "We were coming back here, and about a mile east of here caught the scent of wolf. There's an apartment complex, run down and abandoned looking, absolutely saturated in the scent. We counted six wolves, all females. I left Henry and Danny keeping an eye on it."

"Well let's go! There's eight of us right here, you said there are two more at the complex, and only six of them." Bella jumped up, ready to have some answers.

"You won't be going, La Mia Bella love." Jack said quietly. Bella slowly crossed her arms and cocked her head at him.

"Can I talk to you for a moment in my office, Jack?" Bella bit out and then stalked away, allowing him to follow or not.

Jack walked into the office and Bella closed the door behind him very quietly. "Number one, I could have slammed that, but I didn't. Remember that. It's important. Number two, don't ever, do not ever tell me what I will or will not do. Got it?" Bella vibrated with rage. Jack stalked toward her, and she held up her hand at him. "No, you don't get to stalk toward me like that. Your eyes are not going to go all amber on me, you will not intimidate me, and you will not seduce me. This is too important."

"Damn right it's important. This is about your safety. Damnit Bella! And I am the Primo here. I will give the orders." Jack stopped about a foot away from her, and Bella felt him fighting to control his emotions.

"You are the Primo for your wolves, Jack. You are not my Primo. Get that straight right now. I might be your lover, that's not set in stone yet, I will be your friend, I am apparently your partner in the pack, but I do not answer to you." Bella emphasized each point with her finger in his chest and then placed her palm against him, and finally gave in and rested her forehead against his chest as well. "I'll make you a deal, Jack." Bella looked up at him. "You don't ever order me to do something I won't do, and I won't ever tell you no in front of them." Bella fisted her left hand at his waist, while her right hand kneaded his chest over his heart. "Work with me Jack, please?"

"Bella, damnit." Jack growled and crushed her to him. "Don't ask me to put you in danger." Jacks hands roamed over her hungrily as his body responded to having her in his arms.

"You are telling me that you and eight of your wolves aren't enough to protect me from six measly rogue females? And Jack, not to brag, but my tiger is a match for any two of your wolves. Hell, might be a match for you. I shift faster and smoother than any of you. Are any of your wolves bigger than you in wolf form?"

"No." Jack bit off.

"Then explain to me-"

"Damnit Bella." Jack interrupted.

"You can't keep saying that. Do we have a deal, or are we going to go through this every time something comes up?" Bella tried to hold Jack when he pulled away.

Jack stalked away and ran his hands through his hair. Then he swooped back and swung her up in his arms until her eyes were at his level. Bella rested her hands on his shoulders. "If you get hurt, La Mia Bella, I swear I'll—"

"You'll what, lover-wolf?" Bella laughed, rubbing her nose against his.

"I'll—I'll make you regret it, woman, that's what." Jack crushed her to him and practically ate her mouth in a deep kiss that took her breath away.

"Back at you, lover-wolf, right back at you." Bella gasped as soon as she had half a breath.

BELLA FOLLOWED Jack back into the family room and Jack said a terse, "let's go" to his wolves. Bella had slipped her driver's license into her pocket while they were in the office, and now she handed her car keys to Jack. It took a few minutes far Jack to issue last minute orders to his wolves and then they headed out, Jack and Bella in her Jetta, the other wolves in two SUV's.

Jack was quiet on the short drive and Bella left him to his thoughts. She had a few of her own. They said these were all females. She had some ideas about that. The rogues had come to her, right?

"Hey Jack?" She looked over at him. "When did you guys move in?"

"Hmm?" Jack glanced over at her. "Oh, um, the day before I came to see you, why?"

"Just thinking." Bella was thinking. What if the rogues didn't know about Jack and his pack yet? What if they were investigating Bella?

"I'm sure I'm going to regret this, but what's going through that fertile mind of yours?" Jack prodded.

"Just this. And watch it buddy, I hold the keys to your pleasure over here, and don't you forget it." Jack growled and reached over to tickle her ear. "I don't think the rogues knew about you-all yet. They were investigating me. Either to ask me for help—or for the same reason you were coming to me. Also," Bella continued, speaking as the thoughts came to her, "we fought two males and a female. Why bring a female to a fight? And there are six females at this location, right?"

"Yes. And correct me if I'm wrong, but for some crazy reason, I'm taking a female to a fight."

"You are taking the Primo's mate to a fight, and we aren't intending a fight, not with six defenseless females, unless you aren't the man I thought you were. No, you aren't yet thinking along the same lines I am. What if those two males were the only males in their little pack?"

"Shit." Jack swore.

"Yeah." Bella looked out the window at the sad looking apartment building they pulled up to. There was a realtor's for sale sign out, but the overgrown vegetation and rundown building made it apparent no one had been there for some time. "Hey, Jack? Your whole pack is living at your house next door to me right now, right?"

"Yeah, and it's getting a little tense. Everyone's found jobs just about, but I'm not sure what to do about housing." Jack rubbed his hands over his face tiredly. Bella reached over to hold his hand.

"What about this place? I think it could be fixed up really nice. There's what, at least a dozen apartments here. And you said several of your wolves are mated, so they'd be doubled up. What do you think? And it's not too far from our places." Bella looked around at the quiet neighborhood. The rundown apartment building seemed to be the seediest part; everything else was much better kept.

"I couldn't buy it right now; all of my capital went into the house and surrounding land. It would take me some time to liquidate enough to be able to purchase the building and do the renovations necessary."

"Let me make a call. My accountant has been harassing me about a tax shelter or something. Real Estate is supposed to be good for that sort of thing, right? Give me a minute." Bella reached for a phone that wasn't there and swore.

"Problem?" Jack grinned at her, holding out his phone. "But I couldn't let you—"

"Oh be quiet. They could pay rent or something." Bella called her accountant—after a moment to work on remembering his number—and set him to work, giving him the name and number on the sign. "Okay, I've got another idea, let's go." Bella handed his phone back and got out of the car, joining the wolves waiting on the sidewalk outside of the building.

Jack pulled Bella back a bit. "Maybe you should run this idea past me first, La Mia Bella. Your ideas make me a little nervous."

"Relax Jack. I just think that as a fellow woman, I should be the one to approach them. You are all going to be very intimidating to six very scared, very alone women." Bella did not try to keep her words from reaching the other wolves as Jack had, and Jack growled at her.

"No! Bella—"

"Jack, we've been over this. You will be right here, all of you. Would you trust me please?" Bella reached up and touched her nose to his and then kissed him lightly. "Jack, I'd like to help these women, not hurt them, not be forced to hurt them. If we go barreling in there, that's what will happen. Unless they are completely ignorant, they know we are here, and have since the boys found them. They are scared, don't you smell that? Fear and hunger and illness. We need to help them."

"Bella," Jack growled and shook his head and then lead her back to the others. "All right. We'll do it Bella's way. But we stay close—" Bella made a noise, "—close enough in case she needs assistance. I'm assuming no one else has shown up?" Jack looked at the two wolves that had been watching the building. Apparently getting a negative, Jack sighed. "Okay. Then let's get in there, because Bella is right, I smell illness and hunger, and I want to get them help before any of us rest or eat tonight. Got it?" Everyone nodded, and looked at Bella.

Bella took a deep breath, and headed to the entry to the courtyard. The building was a standard U-shaped apartment building, with eight apartments on each side, four upstairs and four down, with a pool in the courtyard and carports for parking in the back. Bella's looking around served both to assess the property and potential improvements, and get a feel for any possible danger.

Bella could smell that all the apartments were empty except one near the middle on her left, upstairs, so she skirted the pool on that side and looked up.

"Hello!" She called out.

"Yeah, we see you. What do you want?" A weak voice cracked above her, and Bella looked up to see a young girl, about eighteen, with short black hair and vivid blue eyes leaning on the railing above her. She looked emaciated. Bella almost cried.

"My name is Bella. I want to help you and your friends. What's your name?" Bella kept her stance loose and friendly, and her voice quiet.

"We don't want your help. You tell those men they are close enough. Don't let them come any closer!" The girl sounded almost panicked, and Bella looked back to see Jack and Sean inching closer. Bella sighed and waved them back. Jack and Sean froze where they were, but Jack made it clear with a look he wasn't backing up. The other wolves ranged behind them.

"They won't come any closer, and I promise you, they won't hurt you or your friends. Please, let us help you." God, if this young girl was the dominant, the spokesperson, what did the rest of them look like?

Suddenly the girl sat hard on the ground, and let her legs dangle through the iron railings. "It doesn't matter anyway. They didn't come back. It's been more than a day, and they aren't coming back." She sounded so defeated. Bella eased a few feet closer. There was a table placed below the walkway where she sat.

"Who didn't come back? And you never told me your name; I'd like to have something to call you..." Bella eased slightly closer.

"Gordon and Weldon and Mitsy. They went to talk to the local Were, and they didn't come back. That was you, I guess? Did you kill them?" The girl didn't sound accusing, just sad.

"Jack, send someone for some food and supplies, please." Bella tossed over her shoulder, and turned back, making it an order she assumed (hoped) would be followed as she inched one last bit closer to the table. Now she was within leaping distance of the table, which put her within jumping distance of the walkway above. Bella heard Jack's whispered relay of her order and smiled to herself. So he was learning, she thought.

"They attacked me in my home. I had no choice, you understand that, right? It was self defense. If they had come to me, we could have talked, but they broke into my home and attacked." The girl was already nodding.

"Yeah, I figured that was their plan. Gordon kept saying he was going for help, but I've been around him too long to fall for that. If he could have enslaved you like the rest of us, he would have done that, and if you were too strong, he'd have killed you." Bella heard a growl from behind her, which made the girl jump. Bella decided to make her move while the girl was distracted by Jack.

Bella leaped on the table and jumped up, grabbing the bottom of the walkway and swinging her legs up, while pulling herself up the rails until she could climb over them and land next to the girl on the walkway. Bella sat next to her and folded her hands calmly in her lap. It was over in seconds, and the girl was looking at her with her mouth hanging open and Jack was yelling at her from below.

"Jack, just stay put, I'm fine." She waved him back and turned to the girl. "I'm talking to my new friend. Now, what is your name, friend?"

"Alex." The girl was staring back and forth from Bella to Jack. "Who is that?" She pointed to Jack.

"Hello Alex, nice to meet you. Right now? He's a pain in my backside, but usually, he's Jack, my mate. It's kind of a new thing for us. But don't worry about him right now. He's sent someone to get some food for you and your friends. I'm thinking it's been a little while since you ate?" Bella slowly reached her hand out and placed it on Alex' shoulder. Alex flinched, but relaxed a little when she realized Bella wasn't going to hit her.

"We ran out of food a couple of hours after Gordon and the others left. And Mary—" Alex broke off and looked at the apartment door behind her.

"Mary what Alex?" Bella asked calmly.

"Mary's real bad hurt. Gordon had used her last, and Mary was—" Alex fought back a sob. "Mary hadn't really recovered from the last time, so she kind of fought him." Bella heard Jack growl below them, and Bella almost joined him, but she had to stay calm, had to get into that apartment. "And I think Charlie and Traci are pregnant, and they're sick all the time, and—" this time the sob broke through, and Bella took the girl into her arms.

"How old are they Alex? Mary and Charlie and Traci and the others?"

"I think Mary is about twenty-six or something. She's like the oldest, but she's real weak, Gordon called her a submissive I think? Traci is like fourteen. Charlie is I think twelve. I think Lucy is twenty and Sam is about twenty-three. They all look to up me though. Gordon called me the dominant, after Mitsy. Mitsy was practically a man, she was so strong." Alex was sniffing by this point, trying to regain her composure.

"Let us help you Alex, please? I promise you, no one will hurt you. See Jack down there? He's the Primo of the pack, and I told you he's my mate? That makes me the Prima. That means if I say so, they have to obey. And I say no one will hurt you." Alex started shaking when Bella started talking about Jack and Primo's.

"No! No, no, no. Gordon told us all about it. We are all unmated, we belong to the Primo, and he can use us all he wants. We don't want to be used any more, please." Alex was grabbing Bella's arms.

"Alex, listen to me. No one will touch you, if you don't want to be touched. Not the Primo, not anyone. Do you hear me? No one. I promise you. Alex, look in my eyes, I promise you." Bella waited.

"But Gordon said."

"Alex." Jack called from below them. Alex and Bella looked down at him. "Gordon told you the truth—as he saw it. Unmated females fall under the protection of the Pack Primo. Because of that, the Primo has the right to certain—privileges—if he enforces that. And there are Primo's out there that will enforce that. I am not one of them. The reverse of that is, unless the females can find someone else in the pack, they can enforce the same rule, force the attentions of the Primo.

But as Bella has said, our word is law, and if any of you do not wish to be touched, you will not be touched. And no one under the age of consent is ever touched." Jack nodded at Alex and took a single step back, indicating he was turning the situation back over to Bella. His statements gave Bella something to think about—but another time.

"Alex?" Bella asked.

"I have to talk to the others. Will you wait?" Alex stood. Bella looked down and realized the food had arrived.

"Of course, but why don't you take the food in with you? You can eat, and we will wait out here." Bella gestured, and Jack and Sean came forward, which caused Alex to skitter back toward the door, but she didn't go through it. Sean stepped up onto the table and handed the bags of food up to Bella, who handed them over to Alex. Alex took the food and dashed inside.

"Bella, I wish you would come back down here." Jack called up. Bella smiled down at him.

"I'm fine up here, big guy, and I don't think it will be long. They had to be listening, and that food will go fast. They will follow Alex' lead and I think we had her convinced of our sincerity. It helps that we were honest." Bella watched Jack step up onto the table and listened to it groan under his weight. "Don't do that, it won't hold you, I was worried about it holding Sean!" But Jack ignored her.

Jack reached up for her hand. "You are making me very nervous to be so far away from me, and near to unknown wolves, my love." Jack tickled her palm and made faces at her.

"Silly lover-wolf. I'm just fine." Bella made faces back at him, and played at grabbing his fingers. "Now get down from there before you break your neck." She blew a kiss at him, and shooed him down. Jack reluctantly got down about the time Alex came back out.

"Okay, everyone agreed to go with you. But you promised. No one gets hurt, right?" Alex looked from Bella to Jack uncertainly.

"I promise, Alex. We will take very good care of all of you. Now I'm going to need help getting all of you down, unless all of you can walk?" Bella got the feeling that such was not the case.

"Uh, no. Mary can't walk. Everyone else can, but not Mary. We can't, uh, we can't get her free." Alex wrung her hands. Jack growled and Alex jumped.

"Relax Alex. Jack gets very upset when he hears of someone being hurt. Jack is going to take a few deep breaths and relax, right Jack?" Bella gave him a meaningful look. "Okay Alex and then I'm definitely going to need a few of my friends to come up with us, okay?"

"Uh, okay." Alex was trying very hard to be brave.

"Okay, Jack, bring 'em up." Bella stood and started into the apartment, but before she'd taken two steps, Sean was on one side of the door, and Declan was on the other.

"Oh, wow." Alex jumped a foot.

"Yeah, they move pretty fast. Alex, this is Sean, Jack's Secundo, and Declan, Jack's Terzo." Alex led them inside as Bella felt Jack coming up behind her with John in tow.

"Alex, John is our medic. Can you take him to Mary please?" Jack gestured John to go ahead. Alex looked nervous, but nodded, and led John into a room off the main room they stood in. Huddled on the floor before them were three young women, about twelve, fourteen, and twenty. Bella approached them with Jack close behind.

"Hello. I'm Bella. This is Jack. What are your names?" Bella kept her voice pitched low and calm, as the young women were clearly terrified. The youngest, Traci, raised her chin defiantly.

"I'm Traci." She indicated the oldest girl next to her, "this is Lucy, and that's Charlie."

"Hello ladies." Jack said, smiling kindly. "I'd like you all to follow Sean and Declan, here, downstairs to one of the vehicles, okay? I don't want you to worry, no one will leave until we are all together, but let's get started getting down there, okay?" Jack nodded at Sean and Declan, who looked uncertain about leaving us alone in the apartment with only John but Jack was insistent.

Once the five of them left, we continued into the room with the others. The sight that met us turned Bella's stomach. "Oh." Bella stopped, and Jack gripped her elbow to support her, growling his own displeasure. Mary was nearly catatonic with pain and fatigue, and Alex and the final girl were sobbing. John was working at the bindings. Alex rushed to Bella.

"Gordon was so angry with Mary, because she wouldn't—she

didn't—because she was still hurt from last time. She couldn't—she just couldn't." Alex sobbed in Bella's arms. Alex looked up at Jack imploringly. "I begged him to take me instead, and he just laughed and said that would be no fun." Bella choked and Jack had started an almost constant growling. When John looked up, there was a look in his eyes Bella hoped never to see directed at her.

"Its okay, Alex. We'll take care of her now. I want you and, this is Sam right? I want you and Sam to go downstairs. You met Sean and Declan outside. They took the others downstairs already, you two go outside and meet them, and we will be right out with her, okay? I don't want you to worry about anything else. We're here now. Jack and I will take care of everything now sweetie." Bella pulled Sam up and pushed both girls out towards the front door, where she saw Declan coming in. She gestured for him to take the girls outside with him and he nodded. When she turned back to the pallet on the floor, Jack was kneeling next to John, helping him free Mary. Bella went to them and knelt on the other side, waving her hands over them.

"Oh God Jack. What did he do to them?"

"I don't know baby, but I wish he was still here so I could kill him again." Jack was coldly furious. He got the final chain free, and reached for the girl on the pallet, but John stayed his hand.

"No, Primo. She is mine." John gently gathered her into his arms and rose. "If you had not already killed him, I would hunt him for this and kill him twice." John carried her out of the apartment and down the stairs to the waiting SUV's.

"Hey Sasha, we are on the way back now with the girls we found." Bella answered Jack's phone because he was a little over-focused on driving, his eyes still amber in rage.

"You can't take them to Jack's house." Sasha whispered.

"What do you mean? Why not? Why are you whispering, Sasha?" Something in Bella's voice caught Jack's attention.

"Kelly called me all excited about them. Don't let her around them if they are weak, Prima, I'm begging you. I can't say more." Sasha suddenly hung up and Bella looked at Jack's phone in her hand, something in her stomach twisting.

"Did you know Kelly is a lesbian, Jack?" Bella asked, trying to keep her voice unaffected.

"What? Of course not. Werewolves are not gay or lesbian. And I have—" Jack cleared his throat "—personal knowledge that she is not. What would make you say something like that?"

"Then she is bi-sexual. And you most definitely have at least two gay wolves in your pack alone—Nate and Dean—Jeez Jack, I've been in the pack two days, and I've seen this. Sasha is Kelly's lover, and Nate and Dean are lovers.

"But we have bigger issues than your blinders—Sasha is afraid of Kelly, and she just said Kelly is excited about the new girls, and begged me not to bring them to your house, not to let Kelly anywhere around any of them if they are weak. So change in plans. It looks like we are going to my house. Call your wolves." Bella handed the phone to Jack and looked away from his astonished face and out the side window, trying to think fast how best to protect Sasha. When she saw Jack disconnect his phone for the final time as they pulled into her driveway, she turned back to him.

"One more request. No wolves allowed into my house without my express permission. For any reason. This is to protect Sasha, until we can figure out what is going on." Jack just nodded as they got out. Bella thought he looked sick.

CHAPTER 12

*J*ack held the door leading from the garage into the kitchen for Bella and surprised Kelly and Sasha in a tense embrace, although embrace seemed the wrong description. Sasha clearly had tears in her eyes, and Kelly was snarling in her face, her hands wrapped tightly around Sasha's arms, looming over her at the sink, pressing her into the counter until Sasha was bent almost double into it. Kelly jumped when the door opened, and looked up at Jack and Bella, clearly struggling to form her features into something resembling politeness. Sasha used the distraction to back away into the breakfast area and quickly wiped her hands over her eyes to clear the tears.

"Sasha, open the front door so they can take the wounded to the back rooms. Kelly, return home, you don't belong here. There are to be no wolves here without your Prima's permission." Jack barked his orders as he herded everyone to the front door.

"But Primo—" Kelly argued as Sasha moved quickly to the front door to comply.

"Do not argue with me." Jack growled, walking directly behind Kelly until she walked out the front door as soon as Sasha opened it, right before John carried Mary in, leading the others. "Sean, get the supplies John will need to treat Mary and the others, and while you are over there, pass the word that no wolves are allowed over here without the Prima's direct permission. For now, Sasha and I will assist John until you return." Sean looked a little surprised at this but John was already gone, having followed Sasha to the first available guest bedroom next to Bella's office. "For now, all of the new wolves will remain here." Jack continued.

"Yes Primo." Sean responded as he and all of the other wolves returned to the SUV's to return to Jack's.

Jack closed the door and sighed before turning to Bella. "Do you want to tell me why I did that, and what we walked into just now with Kelly and Sasha?" Jack was almost vibrating with suppressed rage, and his eyes were wolf-amber.

"You did that to protect your weakest, and unless I'm very mistaken, your favorite, wolf. And I don't know what we walked into in there, but we need to find out." Bella took a deep breath. She was about to ask questions she really didn't want to hear the answers to, but thought they might help get them in the right direction. "You implied you have had sex with Kelly, am I correct in understanding that?"

"Yes." Jack bit out.

"Have you had sex with Sasha?" Bella closed her eyes, because she really didn't want to have this conversation. It was one thing to understand they had both had previous partners, but to discuss them, and especially to discuss partners they both had to still know and live with was just—icky.

"Of course—" Jack stopped himself and walked over to Bella, taking her into his arms. "I'm sorry baby; this isn't easy for you, is it?" Bella shook her head against his chest and then pushed away from him, and looked up at him. His eyes were the gorgeous sea foam green she was rapidly falling for.

"You were saying, Jack?" Bella's voice was husky from emotion.

"I started to say of course, but no, we haven't had intercourse. A few—a very few I might add—times we exchanged oral sex, but she would always make some excuse to avoid intercourse. It never occurred to me." Jack shook his head at Bella. "I can't believe I didn't realize. Cindy, my fourth unmated female, rarely came to me; she always seems to spend time with Scott I think. Kelly would occasionally come to me, but not lately. Brigit was always badgering me. Thank you for taking care of that, by the way." Bella shuddered.

"Glad she's gone but not happy about my part in it. And I think if you hadn't been badgered so much—" Bella almost snarled it, "—by Brigit, you might have noticed more about Sasha at least. The rest, well, maybe not."

Jack pulled Bella back to him again, and ignored her half-hearted protests. He just needed to feel her in his arms, smell her, and assure himself she was still his. Holding her tightly against him, he leaned down and ran his nose through her hair, his hands running down her back to her delicious ass. A knock at the door interrupted before he could get too carried away.

"Saved by the knock." Bella chuckled, moving away from him and opening the door, ignoring his growl of protest and gesturing Sean inside with the two large duffel bags he held. "Come on Sean, lets see to these kids we've brought home with us."

"Yes ma'am" Sean looked uncertainly between Bella and Jack and then followed her down the hall.

JACK DIDN'T KNOW what to think. He'd never thought of himself as homophobic, but then he'd never thought about homosexuality at all before. It just wasn't a part of their world. Werewolves are born, not made like in the horror stories, and are all about procreation. He just didn't think homosexual wolves, of either gender, would last long— which he supposed could be why they were so secretive about it.

Of course their pack was small because they couldn't have children, and that has been his fault. Without a Prima, there was no one to control the females shifting during pregnancy, and he didn't know if his accidental mating to a non-Were was going to make matters worse or not. Would Bella be able to channel the pack magic to control the shifts of the gestating females? Jack shook his head and followed after Sean and Bella. It was a worry for another day.

~

BELLA WALKED into the first bedroom and found the five ambulatory wolves huddled in the far corner watching John working over Mary on the bed. Sean moved around Bella and placed the bags next to John and began whispering to him. Bella was shocked by a growl from John. Jack was suddenly behind her and then moving into the room.

"Sean, I need you over here." Jack called. "John, do you need assistance?" Bella watched John take a few deep breaths and then look up at his Primo.

"Perhaps our Prima would agree to assist me; I think I could stand that. I'm sorry, Primo, I don't think I could—" John trailed off, shaking his head at Sean, bowing to both of his leaders.

"No problem, John, do what is necessary. Bella, please?" Jack gestured Bella toward the bed and Bella looked up at him in panic.

"I don't know the first thing about first aid or—" Bella started.

"Just do whatever John instructs you to do. It will be okay." Jack pushed her with his eyes and there was a force behind his voice she'd heard before, but never to her. It didn't work on her, not the way it did on his wolves, but she went to John's side.

"What do you need, John?" Bella kept her voice low and calm, understanding that both the injured wolf and the upset one needed the calm.

"We need to get her undressed so I can assess her injuries and then we need to bath her. If we can get the others out, that will help, the smell of their fear—" John looked up at her with the amber eyes of his wolf looking out at her.

"Okay, give me a second." Bella stood back up. "Sasha, send Alex to my bedroom to shower and then break up the others between this one and yours. Before you find them some clothes in my closet, I need you to get us towels and washcloths and mild soap, and a pan of warm water." Bella didn't even wait for her nod before returning to John and began gently removing Mary's clothing.

"How could anyone do something like this?" John growled as he went through the duffel bags, organizing the supplies he would need.

"I don't know John; all we can do is take care of them now." Bella started to croon nonsense words to Mary as she began waking.

"Sean, I need you to walk the house, make sure no one has come back inside, and lock up behind us. Bella is particularly concerned about Kelly. As soon as we figure out exactly what is going on, I'll tell you more." Jack had moved Sean out into the hall, and was barely breathing the words, but Sean heard every word. "Start here, at Sasha's bedroom since we are putting a couple of the new wolves in here, and move around to Bella's bedroom."

"You got it Primo." Sean nodded and moved to the end of the hall just ahead of the new wolves Sasha had directed to her bathroom.

Jack watched the new wolves, he thought their names were Sam and Lucy, follow slowly and tiredly behind Sean. He stepped back into the bedroom after Sasha left to show Alex to Bella's bedroom, and watched the two youngest wolves, also the apparently pregnant wolves, Charlie and Traci; go into the bathroom connecting this bedroom with the guest room next door.

A few moments later, Sasha came back with the supplies Bella asked for to bathe the injured wolf. Jack called Sasha to him after she dropped the supplies off and followed her back to the head of the hall right behind Sean as he checked Bella's office.

"Sash, after you get everyone some clothes, can you put some food together for the new wolves? I can send someone out—" Sasha interrupted him quickly.

"No need, Primo. I had a big stew on, and I put another large pot on when I heard what we had coming. It will be ready when they are. When they get out of the showers, I'll keep them over in the kitchen and out of John's hair." Sasha patted Jack on the arm and smiled tiredly.

"Thank you Sasha. I don't think I say that enough." Jack kissed the top of her head. "Are you okay, Sash?"

"Of course? Why would you ask?" Sasha tried to wave him off, but Jack tightened his hold on her hand.

"Don't lie to your Primo, Sasha." Sasha took in an unsteady breath. "Okay, Sash. Let's get through this, get these girls bedded down, and you and I and Bella will sit down and talk, okay?"

"Yes, Primo." Sasha nodded and then continued on into the rest of the house.

Jack remained where he was at the head of the hallway, where he could look down the hallway as well as out into the family room and further into the kitchen. He watched Sean lock the front door, check the living and dining rooms, move through the obviously empty family room and lock that patio door and make his way to the kitchen.

BELLA FINISHED RINSING the soap from the woman before her and was saddened by the damage done to her. No wonder John was enraged. It was obvious to Bella that he had chosen Mary for himself; she only hoped he allowed her time to choose him in return.

"John, maybe we should have Jack come and force her to shift? Wouldn't she heal faster?" John started growling when Bella mentioned having Jack come in, and he had to rest his head on the side of the bed and take deep breaths. His growling made the young woman try to squirm away from him. Bella moved quickly to still her. "Sshh, its okay, sweetie, we won't hurt you. You and your friends are safe now. I promise." When Mary had quieted again, Bella looked up at John. "John, please—"

"I'm sorry Prima. I'm having trouble with control. My wolf has claimed her, and seeing her so injured—it would be disastrous to have another male around her right now, even my Primo." John shook his head. "Even so, if I thought it would help, I would agree with you, but she doesn't have any broken bones that I can see, though I will have to stitch several of these cuts."

Bella assessed the young woman. She could see beneath the injuries to her delicate beauty. She was tiny—smaller than Bella—about 5'3" and maybe ninety pounds. Long, fine blonde hair and sky blue eyes set in porcelain skin. She was very fine-boned with gentle curves and a tiny waist.

That porcelain skin was currently black and blue with bruises, her right eye completely swollen shut and the left fluttered occasionally as she lost and regained consciousness. There was more bruising along the right side of her jaw. The first of the deeper cuts needing stitching was over her left breast, just missing her nipple. The second ran from below her left breast diagonally across her stomach just above her navel ending just above her pubic-hairline. There were several shallower cuts all over her torso and arms.

When they looked between her legs, it got really ugly. The third deep cut ran through her outer lip area on the right and continued onto her inner thigh, just missing her femoral artery. When they looked deeper, they saw shallower cuts inside, as though the knife was shoved inside, but luckily he was distracted before real damage could be done. There was dried blood caked around her anus, and more shallow cuts on her legs, along with bruises.

"I'll need to shave her here to stitch this." John's voice was husky with emotion.

"I'll do it while you start stitching the others." Bella choked out, the emotions affecting her as well.

"No, I need you to hold her. Once I start stitching, she will wake up. Anesthetic doesn't work on us, so I cannot use any."

"Sasha can help us." Bella responded.

"No! That will be as bad as a male wolf!" John said and then stopped, looking up at Bella as though he'd said something he shouldn't have.

"Of course, I should have thought, I'm sorry. But I need her to bring me a razor." Bella heard Sasha in the hallway. "Sasha!" Bella called out.

"Yes, Prima?" Sasha stopped in the doorway.

"I need a razor, and some shave cream. Actually, I need the special shave cream under my sink in my bathroom, not the regular, and a fresh razor, in the same place." Sasha blinked at Bella for a second, glanced briefly at John and then nodded and moved away.

"Special shave cream?" John choked out, with a strange half grin on his face.

"Don't ask." Bella looked anywhere but at his face, but he just sat there looking at her until she couldn't stand it. "It won't cause razor burn in such a sensitive area, okay?" Bella sounded exasperated.

"Oh." John blinked at her. "Oh. Okay. Thank you for thinking of that."

"You've never had a conversation with her before, and yet—"

"Yes, my Prima?" John smirked at her.

"Yeah, yeah. I got it, but I just have to say this, AS YOUR PRIMA." Bella emphasized the last three words. "Don't take away her choice like mine was. Give her true choice. Get me?"

"Yes, my Prima." John answered quietly. "I—my wolf wants her desperately—can you understand that? I want to protect her—with my life—forever. But if she doesn't want me—there will never again be force in her life as long as I live." John vowed.

Bella reached over and placed her hand over his on Mary's shoulder—rules be damned—and squeezed. "Agreed, I join my vow to yours. For her and her sister wolves." Bella looked up as Sasha walked in, "and Sasha." John looked at Bella in surprise, and then nodded.

"Agreed."

"Prima, the five youngsters are gathered in the kitchen and eating, but are worried about their sister wolf here." Sasha's voice nearly broke on the emotion she was feeling after the vow she'd heard.

"Thank you Sasha. Where are Jack and Sean?" Bella took the razor and cream from Sasha and set them aside.

"Here, La Mia Bella. Sean is keeping an eye on the new wolves. You realize, you eliminated one unmated, and found me six more to worry about?" Jack kept his tone light, and stayed in the doorway, having been just outside the door during Bella and John's discussion of John's intentions.

"Five." John growled. "This one is my responsibility until she tells me differently." John had been steadily bandaging the lesser cuts.

"And I have it on good authority that Cindy and Scott are nearing announcement of their mating." Sasha added quietly as she backed towards the doorway, and Jack.

"Well, Jack, since only two of the five in question are of legal age, I don't think you have much to worry about. Sasha, please let the ladies know Mary will be okay, but warn them we will be stitching soon, and things may get loud. They need to stay where they are. Understood?" Bella started out smiling at Jack, but directed the last seriously at Sasha, who nodded at Bella and returned to the kitchen.

"Everything under control here?" Jack asked quietly.

"Yes, I think we have it. You have our backs?" Bella started preparing what she needed to shave the poor young woman as John moved to block Jack's view, not that he was looking at the young woman. Jack's eyes were on his woman.

"Always." Jack said huskily and then backed into the hallway and out of sight, though both John and Bella were aware he was right there, and if Bella thought back, she'd realize she'd been aware he was there the entire time.

John finished bandaging the smaller cuts and then started preparing his supplies for the stitches while Bella finished the shave. As Bella finished the other side, he looked up in surprise.

"I don't need that area shaved." John seemed very embarrassed to be discussing this with his Prima.

"You want me to leave her lop-sided?" Bella smiled softly at him. There had been bad moments during the shave, as she had to get close to the cut, but she took a deep breath now that she was done, and sat back. "It should grow back more evenly this way. Hopefully."

"Okay. Let's start there, and move our way back up, I guess." John set to work with his needle and sutures.

Bella held Mary as gently as she could at first, worried about hurting her, but as soon as the first stitch went in, Mary woke up with a vengeance. Things got very ugly, and loud. Bella was surprised by how calmly and quickly John worked with that needle, and how gently he crooned to her, attempting to calm her.

It seemed to take forever, but was really only minutes, and the stitching was over. Bella backed off Mary as John took her into his arms and soothed her, rocking her gently in his arms. Bella was surprised that Mary accepted him, after what she had obviously suffered at the hands of other men, but Mary seemed to melt into John's embrace.

Bella gave them a few minutes while she tidied what she could, and then John cleared his throat as he settled her back onto the bed. As Bella was tidying, she found a cotton nightgown Sasha must have brought in at some point. Bella lifted it and gestured at John.

"Let's get her in this." Bella made to put the nightgown over Mary's head, but John stopped her.

"I need to put something on the stitches first. I got distracted, I'm sorry about that. She—I—" John stuttered to a halt.

"It's okay John, do what you need to do." Bella sat back while he put a medication on the stitches, and then bandaged them. John then lifted Mary gently while Bella lowered the nightgown over her head and then gently placed her arms through the armholes. She lowered the gown as far as she could and then John gently lowered Mary to the bed, and John and Bella together arranged the gown over the rest of her body. "Would she be more comfortable with or without panties, you think?"

"Without, they'll just rub." John settled the blankets around her and then set about cleaning up. He gestured for the garbage, and Bella handed over any on her side of the bed, as well as any of the medical supplies that had landed on her side. She gathered the bathing supplies and took everything into the attached bathroom to dump the pan of now cold water, and was not at all surprised to meet Jack there.

CHAPTER 13

"Everything okay?" Jack wrapped his arms around her, and rubbed her back. Bella melted into him gladly and stretched her sore back.

"Yeah, she'll be okay. I don't think we are getting him away from her for quite a while, though." Bella started purring as his rubbing hands started rubbing harder, digging into the knots.

"I was asking if everything was okay with you, but yeah, I didn't figure he was going to be good for much until that situation played itself out one way or another." Jack lifted Bella onto the counter and then stepped between her legs. "Did I mention I love it when you purr?" Jack growled at Bella as he moved into her, his hands cupping her cheeks briefly before moving down to her breasts. Bella tipped her head back and purred some more for him as she felt him weighing her breasts in his hands as his nose ran behind her ear. "Or how much I love your breasts? God, I love these breasts." Jack took her mouth in a deep kiss while his thumbs ran across her nipples, making Bella moan, before his hands ran down her hips to her ass. Bella felt him lift her against him, his hands squeezing. "And this ass, La Mia Bella, I love this ass." Bella was gasping for air as Jack squeezed her and pulled her tightly against his rigid length straining against her.

"Jack." Bella gasped. She rested her forehead against his chin and flexed her hands against his arms, fighting to regain her breath. "You —I—There's a lot to do still, and I—"

"Sshh, Bells. I heard, and I know you believe I pushed you into this—"

"I don't blame you—well, I don't completely blame you." Bella interrupted. "I just need us to take more time, and you just barrel through all my defenses—"

"I know, I'm sorry, I just—" Jack stopped and Bella looked up at him, surprised by his hesitation. Her so-confident wolf was speechless? "Don't push me away baby, I don't think I could survive without you after—" Jack choked and pulled her back to him tightly.

"I'm not saying never, I'm saying let me breathe Jack. I just need to breathe. We don't know each other. You know, your wolves, umm, the Warren's? They stopped me, told me they want children, and how happy they are because now that you have a mate, they can have children because I can keep her from shifting, Jack. How do I even do that Jack? There are children out there, Jack! We are basically now their guardians. I never intended to have children, I mean, hello! I was abandoned when I was twelve! Raped by my first foster father, had to—"

"Raped? What the—" Jack exploded. His hands found their way to her arms, and he squeezed, making Bella squeal in pain.

"Jack, stop it! That was over twelve years ago! You are hurting me, stop it. Calm down, now." Bella hit Jack in the chest and Jack released her as soon as she said he was hurting her and then stepped away from her. Bella jumped down and turned to the sink to clean out the pan. "Do you see, Jack? We don't know each other's stories, yet we are supposedly the equivalent of married! And I can't tell you my story without you reacting that way, my story doesn't get any better; in fact, it gets significantly worse long before it gets better. You need to learn to calm down, damnit!" Bella was angry, and didn't care that she was yelling by the end. Jack came back behind Bella and put his hands lightly on her shoulders and inhaled deeply.

"I'm sorry, La Mia Bella, I'm sorry. When it comes to you, I get—

anyway. You are right, when we tell each other our stories; I need to remember to stay calm." Jack saw the shave cream, and picked it up, raising his eyebrow at her in the mirror at the name. "'Special' shave cream for 'sensitive' areas? I heard that conversation. Where did she need stitches that you had to shave?"

"Umm, you know." Bella lowered her eyes in the mirror quickly then back up, trying to indicate without saying.

"Where?" Jack's eyebrows lowered. Bella pointed to herself and then gathered her supplies, but Jack grabbed her arm to stop her. "He cut her there? How bad is it?"

"It could have been much worse. It looked like he intended to stab her up in there, but the actual cuts inside are shallow, and already healing. The one slice that he had to stitch was on the outer —the outside and running to her thigh—almost to her artery. But she should heal without too much permanent damage." Bella shook her head at the mentality of someone that could do something like that.

"Jesus." Jack turned away from Bella, as though he couldn't stand to look at her right then. Bella shifted everything she was holding, until it was all in the pan, and under one arm, and reached out with the other. "Jesus." Jack turned back suddenly and crushed her to him. Bella saw before she was buried in his shirt there were tears in his eyes. Jacks arms were shaking, "How could anyone do that and call himself a man?" He whispered hoarsely.

Bella dropped the pan and wrapped Jack in her arms and held him. "I don't know, lover-wolf, I just don't know. Obviously, he wasn't a man." Suddenly they went from Jack soothing Bella, to arguing, to Bella soothing Jack.

Jack took a deep breath and squeezed Bella one last time before stepping away. "I'm sorry, La Mia Bella, that is just—"

"I know, but we still have to make sleeping arrangements for five more wolves, and I want to talk to Sasha, and some alone time to just talk to you would be nice. And food would be good at some point. And maybe sleep somewhere." Bella turned and picked up the pan she'd dropped, replacing the razor and shaving cream and soap that had fallen out of it, and they moved back into the bedroom. John was still at Mary's bedside and Sasha was in the doorway.

"Primo, Declan dropped off four roll-aways at the front door. One will fit in my room. We can fit two if we have to in the room next door. It would be best if we can put at least one in here." Sasha spoke quietly from the doorway, but John growled at the mention of putting one of the beds in here.

Bella squeezed Jack's hand in question and at his nod, she responded to Sasha. "Sasha, see if two of the girls are comfortable sharing the double bed next door, and if so, put one bed in there, and two of them in here, John will need one next to Mary here, and I'll want the other for Alex, their designated dominant. I think Mary will be most comfortable with her in here. And thank you for allowing one of them in with you." Bella looked directly at John as she spoke about having Alex in the room with Mary, brooking no argument, and John nodded.

"My Prima, Primo. If the bed is needed for one of the girls, a pallet here will be fine for me."

"Thank you, John. I'm going to leave orders for the others that they not enter, under any circumstances, this room, beyond the visit I'm going to allow them in a few minutes" Jack raised his hand to forestall John's aborted interruption. "Things were very tense out there while you were stitching her. She is their weakest, and their favored because of that," Jack smiled at Sasha. "You know how we are with our submissives. They feel they should have protected her more, though none of them are truly dominant. Sean and Sasha had a very hard time keeping them out." Jack nodded at Sasha, and that was all that was needed for her to carry out the orders already given. "In the meantime, do you need anything?"

"No, Primo, I am fine, but I will need to feed her as soon as she is awake." John had his head down.

"I'm awake," came faintly from the bed. John's head snapped up and his eyes glowed at the sound of her voice. "My name is Mary, not her."

"You will both eat." Jack said, and his voice was an order from the

Primo. John was already nodding. He didn't care, as long as he could talk to Mary more.

"How do you feel? Can you sit up?" John moved closer very slowly to keep from spooking her. "Mary." John's voice was quiet and could only be described as loving as he said her name.

Mary looked around at Jack and Bella then returned to gaze at John. "I know your voice. You spoke to me in that hell, while I was tied up. You promised to untie me. You promised no one would ever hurt me again." She clumsily looked under the gown at the only stitches she could easily see and then looked up at him. John looked so stricken Bella gasped and Jack tightened his hold on her. Mary smiled crookedly at John. "Can you help me sit up?" She asked John.

John nodded and gently raised her up, mounding the pillows behind her and then propping her behind them. "I'm so sorry." He breathed into her hair.

"I was teasing; I know you didn't mean to hurt me, really." Mary took a deep breath while he was still leaning over her. "I know your smell." Mary's wolf moved through her eyes, Bella watched in fascination. "You saved me." Bella heard more in the words. She heard "Mine" She looked at John, and saw his wolf and in his nod, heard the same. Well, I guess that answers that.

Jack cleared his throat. "We'll send Sasha in with food for both of you." Jack started to lead Bella out of the room with a hand at her back, when Sean started in with two roll-away's in tow. After Sean passed them, Jack and Bella walked out. Once they got to the family room, they were inundated with questions. Jack raised his hands for quiet.

"Sasha, would you get some food ready for John and Mary?" Sasha nodded and went into the kitchen. "Thank you. Now, while she does that, we will go, quietly, and see Mary very briefly and then you will break up into your room assignments. Under no circumstances do I want any of you entering that room. Understood?"

Everyone nodded and looked very nervous. Alex stood up to get Jack's attention. "Sir?" Jack nodded at her to continue. "Sasha said I would be staying in the room with her and the man that was doctoring her? Is that right?"

"You are Alex, right?" Jack held out his hand to Alex, and she seemed very confused as to what he expected. Bella gestured at her to shake his hand and Alex smiled at her in thanks, nodding at Jack in response to his question. "I am Primo or Jack. This is Prima or Bella. You had seemed to be the most dominant of the six of you, so we thought that would make Mary most comfortable. Is that right?" Jack gently squeezed her hand and let it go.

"Yes, they seem to look up to me." Alex looked down for a moment, and when she looked back up, there were tears in her eyes. "If I could have stopped him—if I could have saved her—"

"Alex, stop." Jack put his hands gently on her shoulders. "There is nothing any of you could have done. They were evil, it's apparent to me, from the damage—" Jack broke off and backed away, dropping his hands from her. He looked at all of them. "Things will be very different from now on. There is no abuse in my pack, no force, and no misuse of minors." Jack looked intently at the two youngest, and could just see their rounded abdomens indicating early pregnancy.

"Okay, come on, let's check in on your sister wolf." Jack led them in to see Mary, arriving just as Sean came out of Sasha's room, having placed the last bed. As they passed, Bella closed her office door.

"This room is off limits at all times." Bella stated clearly for all to hear. There were several nods. Jack stepped back to allow them into the room and put an arm around Bella.

"We'll get a lock put on, so you can access with a key, okay Babe?" Jack said into her hair as he kissed her temple. Bella nodded as they walked into the room. They moved over to the right, near the bathroom and out of the way. John had backed away, near the door, but was shaking at the need to sweep them all away from his Mary. Jack chuckled and Bella looked up at him in question. "It's just strange to see what I'm feeling so strongly in someone else." Bella looked at him and then back at John and shook her head.

"I think you are both insane. What on earth does he think they are going to do to her? And you? What do you think your wolves are going to do to me? I just don't get it. Insane, the whole thing." Bella just kept shaking her head.

"We are very territorial, Bella. We can't allow anyone near our—"

"So help me, Jack, if you say property, I will kick your ass ten ways to Sunday! And if you start pissing on me to mark your territory, that will be the final damn straw, do you hear me?" They were whispering, barely breathing their words, but John had started to chuckle, and even Sean and Sasha, who were in the hallway were holding back laughter. Bella pulled out of Jack's arms in pique, and Jack tried to stop her, but without making a scene, it wasn't happening. Bella went to Sasha and took the tray of food.

"Sasha, is there enough bedding for these?" Bella handed the tray off to John and turned back to Sasha.

"Bedding was dropped off along with the beds. I'll have them make up their beds when they are finished here." Sasha nodded at the bed, and Bella turned her attention to it. The five girls were piled around Mary, who was bravely trying to stay awake and not to show the pain, but it looked like it was too much.

"Okay, ladies, I think that's enough for now. Mary needs to eat something, and get some rest. Alex, why don't you help Mary eat so John can eat while it's hot? Sasha, would you help direct the bedding assignments?" Bella clapped her hands when it looked like the girls wanted to argue, but once they looked up at Jack, they immediately gave kisses to Mary and filed out, all but Alex, who quietly took the food from John and helped Mary eat. John did not look happy to not be the one feeding her, but couldn't very well argue with his Prima.

As Bella walked past them, she heard Jack and Sean talking quietly, and heard something about a lock, and knew he was following up on the lock for her office door. That made her feel much better. It made her very nervous to have so many unknown people near her office.

Bella felt so tired. It had been such a long day. As she passed her office, she heard a noise and opened the door, realizing it was her cell phone. She'd apparently left it in here, charging on the computer, which is why she didn't have it with her earlier. She grabbed it and left the office, closing the door behind her. She saw she had a voicemail and listened as she walked across the house and then returned the call, walking into her bedroom for privacy.

"Hey Bill, what have you got?" Bella asked when her accountant answered.

"Hey, Bella. Where you been, I've been calling since you called me?"

"Sorry, Bill, I left my phone on the computer charging and have been tied up with other things. What's going on? Were you able to find anything out?" Bella curled up on the oversized chair in the corner of her room near the patio door that she liked to use for reading.

"Well, that property you called about? The owners are really motivated to sell. I've done some research, and even with extensive renovations, I think it could be a good deal."

"Okay, work into those renovation estimates the fact that I'll want to turn probably half the units into town homes, so instead of sixteen units, it will become twelve." Bella heard the door open and looked up to see Jack come in. "And maybe turn the carport into garages, I don't know. Work your magic, let me know. I want to know what the rent would have to be, and be aware, I'll be subsidizing, I'm not worried about any profit, just want it to pay for itself. The interest, whatever—"

"The tax benefits you mean?"

"Yeah, exactly. That's all I'm looking to get out of it." Bella watched Jack sit on the end of her bed facing her with a frown on his face.

"Then you have renters in mind already?"

"Yes, don't worry about that. It will be fully occupied as soon as it's ready. Which would be the other thing. If you decide this is doable, and advise me to go ahead with it, I'll want to move forward as quickly as possible."

"Okay, it looked really good, so I called an architect to look at things, and I've been taking notes. It's too late now to call him back now, but I'll call him first thing in the morning with some of your stipulations, and get an estimate. Once I have that, I'll work the numbers. If they make sense, I'll make an offer on the property. Does that work?"

"Absolutely Bill, you are the best." Bella smiled when Jack growled. "I'll talk to you when you have more news."

"Later, Babe." Now Jack was really growling. She knew he had been listening to both ends of the conversation once he'd entered the room, but wasn't all that worried. If you are going to eavesdrop and then you are going to hear things you don't want to.

"What did he mean, calling you 'Babe'?" Jack growled, stalking in her direction.

"Why, I don't know Jack, would you like me to call him back and ask him?" Jack loomed over her as she sat in the chair and Bella just looked up at him calmly. "He's my accountant, Jack. I've worked with him since I started selling my books. He's closed every conversation I've ever had with him that way." Jack's nostrils were flaring at her. "Jack, he's very happily married with three kids." Bella planted her palms in his face and pushed, hard. "I will not do this every time I speak with someone in my life. Again, you don't know me or my life. Back off." Bella was suddenly angry. "I am not a piece of meat for you to plant yourself over and guard from all the other junkyard dogs. Back off. I'm tired and hungry." Jack allowed himself to be pushed away, and Bella had no illusions that he couldn't have stuck had he wanted to. Bella stalked away from him and into the kitchen. As soon as Sasha saw her come out, she placed food at the head of the table for her, and Bella sat to eat.

A few minutes later Bella saw Jack come out, and Bella watched from under her lashes as he reacted to her position at the head of the table, but damnit, this is her house, and he needed to understand that. Bella just kept eating while Sasha handed Jack his food. Bella figured she thought better of deciding where to put Jack and would let him figure it out himself. Bella watched him flare his nostrils at her a few times before he moved to the seat at her right and sit down.

"I'm sorry, you are right. I need to learn more, and stop treating you like—" Jack inhaled deeply through his nose. "—like a junkyard dog with a bone. Please forgive me?"

"Wow." Bella put her fork down and just stared at him. "Who the hell are you and what have you done with my Jack?" Bella burst out and Jack choked.

"I understand why you might ask that, La Mia Bella, but I'm completely serious." Jack slid his hand across the table, palm up, and waited. Bella looked into his sincere eyes, those sea green eyes she was rapidly falling into, and placed her hand into his. ""My Jack?'" Jack raised his brow at her and she just shook her fist at him. Jack lifted her hand to his lips and kissed it. "I am falling so hard for you, kitty cat, it's scary." Jack paused to close his eyes in a long blink. "Any thought that I could lose you—any thought that you could be taken from me— or there might be a prior claim on your heart—it's unbearable." Jack shook his head at her.

"I don't think I could explain it to you. I don't see you—precisely— as property. I just see you as mine." Bella made a noise and Jack rushed to continue, "not my property, but my heart, my soul, my—every-thing. I'm messing this up." Jack shook his head again.

"No," Bella cleared her throat, "no. I think you said that really— umm—well." Bella pulled Jack's hand to her and rested her forehead on it. "Lover-wolf, that's really close to saying you love me, and there is just no way you could, sweetie, you just don't know me."

"Kitty cat, it's both more and less than love, and I know enough to know I wouldn't survive losing you." Jack rubbed his hand along her face, squeezed her hand before releasing it and tweaked her nose. "Eat baby. We still need to talk to Sasha, and get some sleep."

CHAPTER 14

Sasha cleared the table and then she and Sean joined Bella and Jack.

"Are all of my guests settled for the evening?" Bella looked at Sasha. Sasha jerked a look at Jack, but looked back at Bella.

"Yes, all beds are made and ready. Sam, the next oldest, as well as the next most dominant, is in the other guest room with the two youngest, Charlie and Traci, who, by the way, are in fact pregnant. Lucy will be in my room. Alex and John seem to be getting along fairly well, all things considered." Sasha ran down as she finished her report.

"Sasha's gotten bedding out for me, I'll be sleeping on the couch out here as back-up security, and Nate, Dean and Turner are running special patrols around us all night, just in case. I questioned Alex pretty thoroughly, but as far as she knew, they, in addition to the three wolves you and Prima killed yesterday, were the only wolves from their pack here, but they come from a larger pack. She couldn't give any more information. We can try again later." Sean finished his report, and Jack nodded.

"Sasha, you called Bella and asked her not to take the new wolves next door. Why was that?" Jack's voice was low, but he would have answers.

"I just—I just thought—" Sasha burst into tears. "I figured if they were really skittish, so many wolves in one area would make them nervous." Sasha could barely speak through her tears.

"Sasha, that is too close to a lie. Do not lie to your Primo and Prima. You were specific about keeping them away from Kelly. And then we walked in and found her hurting you." Jack did not make it a question.

"I'm sorry Primo. I—I don't know how to—" Sasha took a deep breath. Bella watched her look around at them. Sasha cleared her throat. "I come from a pack not unlike the one you've saved those girls from. When I left it, I decided I would never allow another man to touch me, if I could help it. When you found me, starving, you promised that none of your wolves would touch me if I said no, that you would protect me. At first, it seemed like it was expected for me to go to your bed. I was able to avoid—well, anyway—I soon realized I could avoid going to your bed completely.

"Kelly is very—strong willed. I don't know how else to explain it. She was going to your bed for the same reason I was, though she prefers not to—she would rather not—she's gay." Sasha took a deep breath after saying that like it was hard work getting that word out. Sean looked shocked, and Jack closed his eyes, but Bella just continued to send calm thoughts to Sasha.

"And are you gay, Sasha?" Jack asked quietly.

"I don't know how to answer that. At first, she was very sweet, and it seemed the answer, I mean, she wasn't threatening, not being a man, and she didn't hurt me as the men always did. And I found I enjoyed it. Well, when she was—well, I mean until I had to—I mean—"

"You didn't like giving." Bella interrupted.

"Yes." Sasha was relieved. "Exactly. Maybe it was her, because since then, there have been—" Sasha's eyes flashed up then back down at the table, and Bella really hoped no one else noticed that flash was at her. "Anyway, I think she knew I didn't really enjoy it, or maybe she got tired of being sweet, and her true nature came out, but she started being mean, domineering. It was like those men, all over again. If I avoided her, it was worse. She would threaten me." Sasha's voice trailed off.

"How long has this gone on?" Jack's voice was quiet. Bella knew when he was really angry, even the growls stopped, and he just got quiet, that much she'd learned.

"Just a few months. The threats have only been a few weeks. It's only been really bad in the last day since I moved over here. I'd hoped, moving over here, she'd just give up, but she would sneak over here—" Sasha shook her head.

"Does anyone else know about this? That Kelly is gay?" Jack was breathing deeply, trying to remain calm.

"No—"

"Yes—" Bella interrupted Sasha.

"Besides you Bella, though how you, in a few hours of observation, can see that as well as—" Jack looked at Sean, "—other things, I don't know."

"I'm not talking about me. I'm talking about John. Or, I should say, John sees Sasha as gay." Sasha squeaked and Bella patted her hand. "I recommended that Sasha come in to assist and he said no, that would be as bad as having a male wolf in the room." Bella looked at Sean. "His wolf is claiming Mary, I'm sure you've caught on to that, right?" Sean nodded, smiling. "He saw Sasha, sexually speaking, as a rival just as he would have any male. I was safe as a mated female, apparently." Bella shrugged.

"So then we don't know if he knows that Kelly is gay?" Jack specified.

"Well, if he believes Sasha is and then why wouldn't he know about her partner?" Bella countered.

"Good point. Okay, doesn't matter so much at this point. Sasha, what do you want done at this point, for crimes against you by your sister wolf?" Jack turned back to Sasha.

"Oh, Jack." Sasha sniffled. Bella found it interesting that when she was most emotional, Sasha became the least formal. "If she will just leave me alone, can we just forget it? You've made the order that she can't come in here. Can we just leave it there?" Jack growled and Sasha jumped.

"Knock it off Jack." Bella snapped at him. "Sasha, are you sure? What if she gets in here? Or gets to you when you are out shopping? Or out on the full moon?" Jack frowned at Bella but left it alone. Bella gave him points for that.

"Can I just think about it?" Sasha asked. Bella looked at Jack and shrugged. Jack shrugged back. "Thank you Primo, Prima. I'll let you know in a day or two?" They nodded and Sasha rose, starting to move into the kitchen.

"Don't worry about that, you've cleaned up most of it, I'll load the last little bit and start the dishwasher." Sean surprised Bella by stopping her.

"Thank you. I'll check on the guests, and then go to my room. Goodnight." Sasha left the room quietly. Everyone took deep breaths until she went down the hall.

"Well." Bella.

"Well." Jack.

"Well." Sean. "What else did Bella observe?" Sean looked from Jack to Bella. Bella looked at Jack and Jack looked back at her. Bella just shrugged at him, it's his pack.

"Kelly isn't the only gay wolf." Jack said quietly.

"Sasha said she isn't really, she just doesn't want intercourse with a man. She doesn't really want sex—not fully—with a woman either. I don't consider that gay." Sean responded.

"I wouldn't either, but I don't know many gay or lesbian people. Actually, I don't think I know any lesbian women. I think it's a better description to say Kelly is a lesbian. Men are gay, women are lesbians." Bella advised.

"And you know this how?" Jack wanted to know.

"I'm a writer. I read. I watch television. I don't know. How do you not know this? And why is any of this a big deal? Why do we care?" Bella responded.

"Okay, back-up. Who else is gay?" Sean wanted to know. "You

looked at me rather significantly, but I know I'm not gay, so whats with the look?"

"Sorry, just didn't want to say anything in front of you or Sasha, but Sasha may well already know, and as my Secundo, you should know.

"Bella believes Nate and Dean are gay." Jack finished in a rush, sounding to Bella's ears very embarrassed.

"Wow." Sean looked at Bella and she shrugged at him. Then he started to stare more intently at her, making her uncomfortable. Bella started to squirm and Jack started to growl. Bella kicked Sean under the table and Sean jerked. "Oh, sorry!" Sean looked over at Jack. "Sorry, Primo. I was just thinking. Now that Bella says that, I realize that they do disappear together a lot. And every full moon, they disappear. It would make sense."

Jack scrubbed his hands up and down his face. "Well." Bella giggled. "What?" Jack growled at her.

"We've said that already." Bella reached over and tweaked his nose. "And don't you growl at me, buddy-boy. I still don't get why it's even worthy of discussion. If they aren't hurting each other or other people, if the relationships are consensual—and I agree, it doesn't appear Kelly and Sasha's was—then what do we care?"

Jack looked at Sean. "Bella, wolves, male wolves, are very heavy on the testosterone, you might have noticed?" Bella waved her hand that she got it. "The men would probably not care one way or the other about Kelly, or Sasha, for that matter, except as it impacts the number of available female wolves we have for mating, but they would not tolerate male wolves—" Jack choked on the rest.

"Jeez, Jack. Use your grown-up words. Men having sex with men. So in other words, they'd get off on the thought of the women going at it together, but because the thought of men going at it together just squicks them out so totally, that's a problem. Again, grow up already. They're adults. If they aren't hurting anyone, leave them alone. It's not against the law or anything." Bella was disgusted by Jack's attitude.

"Actually, my Prima, I don't wish to contradict you, but in several states, I believe sodomy was illegal in the old world." Sean said quietly.

"Well, good Lord. Let's just regulate what people do in their bedrooms, shall we? And this is Faedresse. Do the old laws even apply? I'm going to take a bath, I'm exhausted. It's been a very long day. Good night Sean." Bella smiled at Sean, ignored Jack completely, and walked into her bedroom and avoided slamming the door—just.

CHAPTER 15

*B*ella heard Jack enter her bedroom, but kept her eyes closed, enjoying her bubble bath, and the candles she'd lit, and the soft music she'd set to play. Even with her eyes closed, she could feel him there, leaning against the doorjamb, watching her. She cracked an eyelid to peek at him and caught him smiling at her. She smiled back and shook her head. That seemed to be the invitation he was waiting for, because he pushed off and moved towards her.

Bella shook her finger in his direction lazily. "Uh-uh-uh. I'm having quiet time now. I'm not arguing anymore. Go away." Jack kissed, licked and then sucked the wagging finger into his mouth, making Bella moan. "Stop that. Bad wolf." Jack released her finger with a pop and chuckled.

"I don't want to go away, and I definitely don't want to argue. I want to join you. We can have some sharing time." Bella felt Jack run a finger through the water next to her breast and she shivered in spite of the hot water.

"No, bad wolf I said. And I know all about you and your sharing time. If you got into this tub with me, I doubt we would be doing any talking."

"I promise," Jack held up the universal two fingered "Scout Salute", "if more than talking happens in this tub, it will be because you fail to stop me." Bella squinted her eyes at him.

"You were so not a Boy Scout." Bella scoffed at him.

"Were so." Jack was smug.

"Nuh-uh."

"Ya-huh." Jack nodded, smiling.

"If you were a Boy Scout, I'll eat," Bella paused, eyeing him up and down, "you."

"Well, open wide, kitty cat. I'm an Eagle Scout. My father was our Scoutmaster. We had our own Troop." Jack sat on the wide ledge surrounding the tub and smiled at Bella.

"No way." Bella's eyes were wide.

"Way." Jack nodded. Bella just closed her eyes and slipped under the water. Bella heard Jack laughing at her, but she stayed under as long as she could. She felt his hand in her hair as her lungs started straining, and she burst spluttering out of the water.

Bella spluttered and laughed, trying to catch her breath as Jack wiped the water out of her eyes, and pushed her hair out of her face. Bella finally opened her eyes into Jack's laughing face, and felt really happy for the first time possibly since she was a child. She reached her hands up to his face and pulled it down to hers, and kissed him deeply, making him growl low in his throat. Bella purred in response.

"So you ready to do this?" Jack stood and swept his shirt over his head, toeing his shoes off and unbuttoning his pants.

"What?" Bella asked innocently. Jack stopped before he lowered his pants, and looked at her. Bella sniffed. "Oh, just come soak with me. Rain check, okay? I don't back out of wagers, or—whatever." Bella sat up in preparation of making room for Jack, baring her breasts above the waterline, and distracting Jack. "Jack?" Jack shook his head and looked back up at her face and smiled devilishly and then very slowly lowered his pants and shorts.

Dayum. I could really get used to that view. Bella thought, enjoying the sight exposed to her hungry eyes. Jack stepped into the tub behind her, and settled Bella against his chest.

"You feel so good in my arms, La Mia Bella." Bella shivered as Jack ran his hands up and down her arms, where they wrapped under her breasts, his thumbs brushing under them lightly. Bella felt his long hard cock against her back, and his chin resting on the top of her head. Bella turned her head until her ear rested against his chest just over his heart.

"I have to admit I enjoy being here, lover-wolf." Bella purred.

Jack lifted Bella onto his thighs and she felt his cock rest against her ass, the higher position lifting her breasts above the waterline. Jack shifted her until he rested between her cheeks and Bella wiggled, clenching her PC muscles. Bella closed her eyes as his hands ran back up to her breasts and started tickling her nipples. Bella wiggled some more. "Damnit Jack, you promised." Bella pressed on Jack's hands, but even she wasn't sure if she was pressing them closer to her, or trying to press them away from her.

Jack chuckled, "You're the one who won't stop wiggling, baby. Sit still." One of his hands wandered down her stomach to tangle in her curls, and slipped a finger inside. Bella moaned and wiggled more.

"Jaaack." Bella moaned, drawing his name out. Bella felt Jack plucking at her nipple with one hand as he slipped a second finger deep inside her and started working her clit with his thumb. They were both breathing hard, Bella's hips working rhythmically against Jack's hand as his cock slipped between her ass cheeks.

JACK SWITCHED to her other breast in order to cross her body in an attempt to hold her more still as she neared orgasm, her squirming causing waves in the water. He increased the pressure and speed of his fingers working in and out of her. He could tell she was close, by her movements, they always became more frenzied. He was about to come himself, at her back, from sliding against her. Jack was losing his concentration, so he simply held her breast in his hand, and focused his attention on working her clit and sliding his fingers faster and harder in and out of her until she finally screamed his name as he bucked against her back, spilling himself against her.

Jack felt Bella curl against him, purring, as their breathing returned to normal. Jack lightly rubbed her mound a few more times before sliding his hand back up her stomach then cupping her face and tipping it up to take it in a deep kiss.

"Mmm." Bella settled back against Jack's chest, her ear against his chest. "You promised, talking only. Bad wolf." Bella thumped him half-heartedly on the chest next to her cheek.

"I promised talking only if you stopped me. You didn't stop me. Fair game, kitty cat. I would have stopped if you said no and meant it." Jack stroked her hair away from her face, rubbing behind her ear.

"Well, be good from now on. Talk time now, lover-wolf." Bella snuggled deeper into his arms, breathing deeply. "Hey, did you—you know?" She looked up at him.

"I did. And I thought I was good?" Jack sounded offended. Bella laughed and stretched up to kiss his chin.

"Very good." Bella purred, wiggling lightly against his half-flaccid, but not much smaller cock.

"You too, baby kitty. Just you moving against me was enough." Jack ran his hand along her hip, until Bella curled her fingers with his in self-defense.

"I said be good, lover-wolf. We need some get-to-know-you time." Bella curled the arm attached to the hand she head over her and held his hand next to her cheek. His other hand seemed content to hold her just under her breasts, and was behaving, at least for the moment. "Tell me about your childhood, where you grew up."

CHAPTER 16

"We grew up back east, upstate New York, Old World. I told you my father was Scoutmaster of our Boy Scout Troop? Well, that's because he was also Primo of our Pack. It was a really big pack. Well over 100 wolves. My dad worked closely with the Primo's in the nearest five packs. They had an association, kept each other covered.

"But life as the Primo's son was rough. Everyone wanted a piece of me. I spent my life fighting challenge after challenge." Jack shook his head.

"How much do you know about Were's?" Jack looked down at Bella.

"Next to nothing." Bella shook her head at him.

"We live a very long life." Jack paused and took a deep breath. "How old do you think I am?"

"I don't know, thirty? Thirty-five?" Bella shrugged.

"I'm sixty-three." Bella jerked, trying to come out of the tub, and Jack tightened his arms around her. "Relax, La Mia Bella." Jack rubbed his hands over her soothingly.

"Sixty-three, Jack? I'm twenty-four years old. Jeez, Jack." Bella slumped against him, her nose buried in the crook of his elbow.

"We aren't immortal, but we are long lived. I'll probably live two hundred years or so, assuming—"

"Assuming?" Bella asked, looking up at him. Jack kissed the tip of her nose.

"Assuming something doesn't kill me sooner. And I lo—"

"Don't you say it!" Bella interrupted.

"I am falling hard for every inch of your twenty-four years, La Mia Bella." Jack chuckled, and settled her back against him.

"Better, I guess." Bella grumbled. "God, I'm married to a senior citizen."

"Not yet, but are you asking me?" Bella swatted at him again, making Jack laugh.

"Back to the story. My parents met and mated young. They were thirty when I was born. I was slated to be the next Primo, assuming I survived all the challenges along the way, but my father will remain Primo until he dies, and he has another hundred years, at least.

"Shortly after The Last War, I got tired of the challenges and decided to go out on my own. Too many dominant wolves in the pack, it was crazy. It made my father so angry when I announced I was leaving, but he couldn't stop me. And I think he was a little proud of me, or at least I hope so." Jack trailed off for a few seconds, and came back to himself when he felt Bella running her hand on his arm.

"You okay, old man?" Bella asked with a kiss on his chest.

"Oh, God, don't you start calling me that." Jack reached down and pinched her perfect ass in retribution, kissing her hair. "Yeah, I'm okay, I have my kitty cat." Bella chuckled. "You stop that, woman. You'll get me all riled again, and I won't finish my story." Bella wiggled against him, and Jack made sure she felt his growing cock against her backside.

"Poor lover-wolf, I think you have a medical condition. You always seem to be like this." Bella laughed.

"Around you, yes, now stop that, bad kitty." Jack held her firmly against him. "Now, where was I? Oh, yes.

"About ten years ago, I decided I was going to leave, and form my own pack. My cousin, Sean—"

"You didn't tell me Sean was your cousin!" Bella interrupted.

"Down, kitty. Yes, Sean, as well as John, and much more distantly, Declan. They all followed me"

"Wow." Bella shook her head. "Wait. Sean. Declan. John. Secundo, Terzo, and if I'm following, the next dominant, right?"

"Yes, kitty, you are right. The three most dominant wolves in my pack are all my cousins, and followed me from my fathers pack. The four of us set out to find a territory of our own. We collected the others along our way. My father assumed we would settle nearby, and join the Collective, as he called it, but I just needed out of his sphere, so we came west.

"We've been moving off and on for the last ten years, working construction, which we are uniquely suited to, as well as security, again uniquely suited. I'm good with investments, so I was able to take my inheritance—which my father tried to withhold, but my mother forced him to relinquish—and turn it over a few times until we had enough to buy the property next door."

BELLA RUBBED ABSENTLY at Jack's arm, thinking about what he'd told her. Gah! Sixty-three years old! Bella thought. "Wow, that's some story, but you didn't really tell me about your childhood."

"Sure I did, baby. I fought many challenges, every boy was a Boy Scout, required by the Primo, and I was expected by the Primo, as his son, to make Eagle, which I did by the time I was sixteen." Jack stopped Bella's roving fingers on his arm.

"You were fighting challenges when you were a kid?" Bella was shocked. "I assumed that was once you were grown. Jeez. I'm surprised you lasted until just ten years ago."

Jack tugged her head around so he could look at her. "You think I can't survive a few challenges?" He sounded insulted.

"No, I meant I can't believe you put up with it that long." Bella slinked against Jack, front to front, and slipped upward to kiss him. She felt his hands slide down to her ass and rested her thighs on either side of his waist, rubbing her center against his hot length. "We have been in here a very long time; I think I am turning into a wrinkly prune. And don't I owe you a—favor?" Bella stood up, the water sluicing off her body, her legs straddling his body as she looked down at him. Jack growled up at her, his eyes going amber and Bella smiled.

"Only if I can—return the favor." Jack's voice was husky as he started to rise slowly, stalking her. Bella squeaked as she stepped quickly out of the tub and grabbed a towel. "I'm feeling very hungry for kitty cat." And suddenly Jack was just there, and Bella was against the wall and Jack had her up in his arms and his hand was between her legs and Bella moaned when she felt his fingers moving inside her and he was kissing her deeply and Bella's brain checked out.

When Bella checked back in, her hands were fisted in his hair and she was bucking against his hand. Jack let her slide down his body as the aftershocks swept her, and Bella released his hair shakily. Her legs were like jelly, and she'd have gone down without his hands on her waist.

"Wow." Bella croaked and cleared her throat. "What was that about?"

"I don't know, you were just standing over me, and I just had to—I just had to." Jack snuffled her hair as her legs steadied under her. "You okay?"

"Oh, yeah. Wow." Bella laughed. "I guess I said that." Bella reached up and ran her nose along his jaw. "Wow." Bella leaned down and picked up the towel, and started drying Jack off. She avoided his straining cock, which was practically vibrating in its need for her. Jack took a towel off the rack and started drying her. They threw the towels in the hamper near the door and Bella took his hand.

"Come to bed, wolf, I'm still hungry." Bella's voice was husky, and she licked her lips when she looked up at him. Jack growled and followed her willingly.

Bella sat on the edge of the bed and stopped Jack while he stood in front of her, and took his cock in her hand. It was long and thick and hard. She ran her hand up and down its length a few times before she leaned over it and gave it an experimental lick. Jack shuddered as she ran her tongue up its length to the head, twirling around and into the crease and licking the drop of moisture from the tip. Jack growled again when Bella flicked her tongue at the hole in the tip.

Suddenly Bella found herself lying on the bed with Jack facing her. "I'm hungry too." Jack rasped out before reversing so he was straddling her body. Bella pulled on him until he was positioned the way she wanted him in her hands, so she could reach him with her mouth.

JACK LOOKED down his body at Bella where she worked him with her small hands and mouth. Oh God, she's incredible! He thought. Jack kept himself on his knees in position for her, and bent to her core, spreading her legs for the feast before him. Jack parted her lips and ran a finger along the wet folds and felt her shudder, making him smile. He bent his head and licked.

Jack used his fingers and tongue on Bella and felt her begin to writhe against his mouth. His legs were shuddering from the tension of maintaining his weight above her, and controlling himself against her hands and mouth as she milked him. He felt her do something with the tip of her tongue that made him freeze for a second.

BELLA HAD one hand on his balls, gently rubbing the sack, and the other stroking his length while she sucked the tip of his cock hard in her mouth. She alternated this with dipping the tip of her tongue into the tip of the head of his cock.

He was too thick and long for her to take much of him into her mouth; she had a very shallow gag reflex, so oral sex was very difficult for her. It meant oral sex for her was more manual than oral, and why she spent more time licking the length and sucking the tip while her hand did the rest. Jack seemed to like it.

JACK WAS LOSING IT, so he started working his fingers harder and faster as he sucked hard at her clit. Bella was bucking and moaning, but sill working him manually at least, her head thrown back on the pillow, thrashing as it does just before she comes. He started moving with her hand, and was almost there when his legs gave out. He slid down until he was between her breasts, and she adjusted her hand to continue working him between them.

∾

BELLA BUCKED against Jack's hand one last time and screamed his name at the same time she felt him come on her chest. Jack licked up her orgasm and Bella giggled. Jack collapsed with his face in her curls for a second and then rose unsteadily to turn and look at her.

"What are you laughing at, kitty cat?" Jack growled at her with a smile.

"Uh—" Bella waved at her sticky chest wordlessly. "Uh!" Bella giggled again. Jack stalked up her body, and used a finger to swipe through the sticky mess and held it out to her. Bella took Jack's hand and sucked his finger into her mouth, sucking his essence off, swirling her tongue around his finger. Bella felt his flaccid cock start to harden against her again. "Mmm." Bella purred as she pulled his finger out with a pop. "Finger. Licking. Good."

Jack leaned down to her and kissed the tip of her nose. "I'll be right back, don't go away, baby." Bella watched the muscles in his ass as he walked into the bathroom, completely unselfconscious of his nakedness. Bella loved his ass. Before long, he was walking back in with a warm washcloth in hand, and Bella could watch that glorious cock bob at her. When he paused at the edge of the bed and just stood there, Bella finally raised her eyes to his to find him laughing at her. "You keep looking at it like that, it's gonna grow." Jack leaned over and started cleaning his mess off her.

"Mmm. One can only hope that's all it takes." Bella said and squealed when he tweaked her nipple.

"Be a good kitty." He admonished.

"I thought I was." Bella accused.

"Always." Jack smiled as he headed back to the bathroom. Bella smiled, mmm, repeat performance, she thought. She curled on her side to await the return. Jack walked back in and gestured at Bella. "Scootch over." Bella slid over and Jack laid down in front of her, facing her, his knees drawn up mirroring hers.

Bella smiled when Jack ran his finger down her forehead and nose, following the curves of her face and over her lips to her chin.

"Hi." Bella said.

"Hi." Jack said back. "How are you doing?" Bella closed her eyes and stretched with catlike grace and smiled.

"I'm good." She opened her eyes. "You?" Jack pulled her flush to him and smiled.

"I'm better than good." Bella felt how much better than good he was. The evidence of his hard length against her stomach surprised her.

"I cannot believe you are ready to go again. Was it not good for you?" Jack ran his hands up and down her back, and settled them on her ass.

"It was great, and you know it. But I will never get enough of you." Jack rolled over onto his back, pulling her onto him and squeezing her ass, rubbing his cock against her curls.

Bella climbed up him until she could reach his face. She straddled him, and the tip of his cock just touched her curls as he continued to knead her ass. Her breasts were crushed to his chest as she framed his face in her hands and locked eyes with him.

"Crazy damn wolf." She said huskily before she crushed her mouth on his.

Bella practically ate at his mouth, using her lips, tongue and teeth. She slipped her hands up into his hair and fisted them, holding him in place. Jack kept a hand at her ass and slid the other up to her head. Bella moaned into Jack's mouth. Bella broke the kiss gasping for breath and threw her head back, moaning. Jack lifted her breasts to his mouth and Bella rocked against his chest as he used his teeth and tongue on first one then the other nipple.

"Jack, please." Bella was wiggling and rocking against Jack, and he slid on hand down and slipped it between her thighs. "Mmmm —Jaaack!"

Suddenly Bella was on all fours and Jack was behind her. There was hesitation, and Bella reached behind her for him and positioned his cock where she wanted him and then pushed back as he thrust into her. Jack's hands were on her hips as he thrust into her, hard and fast, and Bella pushed back against him with each thrust. She loved the way he filled her, the way he hit her end on every thrust. She loved hearing the slap of his thighs against hers.

Bella clenched her hands against the sheets as she wiggled, her head starting to thrash, and she felt Jacks hands tighten on her hips as he tried to hold her as she squirmed the closer she came.

JACK STRUGGLED to hold her as she thrashed, and he came closer to his own release. Jack loved the noises she made, and the way she squirmed and wiggled and threw her head around the closer she came. And then she was there, and her contractions pulled his climax and he howled, bucking as he spilled into her.

Jack collapsed behind Bella and pulled her up onto the pillows. Jack rubbed her stomach.

"I need to get a washcloth." Jack whispered hoarsely. "As soon as I catch my breath."

"Mmm. No, I like you here." Bella rubbed her legs together. "My chest, not so much, but here, mmm." Bella purred. Jack's laughter rumbled in her ear.

"I think you may be a little sick." Bella giggled at that. "But I think I lo—" Bella slapped at him at that. "But I think I like you anyway. You really have issues with that word, don't you?"

"Only when you use it too easily or soon." Bella kissed his arm. "Go to sleep, lover-wolf. And don't get used to this. You need to get used to sleeping in your own bed." Bella could almost hear Jack pout behind her at her words.

CHAPTER 17

*B*ella awoke alone and stretched luxuriously. She sniffed the air and smelled Jack and sex, and liked it. But more importantly, she knew he'd showered not too long ago, and was in the breakfast room. She hopped up to shower and something fell off her chest.

Bella looked down at the bed and found a key with a note tied on it with a blue ribbon. The note read, "I wish I could say this was the key to my heart, but it's actually the key for your office I promised you. I love you. Jack." Bella's hands shook as she read those three words she'd fought to keep him from saying. It's too soon! Bella thought to herself, but it didn't stop her from holding the key and the note to her chest tightly.

Bella shook her head and untied the note, placing it carefully in her nightstand and then left the key on top and then went in to take her shower.

~

BELLA WALKED out of her room and found the new wolves, including Mary, in the family room watching television. Jack, Sean and John sat at her table, and when Bella saw that Jack sat at the head of the table, she almost growled. She managed to keep from snarling, but barely, but she did frown at him, and crossed her arms, not leaving the doorway. She remained in that position until he looked up and figured out what the problem must be.

Jack straightened up and raised his eyebrows at her and Bella started tapping her fingers on her arm. Out of the corner of her eyes she saw Sasha start to bring her breakfast, and stop when she saw the problem. Sasha went back into the kitchen quietly. Jack flared his nostrils at Bella, and Bella raised her eyebrow at him.

Sean and John looked at each other and then at Jack and Bella, and Sean moved out of the customary spot for the Primo's mate and gestured Bella toward the seat, but Bella ignored him, her eyes remaining on Jack in her seat. Jack finally huffed out a breath and went to her.

"Did you get my gift, mate?" Jack asked quietly, his hands on her cheeks. He tried to lean in for a kiss and Bella evaded. She held the key she'd taken off the nightstand and slipped into her jeans pocket and waved it at him. "Did you read my note?" He lowered his voice even more, lowering his head as well to look into her eyes.

"I did, thank you Jack, I—" Bella looked away and cleared her throat. "I asked you not to—" she shook her head. "Not now. Why are you in my seat? I've made it clear—"

"I am—" Jack started very loudly and Bella interrupted him.

"This is my house, Jack. If you want to have a big time meeting, take it next door, where you are free to play chief of the mount." Bella kept her voice very low. "Don't make this a pissing contest with me in my own house. You. Will. Lose." Bella bounced her head against his chest. "I was feeling very good when I woke up, and then I found the—I was feeling very good when I walked out, and then— Jack, you need to show me respect in my house. You all act like I'm supposed to just accept," Bella's hands waved around at him, "all of this. This is all new to me." Bella put her hands on his waist and rubbed her nose against him. "Just, you know what? Just do what you want. I give up. I'm going to my office. Take over the whole damn house. I don't give a damn." Bella pushed away from him and stalked across the house.

"Bella!" Jack called to her, but Bella ignored him as she let herself into her office and locked the door.

Bella curled into the oversized chair in the corner, the match to the chair in her bedroom, and cried. She wasn't sure why it mattered, or why it bothered her so much. Bella smelled Sasha at the door with her breakfast when there was a knock a few minutes later, and she ignored it.

A few minutes later she heard a key in the lock and watched Jack carry a tray in with her breakfast. He closed and locked the door, and pocketed the key before turning to her. Bella watched him through teary eyes and anger. Bella held her hand out for the key.

Jack walked forward with the tray, and Bella waved it way, keeping her hand out for the key. "I want the key to my office. This," Bella gestured around, "is my livelihood, my last sanctuary. You've taken everything else. I won't give up this room. Give me the key."

"Bella," Jack objected. Bella just stared at him with her hand out. Jack closed his eyes, but pulled the key out of his pocket and placed it in her hand. Bella put the key in her pocket next to the other one.

"Are there others?" She asked quietly.

"No." Jack answered just as quietly. He squatted in front of her, holding the tray to her. "Please eat, if not for me, for Sasha. She'll hurt me." Bella choked on her spurt of laughter then snuffled. She hated how she snotted and got red when she cried. It was never pretty. She waved her hand at Jack.

"Just go away, Jack." Bella looked around for the box of tissues she'd grabbed, and grabbed several, blowing her nose loudly.

"Not happening, kitty cat. You've made some accusations here I need to address. I'm not going anywhere until you've eaten and we've discussed this." Jack looked like he could stay squatted before her chair for hours holding that tray.

Bella tossed the tissues in the wastebasket next to her chair and sighed, closing her eyes briefly. "Give me the damn tray." Jack handed her the tray and Bella settled it on her lap while Jack moved the ottoman in front of the chair and sat on it, facing her, his elbows on his knees and his hands clasped.

"What's going on, baby? I know you are a little sensitive about me moving in, and you made a point in sitting there yesterday, but I don't understand what just happened out there." Jack moved a piece of her hair out of her face, and anchored it behind her ear. Bella shook her head.

"I don't know. My moods are all over. I'm happy, I'm angry, I'm sad." Bella kept her gaze on the plate. "Now I'm so hungry, I could eat a damn cow."

"I'm fine Jack." Bella answered tiredly. Tears leaked out of the corners of her eyes as Bella looked up at him and she held her arms out to him. "Hold me?"

"Always." Jack picked her up and sat in the chair, arranging her across his lap. Bella curled against his chest and closed her eyes.

"I'm sorry Jack, this is all just overwhelming." Bella spoke quietly into his chest.

"I know, La Mia Bella. I just kind of moved in and took over, didn't I? I'm sorry baby. Once the mating happens, all bets are off and things are set in motion that can't be stopped." Jacks hands rubbed lightly up and down her back.

"What does that mean Jack? Because we accidentally mated, now you have no choice but to go all medieval protector knight on me? Because of the mating, you think suddenly you love me? Do you see why I have issues with this?" Bella leaned away from his chest to look up at his face.

"Falling in love with you has nothing to do with the mating bond. I'll agree that I'm—protective—but you are my mate." Bella groaned. "Bella, be reasonable."

"You take possessive and protective to new heights, Jack. Be reasonable, really. Why don't you try to be reasonable? And how do you know that what you feel for me is real and not artificially tied to this bond?" Bella searched his face for answers.

"Why don't we agree to disagree, Bella? I love you. Doesn't matter that it happened fast, it happened. Accept it. I'm here to stay, baby.

And good or bad, I come with a whole lot of baggage." Jack leaned his forehead to hers. Tears leaked from her eyes again.

"The pack." Bella said quietly, and Jack just nodded.

"They love you too." Bella snorted, "Most of them do already, and the rest will too." Jack insisted.

"I don't know how to be loved, Jack. I don't know how to do any of this." Bella sobbed, burying her face in his shirt again. Jack rocked her and murmured soothingly. Bella snuffled. "Oh, great. I'm snotting again." Bella looked around for her tissues and swatted at Jack when he laughed at her. "Don't you laugh at me. Don't even look at me, I'm hideous when I cry, why do you think I don't let myself do it?" Bella snatched the tissues from his hand and blew her nose.

"Bella, look at me," Jack lifted her chin, "You are the most beautiful woman in the world, La Mia Bella, crying, snotting, raging, smiling, sleeping, I don't care." Jack kissed her tenderly.

"You are blind, it's very sad, a blind wolf, we'll have to put you down. A blind, lying wolf." Bella sighed, and smiled through her tears, "but I'll take it." Bella settled back against his chest again.

"So, my poor, blind wolf, what do I need to worry about? What are my responsibilities?"

"Stop that, silly kitty, I am not blind." Bella poked him in the belly, and Jack chuckled. "Primarily, you help me take care of them. If I'm not available, you make decisions, hopefully the same decisions I would have.

"In addition, the magic of the Prima is to calm and control the female wolves during pregnancy, to keep them from losing the babies."

"How do I do that?" Bella looked up at him. "You can force their shift. Wouldn't it make more sense that you would have the power to force them not to?"

"No, because I have no more ability to avoid the shift at the moon than they do. I'm powerful enough to shift at any time, and to force them at any time, but I think to offset that power, the Prima is given the power to hold back the moon to protect the babies.

"As for how, I'm not sure. My mom, when I was leaving to form my own pack, met with me because she knew I would need to know. She said my mate would have the power, that she would just refuse to shift at the moon, and remain calm, and her calm would calm my wolves." Bella looked at Jack incredulously.

"You're joking, right? That's not cryptic at all." Bella snorted.

"Look at it this way, since you don't feel the call of the moon, it shouldn't be a problem, right?" Jack chucked her under the chin. Bella pushed off his lap in frustration.

"Okay kitty." Jack tried to distract Bella. "You know tonight is the full moon, right?"

"I don't really keep track. Is it really? Okay." Bella waited for the point.

"John told me earlier he thinks Cindy is pregnant." Jack waited for Bella to respond.

"Oh, that's nice. Who is she mated to?" Jack loved that smile she gave him, so sweet. He enjoyed it for a beat before he said the next.

"She doesn't have a mate." Jack felt the moment that sank in for her as her hand pulled out of his. Jack shifted quickly to block the door before she could escape and watched her shut down, as her arms crossed and her brows lowered.

"She doesn't—that means she's one of yours." Bella bit the words through clenched teeth. "That means the baby is yours." Jack watched the emotions cross her face and wanted to reach for her so badly, but knew she would go off even faster if he did. He had to play it out as calmly as possible because her temper was as bad as his, though she'd never admit it.

"No, it's not—" Jack held up a hand when she would have interrupted. "It's not. She hasn't been in my bed for more than six months. Sean tells me she and Scott have been together for most of that time." Bella's eyes came up to his, hope flaring. "I promise you, there is no one in the pack that could be with pup by me. Brigit was the only one in my bed since the last full moon, and only because she forced it." Bella looked away for a moment and Jack was afraid for a moment she didn't believe him, but she stood and stepped into him and wrapped her arms around him.

"I'm sorry. I overreacted again, didn't I?" Jack slid his hands down to her luscious ass and lifted her up to his mouth.

"I might be convinced to forgive you." He breathed against her lips before kissing her deeply.

~

BELLA WRAPPED her legs around his waist and slid her arms up his chest. Bella grabbed his ears to get a chance to come up for air.

"Wolfie, some of us have to breath." Bella gasped, laughing. Jack chuckled.

"Yeah, so do I, but I tend to forget that when I get my hands on you." Jack's voice was hoarse, but the break allowed Bella to think again.

"Ah, hell. Full moon and a pregnant wolf. I have to work already. Damnit." Bella slumped against Jack in defeat, making him laugh.

"Relax. My mom made it seem like the magic would be automatic." Jack paused. "Speaking of pregnant wolves."

"Yeah. Those children." Bella looked at him. "Maybe we should stay in here, and call them to us, give them some privacy?"

Jack made the arrangements. Jack placed the ottoman next to her chair for him to sit on and Sean moved a couple of the kitchen chairs in.

CHAPTER 18

"Hello Sean, Alex. How are you?" Bella smiled at them both. She saw Jack sitting next to her on the ottoman, knees spread wide in that man's man way they seemed to have, like they had boulders between their legs or something. Bella smothered a snicker at the stray thought. Jack had his elbows on his knees, hands dangling. Sean's posture was nearly a mirror of his Primo's.

Alex was huddled nervously on the straight-backed chair. She tried to smile bravely at Bella, but her fingers were fidgeting.

Bella tuned out most of the questioning, thinking instead about how to go about calming a pregnant wolf in order to control the shift. Bella focused on her breathing, keeping it slow and even. She had noticed the wolf behind everyone's eyes she'd seen so far, ready to rise at a moments notice. She realized it was because the moon was so close and they could feel her call. So she decided she would calm them.

She focused on Alex, on controlling Alex' breathing, timing her breaths with Alex'. Bella watched as Alex' hands unclenched and her face relaxed. Her words came more smoothly as she answered Jack's questions. Alex sat straighter on the chair.

~

JACK HAD BEEN QUESTIONING Alex for about ten minutes before he realized Bella had checked out completely. Once he realized that, he also realized Alex had relaxed completely and seemed more comfortable, more confident. He looked at Sean to see if he was noticing the same thing, and caught his nod to Bella.

Jack looked at Bella and realized her entire focus was on Alex. Her breathing matched exactly to Alex'.

Jack looked back at Sean and raised his eyebrows. Sean mouthed 'Wow' at him.

"Bella" Jack said quietly.

"Yes Jack?" Bella answered just as quietly.

"What are you doing?" Jack whispered.

"I don't know. Why are we whispering?" Bella asked.

"Can you stop doing it?" Jack continued whispering. Bella took a deep breath and shrugged.

"Sure. Can we stop whispering?" Bella said in a normal tone of voice, turning her head to smile at Jack. And just like that, Jack felt the invisible band connecting Bella to Alex snap.

"Alex, are you okay?" Jack asked, looking at her closely.

"Yes." Alex took a deep breath, and shrugged.

"I think Cindy is going to be fine." Sean said into the silence. Jack just stared in awe at Bella.

~

"STOP LOOKING at me like that, Jack." Bella told Jack while they waited for Sean to send the two young pregnant wolves, Traci and Charlie in.

"I'm sorry kitty cat. I've never seen anyone but my mother do that. It was—" Jack cleared his throat. "—incredible. I think Sean's right, and Cindy will be okay."

"Just call me the wolf-whisperer." Bella snarked.

"Bella." Jack chided her. Bella looked up at him, and Jack swooped in. The kiss was one of his breath-stealers. Bella gasped when he released her mouth.

"Jack, you are a cheat." Bella smiled to take the bite out of her words.

"All's fair in love and war, kitty cat." Jack smiled.

"And you are fighting to make me fall in love with you." Bella accused.

"You bet I am." Jack's smile grew, "and if you would just admit it, I could claim my winnings, and we could move on." Bella just shook her head as they heard Traci and Charlie walking in.

BELLA PRACTICED her calming technique on them, to see if she could focus on more than one wolf at a time, and it worked just as well. Both girls agreed they would rather not be pregnant at this time. Bella personally had issues with the whole conversation. She was pro-choice; everyone had a right to their opinions and their choices for their bodies after all. And definitely in these instances, these girls were too young to be mothers, being still children themselves, not to mention the fact that the pregnancies were basically the result of rape. Regardless of all of that, she didn't know how she felt about practically intentional abortion. Bella shook her head. Thoughts for another time perhaps.

Bella "released" or whatever it was she was doing, and tuned into the conversation as Jack was making clear to them that they would return to being normal pre- and post-adolescent girls, sans sex, and watched their reactions.

Traci was the older girl at fourteen—God, fourteen years old, and used and abused and left pregnant, Bella thought—and looked so relieved. Charlie, at twelve, not so much.

"All of the wolves will be under orders, and they will obey my orders rest assured, that you are both off limits. It's my hope that some part of your childhood can be restored." Jack's tone was firm.

Bella watched the girl's closely, and Traci closed her eyes in relief, and Charlie simply smirked. Now, what is that about? Bella wondered.

"Beeellla" Jack called. It sounded to Bella like it wasn't the first time. Bella looked up at him.

"Mmm?" Bella asked. Jack laughed. Bella was picking at her breakfast tray.

"La Mia Bella, my gorgeous little kitty cat, you love your food, don't you?" Jack tapped her nose. "How do you stay so tiny, eating the way you do?"

"Tiny?" Bella rubbed the very obviously not flat stomach of hers, "I've never been tiny. But I do have a very high metabolism." Bella squealed and giggled as Jack suddenly lunged at her, swinging her up into his arms and plopping her into his lap.

"You are tiny and perfect and you know it, kitty cat." Jack growled before licking crumbs from the corners of her mouth.

Bella swatted at him playfully. "Ack! Help! I'm being attacked by the Big Bad Wolf!" Bella cried just before he silenced her. Bella broke the kiss. "No, no! Cats don't like wolfs! Bad wolf. Stop that." Bella laughed.

"I'll show you, silly kitty." Jack growled in her ear. Bella started wiggling and giggling madly when he started tickling her.

"Stop! Stop!" Bella gasped. "I can't breath. Stop!" Bella was laughing too hard to catch her breath.

"Do you give?" Jack breathed in her ear. Bella shivered. She loved his deep, husky voice and his breath in her ear.

"Give what?" She breathed back.

"You." Bella nipped his nose, taking him by surprise enough to loosen his hold so she could hop up. When she got to the door, she opened it, looked back and grinned.

"Catch me if you can!" Jack growled as she raced through, and he chased.

Bella came around the corner into the family room and froze. How could she have forgotten her house was full of people? Jack grabbed her from behind and then growled.

"Down, boy." Bella slapped at him. "Sorry." Bella told him. Jack ignored her and picked her up.

"I won." He told her. Bella looked up at him and saw his eyes were wolf-amber. "Excuse us." He growled at the others in the room as he stalked with her across the room and into her bedroom, slamming the door behind them. He turned the lock savagely and strode to her bed, dropping her on it. Bella watched as he stalked away from her toward the windows, as far from her as he could get, Bella's head was twisted around watching him. She must have made a noise because he started, and turned to her. "I'm sorry. You have to be careful so close to the moon." Jack's voice was quiet as Bella watched his struggle to put the wolf away again.

Bella slowly slid off the bed but stopped when Jack backed up and held his hand up to her. Bella sat on the end of the bed for a moment. "I'm sorry Jack. We were having fun, I didn't think. I forgot the house was full of people, I forgot about the moon, I—I just didn't think. I'm sorry." Bella kept her voice quiet and calm. Then she thought about it, and decided to try that calming thing on him. She leveled her breathing and stretched it out to Jack, and as soon as it touched him he looked at her sardonically.

"Doesn't work on me, kitty cat." Bella shrugged and stood up slowly.

"I'm going to go get something more to eat. Are you okay?" Jack waved at her and turned around. Bella moved slowly to the door, unlocking it, and walked out, carefully closing the door behind her.

CHAPTER 19

hen she turned from the door, she found Sasha, Sean and John all gathered near, watching her worriedly. She jumped when something smashed against the door and then closed her eyes tightly.

"Yeah, okay." Bella had to fight every instinct she had not to go back into that room. She pushed past them into the kitchen and opened the refrigerator instead, hands shaking. She heard murmurs behind her and ignored them. She felt Sasha come up behind her.

"Are you okay, my Prima?" Sasha asked, putting her arm around Bella.

"Yeah, I'm okay. Not so sure about Jack, though. I really fucked up, Sash." Bella leaned her head against Sasha.

"Don't worry, our Primo is tough. Why don't you go sit down, I'll bring you something to eat, you are hungry again?" Bella nodded as she turned from the refrigerator and then froze.

"I smell blood." Bella moved toward her bedroom, but Sasha stopped her.

"Yes, but it's not a lot. He's fine. Let him calm down. We all need to calm down. He'll be out in a few minutes." Sasha squeezed her arm and Bella looked at her, wanting to argue and then just nodded again and went to the table.

Bella hesitated at the head of the table before taking the one to the right. Bella slumped at the table with her eyes on the bedroom door. It opened as Sasha brought a sandwich over, but Bella kept her eyes on Jack's as he walked out. He had a bandage on his hand.

Jack walked over to her and leaned over her at the table, his hand on her cheek. He looked from her to the seat at the head. Bella shrugged sheepishly at him and asked quietly, "what happened to your hand?"

"It's nothing, I owe you a lamp. Are you okay?" Jack breathed at her lips.

"Am I okay? You're the one with a bandage! Screw the lamp. Are you okay?" Jack chuckled and licked her lips.

"I so am not screwing that lamp, look what it did to my hand! I'd much rather screw you." Jack groaned the last as he kissed her deeply. Bella pulled away with a gasp.

"Can I eat my sandwich first? I might need the energy, lover-wolf." Bella's voice was unsteady. Jack laughed as he kissed the top of her head.

"Eat your sandwich, kitty cat. You will most definitely need the energy." Jack walked around her and sat in the chair at the head of the table.

Bella reached for his bandaged hand, apology in her eyes, and Jack shook his head. She raised his hand and kissed it anyway and then set to work on her sandwich.

"La Mia Bella?" Jack nodded his thanks to Sasha when she placed a cup of coffee in front of him, but declined a sandwich when she pointed to Bella's.

"Mmm?" Bella paused after swallowing.

Jack rubbed his thumb along her full lower lip. "I love your smile." Bella opened her mouth to lick his thumb and burped. She clapped her hand over her mouth and gasped.

"Oh dear God, how disgusting! I'm so sorry! How mortifying."

Bella slouched down in her seat. Jack laughed and Bella heard laughter from the family room.

"I don't think I've ever been burped on before." Jack teased.

There was a commotion in the family room as Charlie was shushed. Bella thought she heard her say something like, "she'll do more than that before she's done," but couldn't be sure.

"Don't tease me; do you have any idea how embarrassing this is?" Bella pushed the plate away and put her head down.

"Oh, La Mia Bella. My beautiful little kitty cat." Jack got up and leaned over her. "You can burp on me any time." She felt him pull something from his pocket and push it under her hair where it surrounded her face. "Now would you answer this damn phone? It's been ringing non-stop since I found it in your room a few minutes ago and then, remember my plans for us before moon-rise?"

Bella looked up at him. "I don't know, it may not be safe." Bella picked up her phone, looking at the readout.

"I'll risk it." Jack kissed her forehead as Bella answered the phone as it started to ring again.

"Hello, Kayla. What's going on that you have to call a dozen times this morning?" Bella watched Jack sit back down, knowing he'd hear both sides of the conversation.

"Bells, where have you been? You don't answer the phone anymore? What's wrong with you?"

"Take a pill Kayla, I left my phone in my room, Jack just found it. What's up?" Bella rolled her eyes at Jack.

"Fine, fine. You don't want to tell me, whatever. I was calling because I got your check, made reservations, usual place, tonight, eight."

"Sorry, Kayla can't make it tonight. I have plans."

"Change them. This is tradition. Can't mess with tradition. And do you know what I had to do to get that table for tonight?"

"Sorry, Kayla. Can't change these plans. Do whatever you did again, and get the table for another night."

"You are really getting bitchy, Bells. What the fuck?"

"Kayla." Bella frowned at Jack when he growled at the phone.

"Fine, fine. I'll call you with the new plans."

"Text me, Kayls. I've got plans, remember?"

"Whatev."

Bella hung up the phone and ran through the rest of the calls, all from Kayla except one, with accompanying voicemail, from her accountant Bill.

"Hey, Bella! Bill here. I went ahead and made the offer on that apartment building we talked about. The numbers really work, and the sellers were totally motivated to sell. I mean desperate. Got it for a song. I'll set an appointment in a few days for you to meet with the architect. Okay? Later babe."

Bella heard Jack growl and she shook her head as she put the phone in her pocket. She picked up the plate and carried it into the kitchen. "Thanks Sasha. I'm going to lie down for a bit." Before she could open the door, Jack was there.

"Are you wearing shoes, La Mia Bella?" They both looked down at her bare feet and Bella laughed.

"Ahh, no, I believe we can both see those are my bare toes there, why?" Bella grinned up at him.

"I don't want you to cut your feet. I picked up the big pieces I could find," Jack waived his clumsily bandaged hand, "but until we get the carpet vacuumed thoroughly, I don't want you walking around through here barefoot." Jack swept her up in his arms, a la Rhett Butler, and carried her into her room.

"You know, Jack, last time you did this, you threw me on my bed, and I ended up with one broken lamp, and you ended up cut." Jack lowered her gently to her bed and went right down with her.

"You had your sandwich kitty cat," Jack growled, "I'm hungry for kitty cat."

"Is that really a good idea, this close to moon-rise?" Bella gulped. Jack ran his nose along her ear, causing Bella to shudder.

"Definitely not. I need to keep my mouth from—" Jack inhaled deeply "—sensitive bits. But you taunted me earlier, and my hands are going to follow where that finger teasingly led, La Mia Bella." Jack suddenly took her mouth in a crushing kiss and pressed her into the bed, grinding between her legs.

Bella wrapped her legs around his waist, grinding against him in turn, her hands pulling on his tight ass. Jack held her head immobile between his hands as he kissed her, his tongue stroking her, his teeth grinding against her lips.

Bella gasped as Jack pulled away briefly. "Too many clothes." Bella started tugging at the button on his pants as Jack started tearing at her shirt. Before Bella realized it, she was kneeling on the bed naked in front of Jack, breathing heavily. Jack stood just as naked in front of her, breathing just as heavily.

Bella squeaked as Jack grabbed her leg and pulled her toward him, running his finger from her knee up the inside of her thigh to her curls. Bella lifted her hips toward his questing finger. Jack slipped the finger inside her and stroked, bringing a moan.

"Jack!" Bella cried.

Jack flipped Bella over and raised her hips. "Bella, I need—"

"Oh, yes, Jack. Please, yes." Bella moaned. Bella felt him take her in one smooth thrust and she screamed, throwing her head back, panting and rocking against him. She was wet—she always seemed to be wet for him—but there hadn't been any foreplay, so she wasn't ready for him, and he just slammed into her. There was pain for an instant, and then he was moving and she was stretching to accommodate him.

His grip on her hips was tight as he continued slamming into her, hard and fast and Bella panted with her efforts. Bella fought to rock back and meet him thrust for thrust. Every thrust slammed into her end, bringing her closer to orgasm. "I love your dick. Iloveyourdick-IloveyourdickIloveyourdick!" Bella screamed her climax on the last, and Jack followed as her contractions milked his cock.

Jack collapsed behind Bella and groaned. "I'm sorry, baby. There was no finesse, nothing." He chuckled into her hair, "but God, you are wonderful, baby." Jack rubbed her ass then reached up and pinched a nipple.

"Did you hear me complain?" Bella slapped his hand away, "and did you just call me a wonderful piece of ass?" She turned a baleful eye on him.

"No, you definitely weren't complaining." Jack chuckled, tapping her nose. "And wonderful, yes, piece of ass, no, but apparently, I'm just a dick to you." Bella laughed at his raised brow. She turned in his arms and kissed that brow.

"Yep." She leaned down and kissed the dick too for good measure. "Now be a good dick and let me take a nap."

Bella started to crawl around him to the pillows and he caught her, kissing her soundly. "I'll let you take a nap, but only because I love you madly, and I've just used you—badly." Bella laughed at the bad rhyme. "Take your nap, La Mia Bella. I'll wake you with plenty of time to head over to my house." Bella paused as she started to settle into the pillows.

"Wait, what? Why do I have to go to your house?"

"Did you forget Cindy? The full moon? All of the wolves will be running in my yard." Jack laid down facing her.

"So, Cindy and I could stay here. No reason for us to be there." Bella shrugged.

"I want you close, baby." Jack tapped her nose, ran his finger down to her lips and she kissed it. "No arguments." Bella growled. "Please?"

"Only because you just used me—wildly" Bella grinned.

"Go to sleep, kitty cat."

CHAPTER 20

"*P*rima?" Bella ignored the voice and burrowed deeper into the pillow. "Prima, it's time to wake up."

"I don't recall leaving a wake up call, Sasha." Bella snarled.

"We need to go to Primo's for the full moon, Prima." That raised Bella's head. By the looks of the window, it was about an hour to dark. Bella groaned.

"Why didn't Jack wake me?" She whined.

"He thought if he came in here to wake you, and found you like that," Sasha cleared her throat, "all warm and sleepy and naked, it may delay things." Sasha answered. Bella looked down at where the sheet had slipped to her waist and up at Sasha averting her eyes. Bella grabbed the sheet.

"Yeah, I can see where he might think that. Okay, so I've got about an hour to get over there?" Bella watched Sasha move toward the door shakily.

"Yes, Prima." Sasha was at the door.

"Sasha, it's okay." Bella said quietly.

"No, Prima." Sasha said just as quietly and then went through, closing the door behind her.

AFTER A QUICK SHOWER, Bella dressed and packed an overnight bag and went into the kitchen to find Sean waiting for her.

"Where is everyone?" Bella put the bag down in the family room on her way to her office, checking her cell phone. She'd gotten a text from Kayla moving their dinner to a next night week at seven.

"Next door. Jack didn't want to leave the new wolves without either of you so he left me to take you over. We need to hurry; he wants to have the oath ceremony before the moon rises." Sean followed her into her office.

"No problem, I just want to grab my laptop in case I decide to do some writing—I never know when the muse will strike--and maybe a book or two, in case I want to do some reading. I have a feeling I'm going to be very bored." Bella smiled back at him as she went to her bookshelf and grabbed a couple of books she'd bought but hadn't had time to read yet and then picked up her laptop case next to her desk, making sure the computer and charger were in place.

Turning, she indicated she was ready to go. Sean offered to take the laptop, but she refused. "Sorry, this is like my life. You can take the books and slip them in my overnight bag, and carry that if you like. Is the house closed up?"

"Yes, we'll go out through the garage and take your car, if that's okay?" Sean hesitated at the doorway and let her go through first.

"Sure, I left the keys on the kitchen counter." Bella led the way to the kitchen, Sean pausing only long enough to grab the overnight bag.

BELLA WALKED into Jack's house and looked around curiously. It was big, probably three times the size of hers, two stories, a lot of granite and wood. Bella felt like the poor cousin from Hicksville being "brought up" in the world.

Sean marched her directly to Jack and handed him her bag, and seemed relieved to hand her off. They were in a huge great room with a massive stone fireplace topped by an equally large flat-screen television, and lots of oversized comfortable sofas and chairs arranged in various seating areas.

A wall of windows looked out on the large park like yard where Bella saw the wolves assembled, prowling excitedly awaiting the moonrise. The French doors were thrown wide open. Sean joined them outside, leaving Bella alone inside with Jack and two other wolves. Bella turned to them.

"Hi, Cindy, I understand we'll be spending the evening together." Bella smiled calmly at the nervous young woman and then turned to the jittery dark haired man standing behind her. "You, young man, are going to kiss your young lady, and leave us. You are about the furthest thing from calm I can imagine. I think your eyeballs are vibrating." He looked like he was about to argue, and Bella just waved her hand at the door. "Bu-bye now. We're going to have some girl time, denigrate the male of the species, you know, the usual. You really don't want to be here for that." Jack snorted behind her and Cindy smiled.

"Go now, Scottie. Have fun. I'll see you later." Cindy pulled him down for a long kiss then pushed him away. Scott stumbled his way outside.

Bella patted Jack before moving over to Cindy. "Cindy, you find something very soothing to watch on television, I'll be back in a few minutes. You start feeling stressed, you give out a holler, you got it?" Cindy nodded. Bella spent a few seconds controlling her breathing, and when she was sure Cindy's breathing was slow and steady, she moved over to Jack.

"Whatchadoin', Jack? You didn't come wake me up like you promised." Bella leaned into Jack's kiss.

"I knew we'd never make it over here, and it would be disastrous if the moonrise had caught me in your bed." He rubbed his nose along hers. "We need to get outside so the new wolves can swear oath to us and become part of our pack before the run. I'll not have outsiders running with my wolves."

"Okay, but we have to make it fast, I need to be in here for Cindy, but Jack, you need to keep an eye on Sasha, and I'm worried about what Kelly might do, since we've kept her away from her."

"Don't worry, I'm planning on staying right outside this door all night, protecting you and Cindy, and Sasha will be right beside me. Sean's job is to stay on Kelly's tail and making sure she stays away from the girls. I have a feeling John will be on Mary's—ahem—tail." Jack cleared his throat with a smile.

"Well that doesn't sound like fun, why aren't you going to run? I'll just close up these doors, we'll be fine." Bella complained.

"No, I have to keep Scott from Cindy. His wolf will sense the baby; the most dangerous part of this is keeping the daddy wolf away. His wolf too close can bring the change, which isn't his intent, he just wants to protect her, but he doesn't get that, he just senses his pup, and needs to protect."

"Wait, his wolf can sense the pu—baby, even if he doesn't know she's pregnant?" Bella asked, nearly panicked.

"Yes, it's a smell thing, why?" Jack looked concerned.

"Nothing, just, um. You have a lot of control over your wolf, right?" Bella asked, her fingers digging into his arms.

"The best, of course. I would never hurt you, baby. What's wrong?" Jack held her hands now.

"Nothing, nothing. Promise me, no matter what; don't come into the house, Jack. Don't cross the threshold. Control your wolf. I'm fine, as long as it's just Cindy and me, we are fine, no danger, just stay right outside like planned. Can you do that?" Bella looked earnestly at him.

"Okay sweetie, no problem, I promise." Jack kissed her lightly on the lips. "Now come on, we have some new wolves to accept into the pack."

"Okay." Bella said quietly. She looked back at Cindy who was watching quietly from the couch. Bella followed Jack outside and looked around. She smiled at the wolves she remembered, trying frantically to put names to faces. She saw a weasely faced man talking to Declan. "Jack, who is that guy talking to Declan?"

"Mmm?" Jack looked around, "that's Leroy, why?"

"No reason." Cuz he looks like a weasel. Bella thought.

~

BELLA WALKED BACK INSIDE and closed the doors. She'd won that argument with Jack. She told him she didn't want to compete with barks and growls in her attempts to keep Cindy calm.

"How you doin'?" She asked.

"I'm okay. I think. How are you?" Cindy smiled.

"Just fine and dandy." Bella sat on the chair across from the sofa Cindy had chosen, both with a view of the television. "What are we watching?"

"I don't know something with vampires or something, supposedly a love story." Cindy scoffed.

"Yeah, because vampires are all about the love." Bella grinned. "Okay, time to get to work." Bella pulled her laptop and bag close to her. She placed her books next to her in the chair and sat the bag aside for later, and put the laptop on the coffee table.

"I want you to look at me Cindy." When Cindy was looking at Bella, Bella opened whatever it was and stretched it towards her. She slowed her breathing and watched Cindy's match hers. Bella heard the others shifting, and had a view over Cindy's head of the yard and saw Jack begin pacing in front of the windows in his wolf form. There was a tense moment when Cindy stiffened and started to turn and Bella tightened her hold, focused harder, and Cindy was back, and relaxed, and then she curled up on the couch like it was any other evening.

Bella smiled triumphantly and looked up at the windows right into Jack's eyes and froze. He was frozen in place staring at her. Bella blew him a kiss and it seemed to break his trance. He shook his head and lowered his muzzle, rubbing a paw across it before turning away as Sasha walked up in her beautiful white wolf form. Sasha lay down across the doorway and put her muzzle in her paws. Jack turned so he could look out at the yard and also into the windows, and sat on his haunches.

Bella sat for a few moments just enjoying looking at him. The last time she'd seen him in wolf form—the only time she'd seen him in wolf form—they'd been fighting three rogue wolves and she hadn't paid any real attention to what he looked like. Bella was going to take this opportunity to look her fill.

His wolf was beautiful, large, muscular, and graceful. Rust colored with black points at the tips of his ears, tail and feet. She could better see the white tattoo on his right front flank that matched the tattoo on his right shoulder blade in human form, and the tattoo on hers once they'd mated. It was the outline of a wolf's head surrounded by a Celtic knot. It was beautiful. She couldn't see Sasha's, it was on the other side of her body, but she remembered hers was a darker white, like that white on white embroidery you see.

"Hey Cindy?" She looked over, embarrassed to find Cindy had been watching her stare at Jack.

"Yes, Prima." She responded with a smile.

"So everyone in the pack has that same tattoo?" Bella decided she would just give up on the whole Prima thing. They were going to call her what they were going to call her.

"Yes, when you and Primo mated, you got the tattoo, right?" Bella nodded. "Well, it's slightly different from those of us who are unmated —although the pregnancy did what Scott and I hesitated to do formally—have slightly different tattoos."

"Okay, first, how are they different? Second, why and/or how did the pregnancy change that? Third, why did you hesitate?" Bella was fascinated.

"Until you are mated, the knot is—well, untied, for lack of a better way of putting it. Once you mate, the knot—which if you look at it is circular—closes." Bella nodded, encouraging her to go on. "I don't know if Primo told you, but we are all about procreation. It's not a problem to be—"

"Promiscuous?"

"Sure—until you mate. But once you mate—unless you have the Primo's responsibilities—" Bella growled, "—we mate for life and are monogamous. If we mate before we get pregnant, okay, great, if we get pregnant before we mate—presto!—instant mate."

"Wow. So, a disastrous one night stand could land you with a life time—" Bella broke off, it was just too close to home. Not that it was disastrous exactly, she thought.

"Exactly. We try to be very careful with our hookups. Which leads me to your last question." Cindy paused. "Don't get me wrong, I really love Scott, and I know he loves me, but the Primo has to approve every mating, and I was worried he wouldn't."

"Why ever not?" Bella asked, surprised. She looked over and noticed Jack was looking at them, and even Sasha's ears were cocked. Well, that answered that; they can hear them through the glass. Thought so. Bella thought.

"Well, I knew Sasha and Kelly didn't seek out his bed anymore, and I knew Brigit did, but he hated it. I didn't anymore, because of Scott, but I—"

"You thought he would say no so he could force you back to his bed?" Bella was incredulous, and heard Jack's quiet whine. "Ah, Cindy."

"I know, but you didn't know Brigit. She was a ball-busting bitch. She knew he hated her, and just kept demanding he—" Cindy stopped for a moment. "Declan was in love with her, worshipped the ground she walked on, Lord alone knew why, and she treated him like shit. He just went back for more. He would have done anything if she'd sought his bed, but she refused, just kept returning to Jack's. She wanted to be Prima so badly. She was so certain she'd convince him. She couldn't believe he hated her as much as he did. No one could hate the beautiful Brigit." Cindy just shook her head. "Declan would have made her happy, would have spent his life doing whatever it took to make her happy, and she couldn't have cared less."

"And you thought, instead of letting two of his wolves be happy, he'd force you to mate with him so he could get away from Brigit?" Bella shook her head again.

"Well, I kept waiting for him to pick Sasha. It's obvious he loves her—I'm sorry, but it's true—but I guess that's all changed. It was definitely not going to be Kelly, she's—I don't know what she is, but nice isn't it. So, we waited."

"Wow. Well, no more waiting. I wish you would have given him more credit. I've only known him three days, but even I know his people—you—mean more to him than his own happiness. He would have never taken away what you and Scott had found to avoid some harpy.

"And let's be honest, here among us women. He was getting laid regularly." Bella heard a loud bark and ignored it. "He may not have liked her, but his man-brain, trapped firmly in his pants, was enjoying it, I can assure you." Bella took a deep breath and looked over at the doors and found Jack staring at her over Sasha's head.

"As for Sasha? I have no doubt he loves her too, but it's like a sister, or really close friend, and I have no problem with that at all." She watched Sasha blink at her as Jack lowered his head onto Sasha's shoulder. His tail thumped once at her, whether in accusation or acceptance, she couldn't be sure. Bella turned away and picked up one of her books. Bella fell asleep pretending to read.

"HEY, BABY." Jack's voice in her ear was husky, his arms warm.

"Mmm. Hey. How come you have arms again?" Bella opened her eyes to find Jack carrying her up the stairs.

"Moon's set. Everyone's gone to bed." Jack nuzzled her ear again.

"Mmm. Wait! My stuff! I can't leave my laptop!" Bella wiggled to be put down and realized Jack was naked. "Hey, why are you walking around here naked? Put some clothes on before someone sees my man." Bella slapped at his chest. "And I'm not leaving my laptop downstairs for just anyone to mess with."

"I waited for everyone else to shift and go upstairs before Sasha and I shifted, and she's already headed up to my room with your stuff." Jack laughed at her antics.

"Oh. Well, okay then. Wait, why is Sasha waiting in your room?" Bella asked suspiciously.

"Because I'm too tired to return to your house, and I'm not sending her there alone, and I don't trust..." Jack trailed off.

"Okay, but where is she going to sleep?" Bella tried to keep her voice down as they walked down the hall to large double doors at the end. Jack maneuvered her through the doors and closed them, locking them tight for the night.

"My room has a sitting room attached with a couch. She'll sleep there." Jack sat Bella on the end of his huge four poster bed and picked up a waiting robe. They could hear the shower shut off in the attached bathroom.

"I'm going to take a shower when Sasha comes out." Jack waggled his eyebrows at her, "join me?"

"Uh, no, I'm just going to put a nightshirt on real fast before she comes out." Bella started digging through her bag, which she found sitting on the bench at the foot of the bed. She toed off her shoes and unbuttoned her jeans with one hand.

"I locked the door, Bella, and Sasha won't bother us. You don't need to wear anything to bed. You haven't—" Bella found the nightshirt she'd packed just in case and stripped her shirt and bra off quickly, pulling the shirt down and then removed her pants.

"No, there was a moment when Sasha woke me earlier—just no. I'll wear the nightshirt. You had your nooky for the night, wolf boy." Bella heard the bathroom door open and looked up as Sasha came out in a pair of pajamas.

"All yours, hopefully I saved you plenty of hot water. Good night." Sasha smiled and walked around the wall through the archway into the sitting area. God, there's not even a door! Bella thought.

"Bella, if this is about what you were talking about with Cindy, I did not enjoy having sex with Brigit." Jack leaned into her.

"Oh Jack, sex is sex. It's not like I blame you. Now, if you'd gotten your freak on with her after you'd enjoyed all this," Bella gestured down at herself in her silly Mickey Mouse oversized T-shirt, "I'd have to kill you. But what happened before we met?" Bella shrugged.

"My freak on?" Jack choked out, laughing. He pulled her into his arms.

"Go take your shower, wolf-boy. I'm going to bed. And put some clothes on, why dontcha? We aren't alone in here." Bella pushed him toward the bathroom and climbed up onto the big bed.

~

BELLA PRETENDED to be asleep when Jack came out of the shower. She just liked to watch him move. He went to a tall dresser and pulled black silk boxers out of a top drawer, and slipped them on and then padded to the bed. Bella sighed watching that yummy length getting covered up. He was long and hard—of course. He was always long and hard. Yum.

Bella made sure her eyes were still as he climbed into the bed next to her, and felt him shift next to her. She shivered as his hand slowly ran up her thigh to her hip.

"I know you're awake, kitty cat. Come out, come out to plaaay." Jack teased, running his finger along the edge of her panty toward her ass and the inside of her thigh.

"Mmm?" Bella mumbled, knocking against him as though turning in her sleep, pushing him to his back and settling against his chest, hooking a leg over him until his—ooh, yum—cock was lodged firmly against her favorite spot. Bella curled her hand on his chest and tucked her head into his shoulder under his chin.

"Alright then kitty cat, I'll wait until morning for my milking— milk. I love you." Jack kissed the top of her head as Bella snorted. Bella fell asleep listening to him breathing, feeling him rubbing her back. I think I love you too, Bella thought.

CHAPTER 21

*B*ella awoke with Jack's mouth on her breast, his hands roaming over her hungrily. Bella moaned and stretched. She pulled at his hair until her nipple came free of his mouth with a pop making her giggle.

"Sasha?" Bella gasped as he turned his attention to the other nipple.

"Sean took her back to your place a few minutes ago. We're all alone, kitty cat, and I want my milk—ing" Jack laughed and licked her nipple, making her shiver.

Bella was humming by the time Jack worked his way down to her stomach, playing with her navel for a second before settling between her thighs.

"There's the source of my favorite cream." Jack growled before he parted her curls and licked her folds. Bella purred as he flicked and licked and sucked at her. He slid a finger deep inside her and she moaned.

Bella's hands were fisted in his hair, whether to keep him in place, or hold him closer, she wasn't sure. Then she was bucking against him, and because she was afraid of tearing his hair, she released him and took handfuls of the sheets instead. Bella's head thrashed as he brought her moaning with his mouth and fingers.

Once her eyes had stopped rolling in her head she looked down at his cat-that-ate-the-canary grin and watched him lick his lips and then his fingers as he stalked back up her body.

"I love the taste of you on my tongue, La Mia Bella." He said hoarsely into her lips before kissing her deeply. He made love to her mouth, thrusting deeply inside repeatedly, making her moan and writhe against him.

Bella ran her hands down his body until she clasped his hard length in her hand and stroked. "Please!" She begged when Jack let her up for air. She slipped down his body until she could position him for entry and looked up at him. He bent nearly double to kiss her forehead.

"I could crush you, little kitty," Bella lifted her hips and he slipped inside her a small inch and he groaned. "Oh, God! Lift your hips—yes." Bella spread her legs wide, bending her knees and lifting her hips against him as he thrust deep, her hands on his arms where they braced on either side of her head keeping his weight from crushing her.

Bella looked down their bodies and could watch him moving in and out of her as she felt the slide. She rocked her hips to meet each thrust. She slid her hands down his body to the base of his shaft and curled one hand around his balls as she used the other to circle the base and squeeze.

"Aaahh! No, stop. Too soon." Jack gasped. Bella released him and slid her hands around to his delicious ass and squeezed his ass instead, continuing to look down and watch that continuous slide in and out.

Before she knew it, she'd lost the rhythm of the thrusts and was bucking and thrashing. Jack grabbed her ass and held her in place as he increased the pace of his thrusts, bringing her over the edge before following.

"Oh, my." Bella panted.

"Ditto." Jack gasped next to her. "Uh—Yeah. I'm going to take a shower. I think"

"Good. Great. Good for you. You go do that. I'm going to wait for my heart to return to normal over here." Jack chuckled. "Glad you can walk and all that." Bella patted at him.

"You don't want to join me? I think I may just have the strength to help you into the bathroom." Jack said gallantly.

"No, no. You go ahead. I'll just catch my breath." Bella made kissy noises in his direction as he got up and stumbled in the direction of the bathroom.

Bella remained where she was for a few minutes. Slowly, she got up and gathered the clothes Jack had managed to pull off her without waking her—my magic man—and moved to her bag on the bench at the foot of the bed.

Bella pulled out the clothes she'd packed for today and put away her nightclothes. She made sure her books were there—they were—and her laptop and charger were packed in their case—of course. Sasha was nothing if not thorough.

Bella was looking around his room when Jack came out of the bathroom. She started guiltily. Jack narrowed his eyes at her.

"Whatcha doing?" He asked, walking over to her, still naked.

"Nuthin'." Bella spluttered. "My turn in the shower." Bella picked up her clothes, and headed into the bathroom. It was steamy and smelled of Jack.

She'd just stepped into the big shower when he popped his head in the door. "I'm going to head over to your house for a minute, okay? Sasha said she'll have your breakfast ready over there when you get there."

"Okay, can you take my bags with you?" She called back.

"Sure. I love you." Jack closed the door behind him.

Bella finished her shower and dressed. She opened the door and found Kelly lounging in Jack's bed, smelling the sheets right where Bella had been lying.

"What the hell are you doing in Jack's bedroom?" Bella demanded.

"I've spent a great deal of time here, or didn't you know that?" Kelly smirked. She made sure to pat the bed on "here" implying she meant the bed, not the room.

"You're a very bad liar, Kelly. Now get out." Bella gestured at the door. Kelly sniffed at the sheets again.

"Delicious. Just delicious. I was listening. You make wonderful yummy noises. Question, Prima." Kelly slinked off the bed and stalked toward Bella. "Why can't I come over to your house to play?" She tried —badly—to pout.

"None of the wolves are allowed at my house, Kelly. Now quit the crap, and get out. Jack's expecting me, and if he has to come over here looking for me, I daresay, he won't be very happy to find you here. From what I understand, he didn't allow any of you into this room." Bella raised her eyebrows at Kelly.

"Until last night. Sasha slept in here, I know because she didn't sleep in our room, and I smell her here." Bella just pointed at the door until Kelly finally turned and left. Bella took several deep breaths before following slowly.

CHAPTER 22

*B*ella trudged into her kitchen exhausted already. When she walked out of Jack's house, she was happily surprised to find her Jetta outside with the keys waiting for her.

"Hey, sweetie! What took so long?" Jack called from the table.

"I came out of the bathroom and found Kelly sniffing your sheets." Bella told him with a grimace. Bella slipped into the chair next to Jack tiredly.

"What?!?" Jack yelled. There was a crash in the kitchen as Sasha dropped something. Both of them looked over, but she waved them off.

"You heard me. She was lounging on your bed, sniffing the bed where I'd slept." Bella shuddered in disgust. "It was creepy as all get out. I asked her what the hell she was doing in your room; she tried to make it out like she was always spending time there. I shut her down and kicked her out." Bella waved at him to let him know she was over it—not—and wanted to move onto another topic. "I forgot to tell you last night, I got that text from Kayla last night, our dinner was moved to next week, so you'll be on your own for a few hours."

"I'll join you. I'd love to take you out to dinner, La Mia Bella." Jack said.

"No, Jack, this is a special dinner for Kayla and I, a tradition when I finish a book. It's just the two of us. You and I can go out to dinner another time."

"Absolutely not. It's not safe. You are the mate of the Primo of the—"

"Yeah, yeah, the Lupi de Notte Pack. I got that memo, believe me. Along with the tattoo. Hey! I fell asleep. I fell asleep! Cindy didn't shift last night, did she? Oh God, if I fell asleep on the job and she lost her baby because of me, I'll—"

"No, sweetie, she fell asleep about the same time you did, best Sasha and I can tell, she fell asleep because you did. She was just fine, all night long. You have nothing to worry about." Jack smiled at her and then frowned. "And no changing the subject. You have obligations, and responsibilities. And I have a responsibility to keep you safe."

"Jack, I will not live in a bubble. I will go out to dinner on my own. I will go shopping, go to lunch, whatever. Live with it." Bella was insistent. "Let me have my routine, Jack. You have to let me have my life." Bella laid her hand on his tense arm. "It's only a couple of hours. Two, three tops."

"Two. Two hours." Jack said, reaching for her hand. Bella squeezed it with a smile.

"Okay, two hours, lover wolf. Now let me eat my breakfast." Jack lifted her hand to his lips and released it.

"How about after breakfast we get away, just you and me?" Bella asked. "Maybe if you promise to remain calm, I'll tell you more of my story."

IN THE END, it took a few hours before Jack could get away from the pack, but Sasha made them a picnic lunch, and they drove one of the pack SUV's out to the Falls the city was named for. Bella wore a purple one-piece swimsuit—she never wore a two-piece, she didn't feel her stomach was flat enough—under her denim cut-off's and tank top. Jack wore board shorts and a muscle T-shirt.

They parked and hiked closer to the Falls, Bella carrying the blanket and Jack the picnic basket and cooler. The spring air was mild and clear.

"Here." Bella stopped and started laying out the blanket next to the natural swimming hole formed at the base of the Falls. Jack looked around in awe.

"This is so beautiful." Jack looked back at her, "this is incredible." Jack placed the basket and cooler down, and helped her straighten the blanket before anchoring it with the heavy basket and cooler and then he pulled her to him. "But not as beautiful or as incredible as you."

Bella ran her hands up his chest and into his hair as Jack leaned down to her lips. His hands ran down her body to her luscious ass and squeezed, pulling her tightly to him. Jack lowered them slowly to their knees. Bella rubbed happily, purring, against him and then pulled away.

"Jack, public place. People could come out here. Families, with children." Bella stopped him. Jack growled, making her laugh. "Down boy. You are quite well sexed; you are not at all deprived. Settle down now."

"Around you, a saint would be—oh, wait, saints probably are undersexed—oh, well, you probably get where I'm going with this." Jack stole another kiss before he sat back. "Are you hungry, kitty?"

"Are you horny, wolfy?" Bella laughed. "And just for that smirk, you get to sleep in your own bed tonight—alone." Jack started to protest. "It will be good for you. Absence makes the heart grow fonder, or something." Bella crawled to the cooler, pretending not to notice his watching her rump twitch. "Now, what did Sasha pack us?"

"You are an evil, bad kitty." Jack said sternly. Bella gave him a look, "fine, fine. Okay." Bella heard him mutter something under his breath, sounded like a repeat of the bad kitty comment, which she ignored.

"Mmm. Fried chicken. I haven't had home-made fried chicken in— I don't think I've ever had home-made fried chicken! Potato salad, strawberries, whipped cream—mmm—" Bella broke off on a squeal as Jack grabbed her from behind and began nibbling her neck.

"The things I could do with that whipped cream..." Jack trailed off, turning her in his arms to nibble her lips. Bella hummed for a moment before pushing him off.

"Maybe we'll take some to bed when we get home—before you go home for the night—if you're a good boy today." Bella smiled at his growl. Bella put the food down and leaned over to him again. "Let's eat, okay? Then maybe have a swim?" Bella breathed against his lips and then took his lower lip between her teeth, tugging lightly and letting it slip through. Bella looked up at him in shock suddenly. "Oh, dear God! You really are going to make me fall in love with you, aren't you?" She breathed. A slow smile spread across Jack's face as her words registered.

"I'm trying really hard. Is it working?" His fingers traced her faced in wonder.

"Shut up and feed your mate, wolf." Bella's voice was husky.

"Yes, ma'am. That I can do." Jack smiled again and began getting the supplies out of the basket.

BELLA SPENT several hours just being with Jack. First they ate all the yummy food Sasha packed and then they spent a few hours swimming and playing in the water. Bella flopped onto the blanket next to Jack, tired but happy. Jack curled around her, and played his fingers on her stomach.

"You are so beautiful, my little kitty, La Mia Bella." Bella giggled and stilled his tickling fingers.

"You poor, delusional, blind wolf." She told him solemnly. Jack tweaked her nose in response.

"Where did you get your name? Arabella Mia. It's very fitting, my beauty." Jack sighed at her, continuing to run his fingers over her.

"Arabella means 'beautiful eagle' and stop that, if you want answers." Bella slapped his hands and then turned to her side to face him. "I don't know where it came from, my parents—my adopted parents, of course—said it was written on a note pinned to the blanket I was wrapped in when I was found in the hospital lobby." Bella looked up at Jack and found him watching her eyes closely. She reached out her hand, and he took hold of it, squeezing to let her know he was there. "What else?"

"What happened after your first shift—when they were gone?" Jack's voice was husky.

"You have to promise to stay calm, Jack. It's bad. It gets really, really bad." Bella tried to impress on him just how bad with her eyes.

"I promise to—well, I promise to do my best, love. That's the best I can do. How bad is really, really bad?" Jack asked.

"You saw Mary." Bella watched Jack's eyes get wide then hard. "I've met—people," Bella's voice broke on the word, "like Gordon and his crew. Still want to hear the story?" Bella waited. Jack stared at her for several seconds before nodding once. "Okay, but Jack? Remember, I'm right here, okay? I'm here, and mostly whole."

"And in my arms. I'll try to remember." Jack leaned in and kissed her lightly on her lips, nose and forehead. Bella closed her eyes to savor him, and order her thoughts.

"Okay. So, I walked out of my room, and my parents were gone. So was everything. I mean, the whole house was empty. The only room still with stuff in it was mine, I guess because I was in there. I ran outside, and the sun was coming up. There was no sign; even outside, that they'd ever been there.

"I went back inside. I didn't know what to do. I took a shower; I packed my backpack with a few changes of clothes. I had some money I'd made babysitting. This was maybe two years before The War? Yes, that's right. Anyway. I packed all that in my backpack. We lived in what was back then Seattle. I didn't know what I was going to do, but I couldn't stay there, in that empty house. I checked the refrigerator, the pantry; they'd even taken the food." Bella took a deep breath.

"I walked outside and ran into the neighbors, bad luck. Mr. Napier had been out walking their dog when my parents left, told him they were moving. Mr. Napier assumed I was with them, so when they saw me, they were surprised, to say the least." Bella didn't realize she was crying until Jack was wiping tears from her face with shaking fingers.

"I tried to keep walking, but they wouldn't let me. They forced me into the car, and took me to the police, which led to the foster care system. What a joke. I was in the first home a week before the father came into my room and forced me—" Bella's voice choked off and Jack grabbed her to him tightly. He was shaking almost as hard as she was in his struggle to maintain control. Bella took a deep breath.

"I am very well endowed," Bella indicated her breasts and Jack rubbed against them in appreciation. "I developed very early. Very early. He undressed me and fondled me. I fought. Oh God, I fought him. I kicked and bit and hit. I SCREAMED!" Bella was breathing hard and so was Jack, holding her tightly and rubbing her back with hands that shook.

"He laughed." Bella whispered. "Then I realized his wife was in the doorway watching and laughing as well." Bella heard Jack's soft Oh God and had to pause. "But I left them both screaming. He was undoing his pants when I pulled the baseball bat out from under the bed." Bella paused again as Jack pulled away to see her face.

"I'd seen the way he looked at me the day I arrived. I was young, and naive, but not stupid. I stole the bat from the neighbor boy and hid it that same day. I beat him unconscious while his wife screamed at me from the door. When she came at me, I hit her once, she went down. I got dressed, packed what I arrived with, emptied his pockets, her purse, and her coffee tin—where she kept the money the state gave them for me—and didn't look back.

"I was in Portland by morning, and ran into bad luck again, in the form of my first Werewolves." Bella shuddered and Jack's arms tightened.

"Oh, God." Jack rasped into her hair. "Please tell me that was the bad part already over with." Jack begged.

"Oh, sure. That was the bad part. It just wasn't the really bad part, or the really, really bad part." Bella felt Jack's body shaking against hers, and moved to hold his face in her hands. He was sweating profusely.

"Those Weres weren't the really bad ones. They were bikers, traveling southeast. I rode with them for a while. One of them took me—under his wing, you could say. He looked after me, for a while—and for a price." Jack's arms tightened convulsively again.

"What price?" He growled.

"He was—he had unique tastes—and I—took care of them." Bella had to take another deep breath. This was so damn hard, she thought.

"Oh, God." Jack gasped again.

"Jack, I need you to breath, and listen to me." Bella locked on his eyes and held his hands tightly. "He taught me—things."

"What kinds of—things?" Jack bit out. Jack avoided her eyes and Bella squeezed his hands.

"Jack, I need you to look at me." Bella waited until he did. "I'm talking about sex." Jack's eyes closed and she squeezed his hands again until he opened them again. "He taught me every sexual act, except one. I learned to enjoy sex, every part of sex, from being with him. There was only one thing he wouldn't do with me, said I was too young..." Now Bella closed her eyes for a moment. Bella's voice was quiet. "If The War hadn't come, if I hadn't lost him, I might still be with him..." Jack's arms tightened on her briefly and she opened her eyes to him.

"What wouldn't he do with you, Bella?" Jack's voice was husky.

"Straight sex. Vaginal sex. He wouldn't take my virginity. He was saving it for my sweet sixteen, he said." Bella shook her head. Jack's arms convulsed on her again.

"Everything else? You mean—everything?" Jack looked shocked.

"Everything." Bella looked at him very directly.

"And you enjoyed it." Jack couldn't seem to wrap his mind around it.

"Well, not in the beginning, but he didn't force, either. He introduced it kind of—I don't know. But yes, I enjoyed it, I do enjoy it. As in present tense, I enjoy sex, all aspects of it. Is that so shocking?" Bella smiled at him.

"But you've never asked me to—" Jack's voice broke off. He didn't even know how to say it.

"Well, in case you didn't notice, lover-wolf, you're a little repressed. Not to mention, your size is a little intimidating. I'm not so sure I could—accommodate you—there. My previous lovers I've enjoyed that way haven't been so—blessed." Bella laughed at him.

"Bella, my love. I—do you—what can I—I feel like—what do I need to do?" Jack was stuttering worse than a teenager on his first date, and it made Bella smile.

"Lover-wolf, I've never seen you so. You're practically speechless." Bella ran a finger along his lips.

"I feel like I've just found out—I mean you just as much as told me I'm not enough to satisfy you—whatever you need, please, my love." Jack begged.

"Oh, Jack, no!" Bella grabbed him closer to her. "I never said you were less than satisfying to me. You have always more than satisfied me, Jack, every single time. You do everything for me, everything to me, that I could possibly want—"

"But you said I'm too big for—" Jack interrupted her.

"Anal sex is one small part of our sex life. And there are ways. I know better than to suggest bringing someone else into our bedroom," Jack growled, making Bella laugh, "but there are toys, other things we can do instead. I've never brought it up, because like I said, um, repressed much? I mean, it makes you uncomfortable to talk about your wolves alternate lifestyles! How was I going to bring this up?"

"I'm so sorry, my love. You shouldn't have had to be uncomfortable bringing up anything you need to me. Anything! I love you. Please promise to never hesitate to ask for what you need." Jack had his hands on her face tenderly by this point, staring intently into her eyes.

"I promise Jack. Damn you. You really are going to do it, aren't you?" She whispered before she kissed him. Bella felt Jack sink into her kiss with a smile of triumph.

CHAPTER 23

*B*ella came up for air and found Jack smiling stupidly at her.

"You looove me." He said.

"Do not." She denied.

"Do to." He said sappily.

"Shaddup." Bella said. Jack kissed her nose. Bella guessed he decided to take his minor victory in stride for now. She might be halfway—okay, if she were honest with herself, more than—to the emotion, but that didn't mean she was ready to actually verbalize it.

"Where were we in your life story, kitty cat?" Jack asked.

"The biker gang I was riding with had blown into what was then San Francisco with a roar, The Last War just hit, and I lost Eric, the man who taught me so much, and took care of me for almost two years. Somehow I survived that week just after the world was remade, and I was alone again, and it was about to get really, really bad. I was fourteen years old." Bella resettled herself next to Jack, on her side facing him. Jack was suddenly breathing hard again as he realized how young she'd been during all of those sexual acts they'd been discussing.

"Another thing Eric taught me was how to ride, and I took his motorcycle, and his money, and rode away, as fast as I could, because that area was so unstable and falling fast.

"A week later, Faedresse was stabilized, the Fae had been locked behind their dimensional portals, and I was trapped by another group of Werewolves." Bella shuddered. "I didn't make it to my sweet sixteen." Bella looked up at him to make sure he understood what she was saying.

"There were six of them. They passed me around for months." Jack cried out. "They kept me tied up in the beginning, but after several months, they got lax. As soon as they did, and they'd drunk themselves into a stupor, I grabbed some clothes, some money, and snuck off to the nearest bus station. Which if you remember, was hit-and-miss back then. But I got lucky, and for all the money I had, and one sexual favor, which by that point—" Bella just shook her head. Jack was shaking again.

"The bus brought me here. Almost as soon as I got off it, I ran into this guy—" Jack groaned and squeezed her tight.

"No more, I don't think I can—" Bella interrupted him with kisses on his face and was shocked to find tears.

"No, that's what I thought too, and I started out swinging, believe me, but he just slung me over his shoulder like a sack of potatoes, and told me to be quiet, and took me home. To his wife, who took one look at me, put me in a bathtub and then fed me, and put me in a clean bed, but not before showing me there was a lock on the bedroom door, on my side of the door.

"The next morning, I slowly came out of the room to find them at the table. He gestured sternly at me to sit down while his wife got a plate for me out of the stove. His name was Bill and his wife was Marie. He was an accountant, and she was a teacher. He told me that as long as I followed their rules I could stay with them. Schools weren't up and running yet, but his wife taught me.

"I think it was a defense mechanism when I started writing, and it evolved into this career of mine—once the publishing houses got running again, of course."

"Bill the accountant, as in 'Later, Babe' Bill the accountant?" Jack asked, surprised.

"The one and the same. He and his wife saved me." Bella leaned her forehead to his. "They never asked my story, and I never told them, but they suspected some of the really bad parts. I had to look really bad when I came off that bus." Bella sighed. "I didn't have another sexual encounter until about four years ago, I had a couple of partners off and on, and nothing after that, until this crazy, delusional, blind wolf came along—" Bella started giggling when Jack rolled over on her, tickling her.

"Delusional? Blind? I'll show you." Jack growled, running his hands up her sides to cup her beautiful breasts as he settled his weight between her legs.

"What exactly will you show me, wolf-man?" Bella asked, wiggling against him, moving her hands up and down his back.

"Oh, Bella, my love. La Mia Bella, I will show you just how much I love you." Jack sank into her lips. Bella moaned and wrapped her legs around him as she drank him in. Bella pulled her lips away and gasped for air.

"Take me home and take me to bed?" She asked.

"I thought I was sleeping in my own bed tonight?" Jack asked.

"You are, but we have hours yet before you have to go home…and there was mention of whipped cream…" Bella purred. Jack bounced up and pulled her with him, frantically packing everything away.

"What are you doing standing around, woman? Let's go! There's whipped cream!" Jack exclaimed, and Bella laughed to see his exuberance.

CHAPTER 24

*J*ack and Bella swept into the house through the garage, and Bella stopped briefly at the refrigerator to look for more whipped cream, which she hid in the blanket she carried into her room while Jack dropped the basket and cooler off with Sasha and thanked her for the picnic. Sasha just smiled knowingly, and Jack knew she knew exactly what Bella took into the bedroom with her.

Bella was on the toilet when he swooped into the bathroom. "Hey!" She yelped. "A little privacy here!" Jack leaned over Bella and spoke into her lips.

"I've been over every inch of your body, kitty cat. With my hands, with my tongue, every inch many times." He kissed her and straightened. "Now hurry up, I can't wait for that whipped cream you promised me!" Bella laughed and watched him move to the other toilet before starting the shower.

AFTER THEY QUICKLY SHOWERED, they raced to the bed, where Bella had left the whipped cream, and Bella shoved him down on the bed, shaking the can in her hand with an evil glint in her eye.

"What are you thinking of doing with that, kitty cat?" Jack asked with a smile.

"Why, I sure don't know wolf-man. Any ideas?" Bella squirted a little of the cream in her mouth with a smile. Then she stopped smiling. "Alright. No more Ms. Nice Kitty. Get up there, on the pillows, flat on your back. Arms up, spread eagle. Pretend you're tied down. If you don't pretend properly, I'll go get the real thing, got that, wolf-man?" Jack just looked at her, but Bella stared him down until he slowly complied.

"O-kaaay." Jack said slowly. "Do I want to know why you have restraints?"

"You've never asked what my novels are about, have you?" Bella shook her head. "Silly, silly wolf. I have a lot of—research materials—in my office. I've never actually used any—well, okay—most of it, but I have it."

"Oh, Lord." Jack gasped as Bella slowly climbed onto the bed between his legs.

"Mmm. Such a yummy smorgasbord of manly goodness. Where to start?" Bella ran her eyes from his crotch up his chest to his eyes and watched them go from the sea green she loved to the amber she adored. Bella shook the can again in one hand and then reached for his long thick hard cock with her other and licked her lips. "Who am I kidding? This is my favorite meal right here."

Bella sprayed the cream along his length and around the base and then set the can aside. Bella leaned down and ran her tongue up that length, licking the cream and felt him shudder against her. She continued to lick and suck and then took him in hand and worked him manually as well. Jack bucked against her, and she felt his hands on her head and she looked up at him in warning and he returned his hands to position quickly as he growled. She laughed and went back to work.

"Bella, I'm going to come!" Jack gasped out.

"Go, baby. That's what I'm working for here." Bella went back to working him manually along his length while she sucked at the head of his cock. Bella heard the sheets tear as he fought to keep his hands where she'd ordered him, while he bucked against her in rhythm with her sucking and hand motions.

Bella knew he was close, and took a second for a deep breath and to swallow before renewing her attack in time for his explosion. She took all of it in, swallowing convulsively and then licking him clean before resting against him as their breathing returned to normal.

JACK REACHED DOWN and lifted Bella up into his arms, turning her onto her back before kissing her deeply. He tasted himself on her, along with whipped cream, and sighed. He brushed her hair from her face and smiled down at her.

"Mmm." He tried.

"Yeah." She responded.

"Wow." He said.

"Mmhmm." She returned. Jack laughed.

"Words." Jack said. "I'm trying." He sighed, "Wow."

"You said that." She giggled.

"I thought it bore repeating." He smiled at her again.

"Ooh, five words all together." Bella smiled back.

"You realize it's my turn now?" He grinned at her.

"I thought that was your turn?" She smirked at him.

"You know exactly what I mean, kitty cat." Jack levered off her and grabbed the can of cream. "Assume the position. Remember the rules, no more Mr. Nice Wolf." Jack ordered sternly. Bella laughed silently and assumed the position she'd ordered him to, wiggling enticingly to get there. Jack smacked her flank lightly.

Jack settled between her legs after spraying the cream around and over her breasts, concentrating on her nipples and then began lapping it up, licking and nipping, sucking and biting, until Bella was moaning and writhing on the bed, clenching the sheets as he'd been in order to keep in position. Once she was bucking uncontrollably and he'd licked her breasts clean, he slid down until he faced her curls between her legs and held up the can of whipped cream before looking at her with a smile.

"I prefer the taste of my kitty's cream." He said, tossing the can away, and settling down. In moments, she was bucking against him, her knees drawn up and open wide to him while he licked at her. He held her wide open to him as he thrust his tongue deep and she rocked her hips into him, moaning.

"Jack!" Bella called. "Please!"

"Come for me baby, and I'll give you whatever you want." Jack told her.

"I am! I have! I will! Please, Jack! Please, now, I need you!" Bella was thrashing, her head rolling on the bed as Jack sucked on her clit and he slipped two fingers deep inside her and started stroking. Bella rocked her hips against his thrusts, once, twice, three times and she came with a gush over his fingers with a scream. Jack lapped at her and then sat up licking his fingers while she stared at him, panting for breath.

Jack looked down, and tasting her, as always, went a long way to bringing him back, but he wasn't quite ready for her, and Bella saw immediately the problem.

"You drained me quite thoroughly, baby." Jack said sheepishly. Bella sat up quickly and grabbed him, working him roughly back to hardness. Jack threw his head back and then turned her over and thrust into her in one motion.

"OH GOD YES!" Bella yelled as she felt Jack's hands on her hips gripping tightly as he thrust deep. Then Jack's hold changed, his left arm crossed her body and gripped her right shoulder to hold her in place while his thrusts never faltered, and his right hand moved over her hip, caressing her ass. "Please, yes." Bella panted as Jack's hand continued into her crack and caressed up and down before he slid one finger slowly inside her anus, making her buck against him.

Bella's breathing got faster as he slowly stroked his finger—oh, God!—deep inside then slowly back out while he continued thrusting deep and hard. "More. Moremoremore. Please ohpleasepleaseohplease." Bella chanted as Jack slid a second finger in and increased the tempo of both thrusts. Bella's thrashings got wilder and her chanting became wordless pleas until she was suddenly there and Jack thrust a last time and convulsed inside her. Bella felt him kiss her tenderly on her neck before he lowered her to the bed.

"I love you." He whispered into her hair.

"I know you do." She whispered back. She turned into his arms so she could face him. "You are incredible, wonderful, and awesome. You know that, right?" She ran a hand along his face.

"I take it I did good?" He asked shyly.

"You crazy, wonderful, delusional wolf!" Bella rested her head on his shoulder. "You did so very very good." Bella sighed. Bella looked up at him again. "We had a good day, didn't we? A day just for us?" Bella asked hopefully.

"Yeah, we had a good day." Jack looked down for a second and then back up at her. "Are you really sending me next door for the night?"

"Jack, don't ruin the day, please, don't be difficult. We're doing good here. Getting to know each other, enjoying each other. I'll see you in the morning, I'm sure." Bella looked imploringly at him. She needed this. She needed him to understand this.

"Okay." Jack sighed. "Okay, but soon, my perfect little kitty cat, we will be addressing this living apart business." Jack kissed her nose. "Are you in bed for the night?" he asked.

"Yes, someone exhausted me." Bella smiled.

"Well, I'll have to track him down." Jack kissed her tenderly again. "I'm going to use the bathroom and then leave instructions not to disturb you and then head next door. Call me if you need me, or want me..." Jack looked at her hopefully.

"Go, get!" Bella pushed him out of bed.

CHAPTER 25

*B*ella woke and stretched with a smile. She rushed through her shower and headed out of her room. It was earlier than she was usually up, and she saw a surprised, and was that a guilty look on Sasha's face? Maybe it was because breakfast wasn't ready.

"I've got some ideas I want to put down. I'll be in my office for a few minutes." Bella called to Sasha as she passed through quickly. She came to a sudden halt next to the sofa and stared down at the rumpled bedding. "What's this Sasha?" Bella looked over at the kitchen and caught the flash of panic and now definite guilt on Sasha's face.

Then Bella got it. After the first night, Lucy had moved out of Sasha's room and in with Mary and Alex, and Bella had kicked John out of the house and back to Jack's. Apparently, he'd been sleeping on the couch, and Sasha was feeling guilty about keeping it from her.

"Ahhh, John's been sleeping here, hasn't he?" Bella just smiled and shook her head as she kept walking. But then the scent reached her, and the scent was one much more familiar to her. Almost as familiar now as her own. And the smell was getting stronger as she moved to the hallway. Bella paused and looked back at Sasha and saw the stricken look on her face and Bella knew.

Bella followed her nose all the way to the end of the hall to Sasha's room, and heard the shower running in her bathroom. Without thinking, she crashed in and found Jack.

~

JACK LOOKED up when the door crashed into the wall and saw Bella in full rage. "Bella." Jack breathed. He rinsed quickly and shut off the water, stepping out of the shower and grabbing a towel, holding it like a shield. "I can explain."

"What the FUCK!" Bella screamed and shoved him into the wall. Jack dropped the towel—lousy shield anyway—and grabbed her arms to stop her blows. "You. Don't. Fucking. Live. Here. Damnit!" Each word punctuated by a blow before Bella spun out of his arms.

"Bella, please. Listen to me. Please listen to me, love." Jack begged.

"Listen to you? Why? So you can lie to me some more?" Bella had walked away from him, but stalked back and punched him full force in the jaw, closed fist. Jack rocked back two paces before catching his balance as Bella screamed, clutching her hand to her chest.

"Bella!" Jack ignored the throbbing in his jaw and reached for her hand. "Let me see your hand, baby. Please let me see."

"Don't touch me!" She yelled. "You liar! Don't touch me!" Bella backed away from him, tripping on the corner of the bed until she fell on her bottom. Tears poured down her face.

"Please don't say that. I've never lied to you. Please let me see, we need to get your hand looked at, please love, please baby. Let me see it." Jack begged as he kneeled next to her.

"You did! You lied! You said you were going home! But you didn't! You slept on the couch, you lying piece of shit!" Bella sobbed. It tore Jack's heart to see her pain.

"No baby. I never said I was going home. I am home. Right here, with you, wherever you are, is home." Jack carefully placed his hands on her face and tilted it up to his, using his thumbs to wipe her tears.

"You said you were going next door. But you didn't. You lied." Bella hiccupped.

"I tried, I really did. I went to the door, I even opened it, but I

163

couldn't leave." Bella snorted, and Jack leaned into her, resting his forehead on hers. "Baby, I couldn't leave you. I'm sorry. I tried, but I couldn't. I thought—I don't know what I thought. I guess I should have just come back into the bedroom and told you."

Bella hadn't pulled away from him, so Jack pulled her into his arms and gently took her injured right hand into his, straightening and flexing the fingers experimentally. Bella hissed her breath, but didn't making any other noise.

"If I hadn't caught you, you would have kept it from me. And you had Sasha ready to lie for you." Bella said quietly.

"I don't know. Probably. I'm sorry. But not for long, I did warn you, my kitty, we'd be addressing this soon.

"I don't think it's broken, baby kitty. Just badly bruised. Please don't hurt yourself again. If you want to punish me again, use something other than my precious love kitten, please?" Jack kissed her hand tenderly. Bella shook her head and pushed out of his arms.

"I—I can't. I just—" Bella waved her uninjured hand at Jack and walked away from him as his heart shattered. Jack threw on jeans so he could go after her.

BELLA IGNORED everything and everyone as she walked through the house back to her bedroom and climbed back into bed, tears pouring silently down her cheeks. Bella heard Jack come into the room but ignored him, her back to the door. She felt the bed dip before he slid behind her and then his arms were around her. He tenderly took her right hand in his and put ice on it.

"Talk to me, baby." Jack begged. Bella just shook her head, curling tighter around her injured hand. Jack curled tighter around her. "I love you baby, please."

Bella couldn't speak. She wasn't even sure why she was so upset. Why it was so important that he not move in, why he was supposed to sleep somewhere else last night. But it was, and he didn't. And now she'd lost it and she didn't know how to fix it, or even if she should.

When it felt like he was going to leave her, she pulled his arms into her and tightened her arms around them. They stayed that way until Bella cried herself to sleep.

~

BELLA WOKE with Jack's arms still around her, and Jack brushed her hair out of her face. He was handling her so tenderly, she could have cried again, but there were no more tears. Bella turned in his arms and looked up at him. She could practically see the love shining from his eyes, and she couldn't take it. She tucked her head into his chest instead.

"I'm sorry." She mumbled. Jack chuckled.

"For what, baby? For calling me on being a domineering asshole? Don't you dare. Now, if you want to apologize for damaging your beautiful hand and then by all means." Jack lifted her face to his. "I love you, and I won't apologize for that, or for not being able to be away from you. I can't. You became my life when I walked into this house and turned around and saw this beautiful creature walk out of this room—there's no coming back from that." Bella squirmed and then tapped her forehead lightly against his.

"You know," Bella had to stop and clear her throat; it was rusty from too much emotion, "you know, my emotions have been all over the spectrum since I met you. You make me so damn angry, I bust my hand on your jaw—don't you laugh at me!—and then you say something so—you say something that just completely melts me. How am I supposed to defend against that?"

"Why are you fighting this so hard, La Mia Bella?" Jack asked.

"Because you blew in here and just took. You just took me, you made me yours—"

"Baby, you take me with every look. You take my every breath. You were mine the moment you opened that door over there, but yes, in a perfect world, I would have given you a chance to choose me too." Jack's hands shook as he ran them over her face. Bella closed her eyes as she leaned into his touch.

"Do you know what I think scares me the most?" Bella asked before she opened her eyes and stared into those beloved green eyes.

"What, my kitty love?" Jack smiled that smiled she'd fallen in love with.

"You take me with every look. You take my every breath. And I have chosen you." Bella ran a finger lightly under his beautiful eyes. "You damn, delusional, blind, possessive, overbearing, overprotective, domineering wolf, you went and did it, didn't you? You made me fall in love with you."

"Score!" Jack grinned, and kissed her.

They didn't come up for air for a few hours. Their lovemaking was sweet and slow, long and tender and then wild and frenzied. Jack whispered words of love over and over.

As they collapsed, Bella panting under Jack, she gasped, "I'm going to walk funny for a month." And Jack laughed, rolling off her and pulling her across his chest.

"Oh quitcherbitchin, my crazy, beautiful, perfect little kitty cat." Jack squeezed her tight. "I love you."

"I know, you told me, repeatedly, while you pleasured me, again, repeatedly." Bella purred in his ear. "And who said anything about bitching? I was just saying. You were a wild man. I didn't know you could go so long—" Bella broke off as Jack began tickling her ribs. Bella broke away and raced into the bathroom just ahead of Jack. They laughed all the way through their shower.

"WHERE IS EVERYONE?" Bella asked as they walked into the kitchen.

"Well, this note says Sasha and John took the girls to the apartment complex to clean. They were meeting all of the couples. I guess they thought since they were going to be getting first pick of the apartments, they owed some work." Jack responded, picking up a piece of paper left on the kitchen island.

"Really? When did this get planned? Why didn't I know anything about it? You know, I really hate—" Bella was really working up a head of steam when Jack stopped her with a kiss.

"Bells, stop. Apparently, your Bill called yesterday while we were on our play date. He spoke with Sasha, and she made the plans without us then. Looks like we have plans today too. Bill is bringing the architect over, along with lunch, in—" he was interrupted by the ring of the doorbell.

"Thank God! I'm starved." Bella exclaimed. "Get the door, would you? I'm feeling weak, someone's exhausted me again, and he didn't even feed—" Jack interrupted her mock-tirade again with a quick kiss before heading for the door with a laugh and a shake of his head.

"Someone is lucky she is well loved." Jack called over his shoulder as he opened the door.

Bella muttered "Someone is getting cocky," quietly as she walked up behind him to greet her surrogate father. "Bill!" She called as she gave him a big hug. "Come in, please. This is my—Jack." Bella looked up into his laughing face in chagrin. She just didn't know how to introduce him. Jack's arm came around her as he held out his right hand to Bill.

"Her fiancé. Jack Kincaid, pleasure to meet you, finally." Jack kissed her hair while he shook the hand of the man who rescued her ten years before.

"You know, you say that to people, and yet, you have yet to ask me. It's annoying." Bella smacked him with her good hand.

"I haven't had an opportunity to ask Bill's permission yet, Miss Kitty." Bella shook her head at him.

"Always with the smooth answers, buddy-boy." Bella gestured Bill and the architect, who he introduced as Rick Manning, into the kitchen, and they laid out the lunch they brought.

CHAPTER 26

*T*he next morning Bella woke up alone. After a moment's shock, she realized he just woke up ahead of her. When she stopped to think, she found she could hear him talking in the kitchen. She smiled and headed for the bathroom.

IT TOOK LONGER than usual before she made it to breakfast, but finally she joined Jack at the table, and even managed an almost smile as Sasha placed a plate in front of her. After a few bites though, she kicked back the chair and raced for the bathroom. She barely made the toilet. Again.

Jack was right behind her, holding her, sweeping her hair out of her way. "Baby, are you okay?" Bella thought Jack sounded half panicked. After a few dry heaves, Bella allowed him to pull her back into his arms and shook her head weakly.

"I think so. I just need a minute. I was in the shower, and got so damn nauseous, I had to get out and run for the damn toilet. I almost didn't make it before I was sick. I can't remember the last time I was sick. Can you—" Bella gestured at the open toilet. "The smell. Please."

Bella closed her eyes. Jack flushed the toilet and she heard him move swiftly to the door.

"Sasha!" Jack called urgently after he'd opened the door. Sasha was at the door before he made it back.

"Yes Primo?" Sean and John were behind her, worry clear in their eyes. They could smell the vomit.

"Bella's sick, I need—" Jack broke off, not really sure what he needed, but Sasha did.

"Right away, Primo." Sasha rushed past him into the bathroom. John stepped to the doorway.

"What's going on?" John asked.

"She said she threw up the first time in the shower this morning and now again after eating a little bit. I don't know. She's sweating. I'm worried." Jack looked back at her. John just hummed a bit.

"I'll talk to Sasha. I wouldn't worry too much. Probably just too much going on." John clapped him on the shoulder and went back to the kitchen. Jack went back to Bella and put his hand on her leg.

"How are you feeling, baby?"

"M'okay." Bella mumbled. She held his hand in hers. "My head hurts. I think there's some ibuprofen in my nightstand, would you get it?"

"No!" Sasha said sharply, causing Bella to jerk. "No ibuprofen. I'll get you something else." Sasha moved in and wet the washcloth in the sink, ringing it out before bathing Bella's face.

"Really, Sasha, the ibuprofen works best. This is probably just one of my migraines, and nothing else works." Bella argued. What's with the no ibuprofen? Bella thought to herself.

"Jack, can you give us a few minutes?" Sasha looked up at Jack and he growled at her. "Primo, please." She squeezed his hand. "Let me take care of our Prima."

"A few minutes." Jack said reluctantly. Jack bent over Bella and kissed her hair. "I'll be in the kitchen. Five minutes. I'll be back." Jack's voice was husky, and he looked significantly at Sasha, but she just gestured him out of the room. Sasha followed him and locked the door.

"Bella, are you feeling moody?" Sasha asked her when she came back, rinsing and wringing the washcloth for another cooling pass.

"Yeah, why?" Bella squirmed away from Sasha and sat up, wincing when it made her head and stomach hurt.

"I don't want to give you ibuprofen if you might be pregnant. Are you on the pill?" Sasha asked quietly. Bella's eyes got big as she shook her head mutely. Sasha nodded. "Are you and Jack using condoms? Not that they work real well with us."

"No. Wait, what do you mean they don't work?" Bella grabbed Sasha's hand. "Sorry. Damnit, I can't believe I've been so irresponsible." Bella closed her eyes.

"Were's are all about the procreation. That means we are really fertile, really strong swimmers, you know?" Sasha smiled at her.

"Oh, God. I was probably pregnant from the first time." Bella groaned.

"Well, you might have been, but it wouldn't have taken, because you shifted for the challenge fight, remember. But you haven't shifted since then, right?" Bella shook her head. "Then you need to avoid shifting. Unless—"

"Unless?" Bella asked and then looked at Sasha. "You mean, correct my irresponsible mistake by 'oops, I forgot and shifted, so sorry,'? I don't think I can do that." Bella thought a bit more while Sasha handed her some mouthwash. Bella spit into the sink and then thought of something. "Wait a minute Sasha. We've been together, what, a week? And if you are right, and I aborted the first days—attempts—that only leaves a few days. There is no way my body even knows I'm pregnant at this point, assuming I am." Bella was shaking her head in denial.

"Well, we could be wrong about you aborting, you shift so smoothly and quickly, it may not affect the fetus, but beyond that, your body most certainly does know the moment you conceive. And more importantly, it will start reacting much more quickly. What do you know about wolves in the wild?"

"Absolutely nothing beyond what I saw in a school trip to the zoo before—well, a long time ago. Why?" Bella settled back to sip the bottle of water Sasha had handed her.

"Average gestation for wild wolves is sixty-three days, in litters of four to seven pups. Gestation for humans is forty weeks. We tend to come in around sixteen to twenty weeks." Sasha put the washcloth in the sink and waited for that to settle.

"Tha—but that's four to five months! Christ on a frickin' cracker, Sasha!" Then the rest of what Sasha said sank in. "Oh, God, I'm going to have fucking puppies. You made me bust out the actual 'F' bomb, damnit, and I'm having a litter of fucking puppies." Bella pushed off the floor and stalked away before dropping back toward the floor and moaning. "Oh, God, no sudden movements."

"Prima, you are not having a litter of puppies, please stop saying that. Really, it's kind of insulting." Sasha moved over to her and squatted next to her. "You are no more or less likely to have a multiple birth than anyone else."

"Okay and the puppy thing?" Bella was having trouble catching her breath.

"Your baby will be a perfectly normal baby." Sasha reassured.

"Okay." Bella nodded weakly. "Okay. I gotta sit back down." Sasha helped her into her bedroom to her favorite chair. "Okay. First, I need to stop saying okay. Second, we don't tell Jack until I think on this some more."

"I can't lie to him." Sasha objected.

"And I'm not going to tell him I'm pregnant and see just how far he takes this 'put Bella in a bubble' crap. So no telling him. Got that?" Bella wouldn't take no for an answer.

"Well, John told him it was probably just too much going on. I'll just tell him I agree with John." Then Jack was at the door, Bella could smell him, and his anxiety.

"It's been more than five minutes." He called. Bella nodded and gestured to let him in. Sasha walked out, letting Jack in on her way.

"Sasha?" Sasha just kept walking so Jack turned to Bella, closing the door and walking to her, kneeling in front of her. "Bella, baby, are you okay?"

"Oh, Jack."

"You get headaches often, my kitty cat? We don't tend to get headaches, not really bad ones anyway. Not without injury."

Bella froze with one hand on her stomach. "Bella, sweetie, is something wrong? Do you feel sick again?" Jack had his hand on her knee, kneeling beside her. Jack shook her knee, "Bella?"

"Huh?" Bella looked down at him. "I'm sorry Jack, daydreaming. I'm fine, really." Bella leaned over and kissed him, "I guess that's one more difference between us, I get headaches, and you don't." Bella shivered and took his hand where it rested on her knee. "I want to try to eat something."

"Relax in your chair, I'll go talk to Sasha." Jack kissed her hand and then stood.

Bella sat back in her big comfy chair with her legs curled under her while resting her eyes and waited.

"Prima?" Sasha called quietly. Bella's eyes popped open to see Sasha standing in front of her with another damn tray. "I'm sorry Prima, I didn't mean to wake you, but Jack said you were hungry."

"Its okay, Sasha, I wasn't sleeping, just resting my eyes. Why does he get to be Jack, and I have to be Prima?" Bella sat up and waved her hand. "Never mind that, I'm just a little cranky." Bella took the tray and looked down with a frown. "What is this?"

"Dry toast and room-temperature lemon-lime soda." Bella handed the tray back.

"Let's try this again. Slap some butter on that toast, and some ice in that soda and I'll think about it." Bella closed her eyes even before Sasha took the tray. After a few seconds and she was still holding the tray, she opened an eye and looked at Sasha. "What? I'm not speaking English here? What part of cranky wasn't clear?"

"Is she being difficult?" Jack said from the doorway.

"Yes, she brought me dry toast and warm soda. Disgusting." Bella bent and put the tray on the floor since Sasha wasn't taking it, and settled back to close her eyes again.

"I meant were you being difficult, kitty cat." Jack chuckled. "I think this is exactly what my mom used to give me when I had an upset stomach." Bella opened her eyes and glared at him.

"Bully for you, you had a mom." She closed her eyes again. "You can eat it if you like. I'm not."

"Bella—" Bella held her hand up and smacked his face. Oops, Bella thought. She didn't realize he'd squatted so close. She felt him kiss her palm, so she flicked his nose and pulled her hand back to her lap. Bella ignored their rustling and whispers, although it wouldn't take much to hear their words. She knew she was being a bitch, and she really couldn't work up the energy to care.

Suddenly she felt Jack's hands on her face. "Bella, look at me." His thumbs brushed her lips lightly.

"No." She said, snapping at one of his thumbs, making him laugh.

"Kitty cat, look at me, please." Jack insisted. Bella gave a martyred sigh.

"Whaaat?" Bella looked at him and snorted then was forced to chuckle then laugh outright because he was crossing his eyes at her.

"I love you Bella, every beautiful, sexy, difficult inch of you." Jack told her, punctuating his words with kisses on her nose, lips and chin.

"You do not. I'm cranky and unlovable and you said it yourself, I'm difficult." Bella argued. "And I'm hungry and my head hurts and I'm really really cranky." Bella was starting to really hate the whine she heard in her own voice.

JACK BRUSHED the hair back from the most beautiful face in the world and smiled. "I do so. You are completely loveable. And I will spend the rest of our lives proving that to you. Even when you are hungry, and cranky and difficult, when your head hurts, and especially when you are making me feel so hot and hard and as randy as a teenager, I will love you."

"Am I going to get edible food soon?" Bella asked.

"You are killing me."

Bella leaned over and kissed him, sighing. "I believe you believe what you just said, and it was—wow—but seriously. You just like getting laid."

"Baby, I was getting laid before you came along," Jack's breath oofed out when Bella punched him at that, "but I love making love with you."

"Ahhh." Jack smiled at the sweet look on Bella's face. "Seriously." Jack just shook his head and smiled because he could hear Sasha coming back into the hall.

~

BELLA HAPPILY MUNCHED HER—BUTTERED—TOAST and sipped her—iced—lemon-lime soda. She could have used some cinnamon sugar--or jelly--or iced tea--lemon-lime soda was not her favorite—but she'd won as much of the battle as she was going to, she was sure. Jack stood nearby with a large pan ready, scowling fiercely. Bella knew it was all for show, and he was just worried about her, but she was determined not to get sick again.

"Nummmnmmm." Bella hummed as she chewed, bobbing her head. She heard Jack chuckle and looked up at him and watched him drop the stern façade. Bella slowly licked butter off her finger as Jack walked over to the ottoman next to her and sat down. Bella smiled.

"Killing. Me." Jack said. "How's the tummy, kitty cat?"

"This will hold me for about five minutes." Bella licked another finger, she didn't think it even had butter on it, she just liked the way his eyes lightened watching her do it.

"You just keep that in your stomach for five minutes, and we'll talk, how's that?" Jack croaked, handing her a napkin. "And use a napkin before I attack you." Bella ran a hand up the inside of her thigh and purred.

"What would be so bad about attacking me?" Bella's finger circled the apex of her thighs as she watched Jack swallow.

Jack grabbed her hand and kissed it, growling. "I am so torturing you tonight over that!"

"Not tonight, sweetie. I have plans. Tonight's my dinner with Kayla, remember?" Jack growled.

AT SIX THIRTY that night Bella walked out of her bedroom ready to go meet Kayla. She heard a whistle from the family room and turned with a smile. The smile froze when she saw the look on Jack's face.

"Nuh-uh. No way. You go back and put on something else. A-a gunny sack or something. No way are you going out looking like—like—"Jack stumbled to a halt.

"Like one seriously hot babe?" Alex asked. Apparently she was the whistler. John chuckled where he sat next to Mary.

"What? Right! No way. No going out looking like a seriously hot babe." Jack said pointing from Alex to Bella.

Bella laughed. She was wearing one of her few dresses, a green silk knee length with a wrap bodice and flaring skirt. It displayed her assets to their best advantage, as Kayla put it, and Bella felt beautiful in the dress. She'd worn her hair up, and paired the dress with a pair of black stilettos that matched the small black bag she carried.

Bella grabbed his shirtfront and pulled him down for a kiss. "See you later, lover-wolf. You be a good wolf, and I'll give you a present when I get home, okay?" Bella kissed him deeply and then wiped the lipstick off his face. "Bye now." She laughed as she walked away, listening to him splutter his complaints.

BELLA MET Kayla at their favorite Mexican restaurant for tacos and margaritas. They laughed and talked about the book. Kayla left the table to go to the restroom, and suddenly, Bella wasn't feeling well. The room was spinning. Bella started to stand, and stumbled. She knocked the glass over and suddenly the waiter was there. Then she heard a voice, and she smelled wolf. If was a familiar smell...

～

JACK STARTED PACING when Bella had been gone about two hours. "Sasha!" Jack bellowed.

"Yes, Jack." Sasha answered quietly just behind him. Jack turned to find Sasha standing calmly behind him, holding a cup of steaming coffee out to him.

"Oh, thank you, Sasha." Jack took a (hopefully) calming sip. "What time did she say she'd be back?" Jack ran a hand absentmindedly through his already mussed hair.

"I would expect Miss Bella will be here any time. She said these celebratory dinners don't take more than a couple of hours." Sasha eased away from Jack's pacing route quietly. "It's just a dinner. How much trouble can she get into? She and Kayla do this every time she finishes a book."

"I don't like Bella being away from me." Jack growled. "Especially since she hasn't been feeling well." Jack drained the cup and placed it on the coffee table as he passed. Jack missed Sasha's knowing smile.

"She was feeling fine when she left. Why don't you call her and let her know how much you are looking forward to her returning home?" Sasha followed behind him and picked up the cup, returning to the kitchen to refill it.

"Good idea, Sasha. What would I do without you?" Jack pulled his cell phone out and hit speed dial. "Who is this? Where is Bella?" Jack listened intently and then bit out, "When was this?" Jack was frozen in place, and didn't notice Sasha had returned to his side. "No, I'm sure everything is fine. Thank you." Jack stabbed the off button then just as quickly hit another speed dial button. "Where's Declan?" Jack waited for a response and then growled, "Get over here, and bring John. Bella's missing." Jack threw his phone across the room and hit his knees, howling.

When Sean and John walked in the front door, they found their Primo on his knees and Sasha standing before him in tears. Sean strode to Sasha, "What's going on?" Sasha shook her head, she had no clue.

"Find my mate." Jack looked up at Sean, and brought John into his glance, and begged. "Please find my mate." Both wolves hit their knees before their Primo.

"Our lives for our Prima. Tell us what has happened." Sean said. Jack seemed too shaken to speak.

"Miss Bella had her dinner with Kayla tonight. She's been gone about two hours, and our Primo is impatient, so he called her cell phone. Someone else answered—"Sasha didn't have anymore of the story.

"The restaurant hostess answered. Bella had become ill, and two men approached her table. She addressed one as 'Declan'. They offered to bring her and Kayla home. Bella must have dropped her phone. That was over an hour ago. If Declan was bringing her home, they would be here by now." Jack's eyes had gone amber and he fought his wolf. He couldn't lose control, that wouldn't help him find Bella.

"All wolves are accounted for except Declan, Leroy and Kelly." Sean looked up at a sound from Sasha and then turned back to Jack. "We need to start at the restaurant, try to get her scent."

"Let's go." Jack was on his feet in seconds. John stayed him with his hand out, just short of touching him.

"Primo, it would be better if you waited here. Let me do my job. If you walk into that restaurant, and lose control—" John broke off, leaving Jack to figure out the consequences for himself.

"No one knows her scent like I do." Jack objected.

"Let me go into your room. I'm your best tracker. I'll be able to pick up her scent." Jack closed his eyes. He could imagine well John burying his nose in Bella's pillow, in the sheets filled with the scent of her—Jack clenched his fists and broke off the thought.

"Go. Find my mate. Find your Prima." Jack sank onto the couch and dropped his face into his hands. Only then did he notice Sasha standing next to him, crying quietly.

CHAPTER 27

Bella woke to a migraine like she hadn't felt in years. She moaned and reached for her head, only to be stayed by something holding her wrists tightly. When she tried to turn, she found her ankles held as well.

Bella tugged at her bonds and found herself held fast. They seemed to be made of some sort of strong shiny metal, and short of shifting, she wasn't going anywhere, The manacles were chained to posts set in the cement in the four corners of the mattress where she lay, so she was spread eagle on the bare mattress.

Bella heard a noise and looked to the far corner of the room and saw Kayla similarly bound on another mattress. She'd been stripped bare, as Bella had been. Kayla was still unconscious. The noise she'd heard was Declan sniffing at Kayla's body.

"Declan!" Bella tried to infuse power into her hoarse voice, in spite of her pain. "Wait is going on?"

"Silence, false Prima." Declan growled at her, and turned back to Kayla, running his hands over her.

"Ooh, is the little woman awake now?" Bella heard a high, vaguely familiar voice from somewhere behind her. She realized her sense of smell was off, she wasn't scenting anything she should be able to, and turning her head quickly to try to see around her caused dizziness. It was unclear to Bella if the dizziness was a result of her migraine, or if the migraine was a result of whatever knocked her out. The new voice moved around into her line of vision and Bella blinked. It was another of Jack's wolves, Kelly.

Kelly leaned over Bella and ran her nose across the tops of her thighs, and Bella tried to twist away to no avail. Kelly laughed and grabbed her thigh, pushing it away. "Oh, no, no no. I will be tasting the false Prima."

"Enough!" A new voice called from behind Bella. Kelly jerked up, and growled angrily, but pinched once at Bella's clit before moving to join the voice. Bella winced, but made no noise. Bella looked over at Kayla and saw Declan still leaning over her, but looking up menacingly in the direction of the voice, a near constant growl emanating. Bella saw that Kayla had awakened and was trying to squirm away from Declan in terror. Her whimpers brought Declan's attention back to her. "I said enough! Get away from her!" The voice called again, and this time Declan pulled away from her reluctantly and joined him.

Bella listened to them leave, moving up a flight of stairs and a door close before she looked back at Kayla.

"Are you okay, Kayla?" She called quietly.

"What's going on Bella? Where are we? Who are these people?" Kayla was nearly screaming, and Bella tried to quiet her.

"Sshh. Kayla, we need to be quiet. I don't want them to hear us talking. Are you hurt?" Bella tried to keep her voice calm.

"I don't think so. My head hurts, and I have a bad taste in my mouth. That guy, didn't I meet him at your house? He was—"

"I know sweetie. I'm sorry. I think this is about me, and they just grabbed me when I was with you. I'm so sorry. I'll figure out a way to get you out of this. I promise." Bella didn't want to let on how scared she was, she had to stay strong for Kayla. "Jack will come. Jack has to come." Bella whispered.

Bella worked on one of the manacles, and thought if she shifted, she might get free, but there was a problem. She knew Sasha suspected she was pregnant already, and Sasha had told her that

179

female wolves have to be kept from shifting, or they lose their babies. Bella didn't know if the same held true for shifters like her. Also, Bella didn't know how many there were upstairs, or where exactly they were. She didn't want to risk aborting her baby only to lose the fight getting away. And then there was Kayla to think of. Whatever she decided, she had to protect Kayla.

It looked like her best bet was to play docile until the odds were better. But that meant probable abuse for both her and Kayla.

"Kayla?" Bella called quietly.

"Yes?" Kayla turned as much as she could until she could look at Bella.

"Kayla, I don't know how many there are, or where we are, so I can't risk trying to get us out right now. Do you understand?" Bella had to make things clear to her friend.

"Yes, I think so. You could possibly get us free, but maybe not get us out of here?"

"Yes, exactly." Bella sighed. Kayla did understand. "You saw how Declan was acting with you and Kelly with me." Kayla nodded jerkily, "I think you know what is going to happen if they have a chance to come back down here." Bella watched Kayla's eyes close briefly and then open again.

"Yes. They want to rape us." Kayla's voice broke on the end.

"Yes, I think so. It will be worse if we fight them Kayla. Do you understand what I'm saying?" Bella wanted to sob. Where are you, Jack? Bella begged to herself.

"Yes. I'll try."

"Try to rest while you can, Kayls. We need to build our strength." Bella sighed and lay back on the mattress, trying to take her own advice. Where are you, Jack?

∽

"Jack, you need to eat something, get some sleep." Sasha held a plate out, and Jack ignored it.

"I don't know if Bella has eaten, if she is able to sleep, if she's

HURT and you want me to eat? To sleep?" Jack knocked the plate out of Sasha's hands.

"You need to keep your strength up for when we find her." Sasha was kneeling down to clean up the mess. "And we will find them." Sasha whispered. "We have to."

Jack realized what he'd done and pulled Sasha to her feet. "I'm sorry Sasha. I'm losing my mind. She's my entire world. Don't do that, it's my mess, I'll clean it up." Jack knelt down to start picking up the food mess.

"It's okay Jack. I understand. They will be okay. They have to be. Don't, it's okay. I need to stay busy. Please, go lay down. I promise, if we get any word from John and his team, I'll come get you right away." Sasha pushed his hands away.

"They? Oh, you mean Kayla, yes of course. I forget about her in my worry about Bella. She's been so sick." Jack missed Sasha's guilty look as he walked away.

~

BELLA AWOKE AGAIN to find a strange female next to her. She looked quickly over at Kayla and saw Declan was next to her.

"It's okay; he's just giving her food." The stranger told Bella quietly. Bella looked back at her and nodded. "I have food for you also. We can't free you so you can feed yourselves, so we will feed you." The woman worked her way under Bella's head and shoulders to help support her slightly to make eating easier, and gave her sips of water. "The food is drugged." She breathed into her ear. Bella looked up quickly at her. "Wolfsbane."

"What does it do?" Bella breathed back and then nodded a question at Kayla, asking if they were drugging her food. The stranger shook her head and Bella breathed out in relief.

"It keeps Were's from being able to shift." Bella nodded.

"What about, um, what will it do if you're pregnant?" Bella asked quietly.

"It doesn't hurt you, in packs without a Prima, or where the Prima

181

is particularly weak, it's used to control the shift to avoid aborting." Bella nodded, and accepted the food anyway. Maybe they didn't realize she wasn't a Were, or Declan and Kelly didn't tell them? Or they didn't know if it would affect her the same way or not. Bella didn't even know if it would affect her or not.

"Can you get us blankets? It's cold down here. Kayla will get sick." Bella nodded over to where Kayla was visibly shivering. For now, at least, Declan was very tenderly feeding her and not touching her in any inappropriate way.

"I'll try. My master really isn't—your comfort isn't high on his priority list, you know?" The stranger said.

"How many of you are there? What is your name, by the way? I'm Bella." Bella remembered some research she'd done on one of her books. If you personalize the victim to the suspect, it's harder for them to hurt you. Supposedly.

"We know who you are. My name is Staci. I don't think I can help you--" Staci broke off, looking around.

"I've seen Declan and Kelly from my mates pack, any others from our pack?" Bella was barely breathing her questions.

"Just a wolf named Leroy." Staci looked around carefully before speaking just as quietly. "They—want you." Staci blushed and looked away from her. "Except him." Staci indicated Declan. "He just wants the human. But Kelly and Leroy? They talk of nothing but having you. The master won't let them right now, but he may not always deny them, or be here to stop them."

Bella nodded at this news. "And I've heard one stranger's voice, your Master? And now you. How many others? Are you from the same pack as Gordon and Weldon?" Bella brainstormed.

"My master and I are alone here with your wolves, we came to investigate what happened to Gordon and his small pack." Bella nodded.

"You come from a larger pack then?"

"Getting to know our false Prima, little Staci?" Kelly's high grating voice was suddenly behind Bella. "I'll take over. Return to your Master."

"I am supposed to feed her. Master told me to make sure she eats everything." Staci's voice shook, but she held her ground.

"Don't talk back to your betters, bitch! I said I would take over!" Before Kelly could connect with the blow she swung, a very large man was there and grabbed her arm in a forceful grip.

"Staci is following my orders, bitch. Return upstairs. No one told you to come down here." He pushed her forcefully toward the stairs then looked down at us. "Staci, keep taking care of our guest and then return to me."

"Yes Master." Staci gulped. "Uh, Master? Could they have blankets? The human, specifically, is suffering the cold down here." Staci debased herself to her Master and waited for his response.

"Yes, Staci. Good idea. I'll see to it." The man looked around then turned and went up the stairs.

"Thank you, Staci." Bella sighed deeply. She thought she could maybe taste the wolfsbane. "Do you know why they call me false Prima?"

"They say you are a murderess that you murdered to get your position. That you murdered Gordon and Weldon and Mitsy, and Declan's Brigit, who was the only rival for your position of the Primo's mate." Staci said it all in a rush, words tumbling quickly over each other.

"I've never killed in cold blood, only in self-defense or in sanctioned challenge. Your pack-mates, Gordon, Weldon and Mitsy attacked me in my home, and I defended myself. Jack and I were mated, neither of us had prior claims. Brigit challenged me, after attacking me and one of our wolves in my home, and I defeated her. Staci, I am not a murderess.

"Do you know Alex?"

"You know Alex?" Staci realized her voice was too loud and lowered it. "We cannot find what happened to Gordon's females. Are they okay?"

"Alex and the others are fine. Mary is recovering from what Gordon did to her. They've joined our pack. They are very happy. No one is abusing them." Bella looked intently at Staci.

"But your mate—they are now his, right?" Staci looked like she wanted to believe, but she was so broken.

"They are his as all the wolves in his pack are his. But I made the order, and my mate is enforcing it, that none of the females have to suffer unwanted attention of any male."

"Truly, Prima?" Staci started to look truly hopeful.

"I promise you, Staci. You do what you can to help Kayla and me, without endangering yourself, and I will do everything I can for you." Bella heard a scrape on the stairs and Staci jumped up, gathering the dishes.

"Well, the false Prima. Mmmm. Don't you look tasty? I will be having some of that, real soon." Leroy leered at Bella and then made kissing faces. "Alexander told me to bring blankets down." Leroy threw one to Declan, who tenderly kissed Kayla before covering her up, and carrying the dishes upstairs. "Back upstairs, Staci-baby. Your Master wants to see you." Leroy strutted closer with the blanket as Staci backed away.

"But—but." Staci looked from Leroy to Bella. "I'll cover her and then follow you upstairs."

"Nope, sorry babe. Master calls. Better get your butt up there." Staci looked back down at Bella apologetically, and Bella nodded at her. Staci scurried up the stairs, and then Leroy knelt down and dropped the blanket on the mattress next to Bella.

"Just you and me, bitch." Bella's eyes went to Kayla and Leroy scoffed. "She doesn't count, she's just a human." Leroy leaned closer and buried his nose between her legs. "God, you smell ripe." His hands followed his nose roughly, and Bella forced herself to stay still for the abuse. His nose worked his way up to her stomach and he laughed, "gaining a little weight, aren't you, little bitch?" Leroy licked her stomach and was moving towards her breasts, his hands still pushing roughly into her, when the heard the door at the top of the stairs open. Leroy jumped just before they heard the bellow.

"Leroy!" Leroy opened the blanket over her and stomped up the stairs.

"Are you okay, Bella?" Kayla called quietly after the door closed.

"Yeah, thanks, you?" Bella shuddered, and cried to herself for about the hundredth time since first waking up in this nightmare, *Jack, where are you?*

"I'm okay, Bells. He was really kind of sweet, if a little creepy." Kayla settled back on the mattress. "How long do you think we've been here?"

"I'm not completely sure, but I think about twenty hours now. Jack has to be looking for us. How long can it possibly fucking take for him to find his damn mate?" Bella jerked twice in frustration, rattling the chains.

Bella looked around again. She had already determined they were in a basement somewhere. She didn't think they had been taken too far away. She wondered if Declan and they others had completely left the pack, or were still reporting --she'd have to remember to ask Staci next time she had the chance.

"Hey Bella?" Kayla called out. "Why did that Leroy call me a human? And Staci, I think she did too. And they have you all chained up, and I'm just tied with ropes. What's going on Bella?"

"Well, Kayla, this wasn't how I was going to tell you, but everyone you've seen here are Werewolves." Bella didn't want to specify out loud that she wasn't, in case that Alexander could hear and wasn't aware of her differences.

"That's crazy, Bella. There's no such—" Kayla was looking at Bella, and saw how serious she was. "And your new boyfriend? Jack?"

"He's my mate. He's the Primo of his pack. And if he ever wants to get laid again, he'd better hurry up." Bella ground out the last between clenched teeth.

"You aren't making this up, are you?" Kayla flounced back on the mattress. "That's why you are in chains, they are afraid you could break out of ropes. Oh, man. Okay. I can deal with this." Kayla shook her head. "Mmm. Maybe not."

"Rest, Kayla. I have a feeling it will get worse before it gets better." Bella sounded tired.

JACK WAS DREAMING. Bella was home safe and back in his arms. She slithered down his arms to the top of his jeans, and unfastened them. She felt lighter, like she'd lost weight.

She took him in her hands, and stroked him. Oh, it felt good. Then her mouth was on him, but something wasn't right.

Jack jerked awake and reached down and found Charlie kneeling between his legs. "What the hell?" Jack yelled, grabbing her and shoving her off the bed. He was off the bed on the other side and refastening his pants in the next second. The bedroom door opened and Alex was there.

"Primo?" Alex took the scene in with a glance and grabbed Charlie by the arm. "You have done it now, girl. The Prima saved you, and this is how you repay her? What did you think you were doing?" Alex shook her.

"Let go of me. He needs one of us to see to him. You certainly aren't going to do it." Jack was crossing the room to them when Alex backhanded Charlie.

"If I catch you in this room again, I'll chain you myself, do you hear me?" Alex was fairly screaming at Charlie, and shaking with rage. Charlie cowed from her and slunk out the patio doors, where she'd apparently snuck in. Alex turned to Jack. "I'm sorry, Jack. I will try to do better at controlling her." Alex followed Charlie out.

Jack took several deep breaths and ran his hands through his hair. He walked out to the kitchen and looked around.

Jack swiped his hands down his face.

Jack sat at the island and Sasha poured them both coffees. Jack glanced at the clock and noticed he'd only been asleep a couple of hours.

"No word?" He asked wearily.

"No, Sean checked in about half hour ago, John hasn't returned to human form since they left the restaurant, I don't think he will until he finds her, he tracks better as wolf. Turner, Nate and Dean are following, providing backup as needed. John believes he's getting closer, believes he has the trail, but doesn't have her yet." Sasha's hands were shaking.

"It's been more than twenty-four hours, damnit!" Jack swore and then tried to calm himself.

"I'm sorry Jack. I need to tell you—" something in her voice made Jack look up. "Kelly," Sasha's voice caught, "Kelly has been obsessed with Bella since she first saw her. When we were together, those last few times, she fantasized that I was her." Jack growled and Sasha flinched. "I'm very afraid if she's left alone with Bella."

"Jesus." Jack jumped up, knocking the stool back.

"I'm sorry. I will accept any punishment, my Primo, but I only beg that you allow me to remain until we get our Prima back safely." Sasha dropped to the floor before Jack in subjugation.

"Punishment? Whatever for Sasha? None of this is your fault. You have done nothing but take care of her since she came into our lives." Jack lifted Sasha back to her feet before him

"I should have told you about Kelly—" Sasha sobbed.

"We will deal with Kelly when we find Bella. Do you think Bella would forgive me for letting anything happen to you? Do you remember the shape she was in when we met her? Up for two days straight without eating? Sleeping? She needs you. We need you. I don't want to hear anymore about punishment." Jack took Sasha into his arms.

"This is inappropriate, Jack. Bella would kill you, or me, or both, if she were here." Sasha tried to laugh as she stumbled away from Jack and returned to her stool.

"Nonsense. We've established I need to be more worried about you around her than around me. Wait, I don't need to worry, do I?" Jack tried to look mock worried.

"Oh you!" Sasha snapped her towel at him. "Did you get enough rest earlier?" Sasha got up and quickly started putting together a sandwich. Jack ducked and laughed and then sobered quickly.

"Probably not, but I got all I'm going to get for now." Jack scrubbed his hands down his face.

"Well then you are going to eat at least." Sasha placed a sandwich before him and reached for more coffee. Jack looked around in awe, wondering how she could put that sandwich together so quickly.

Jack got no more than a few bites in before the phone rang and Sean told him to meet him at an address a few miles away. John was sure he'd tracked Bella. Jack looked at Sasha with a grin. "Get the house ready, I'm bringing our Prima home."

"Go get our girl, Primo." Sasha called to his back, because he was already moving through the garage.

~

THE NEXT TIME BELLA WOKE, she heard grunting coming from Kayla's corner, and felt a tickling on her thighs. Bella looked over and saw Declan rutting on Kayla, Kayla's eyes closed tightly, tears pouring down her cheeks.

"Oh, look Kelly. Our little bitch is awake. What are we going to do with her?" Leroy brought her attention to him, where he knelt on the mattress near her head. Bella looked down where Kelly knelt between her legs.

"I don't care what you do up there Leroy. I'll be busy with our false Prima down here." Bella felt Kelly's hands become more insistent, pushing her thighs as far apart as the chains would allow. Bella grunted as with one hand, Kelly pinched her clit hard, and with the other roughly shoved three fingers into her. The grunt was the only sound Bella allowed.

Leroy brought her attention back to him when he started to undo his belt. "You bite me, bitch, and I'll kill your little friend over there, do you understand me?" Leroy snarled, pushing his jeans and shorts to his knees. Bella glanced over at Kayla then nodded mutely. "Good. Open wide, bitch."

Bella tried to step outside of herself, tried to distance herself from the sensations. Kelly had replaced her hands with her mouth, and had begun working her with tongue and teeth while Leroy pushed himself into her mouth roughly. Bella fought not to gag. He wasn't nearly the size of Jack, and he was half-flaccid still, but the stench was stomach turning. It didn't take long before she had more to worry about than his lack of good hygiene. He didn't stay flaccid for long, and began moving in and out of her mouth rapidly, barely leaving her a moment to swallow. Bella had to completely ignore what was going on below to concentrate on not gagging.

Dimly, Bella began hearing noises of a struggle from above. At about the point the noises reached the door at the top of the stairs, Bella smelled something even above the unwashed male body moving above her, a smell that made her heart sour. Jack!

Bella heard Jack's howl when Leroy was mid-withdrawal, and Bella bit down. Bella hadn't realized her rage had built until she'd partially shifted and had a mouthful of tiger fangs, which bit right through Leroy like butter. Leroy howled in pain, and blood spurted at the same time Bella yanked her arms and legs out of the manacles, shifting them into claws and raking them through first Leroy and then Kelly, mid-body, eviscerating them before they could make a sound.

Before Jack could make it down the stairs, Bella had made the leap across the basement to Kayla's mattress and ripped Declan off her friend, tearing his head from his shoulders and throwing him against the cement wall.

JACK BURST INTO THE HOUSE. They heard a noise to the left and saw a tiny girl cowering in the doorway of what turned out to be the kitchen. Jack stalked to her and she fell supine to the floor.

"You are the Prima Bella's mate? I will show you where she is. You must hurry, they are with her, they are—please, you must hurry." The girl was crying freely.

Jack picked her up. "Who is with her? Where?" He held her inches from his nose.

"Your wolf traitors. In the basement. She said if I helped her she would spare me. Please. Just there." The girl pointed to a door behind them.

Jack passed the girl to Turner behind him. "Hold her here. You two, search the house for others." Jack indicated Nate and Dean. He gestured to Sean and John to follow him and went to the door.

When Jack opened the door, it took a moment to understand what he saw, but once he did, he began howling. Leroy and Kelly were abusing his mate. Kelly's face was buried between Bella's legs, and he could see one hand stroking her as Kelly's tongue laved her repeatedly. As this was going on Leroy was—the only description for it was fucking—Leroy was fucking Bella's face.

But then Jack saw something overcome Bella. As the door opened he saw Bella jerk and then her hands and feet were transforming into her tiger claws and she was breaking free of the manacles holding her as Leroy jerked free of her and blood was spurting from him where she'd bitten through him.

At the same time her claw-hands were ripping through his stomach while her claw-feet were attacking Kelly, ripping through her stomach, and Jack was only halfway down the stairs. But Bella wasn't finished. Bella threw her kills down and leapt at the mattress where Declan was rutting with her friend Kayla and grabbed him with all four claws, and ripped his head off his body, throwing the body parts against the cement walls. Then Bella stood over Kayla panting as Jack finally caught up to her and Kayla looked up at her and began screaming.

"Well, that was anti-climactic." John said, looking around at the carnage.

Sean moved around Bella to Kayla and began undoing her bonds. "Sshh. Miss Raymond, its okay. You're okay now. You're safe. John, a little help here?" Sean called.

"Bella? La Mia Bella? Baby, please?" Jack called, afraid to touch her for fear of startling her. Bella slowly turned to him and sobbed. Her hands were her own again, but dripped blood and gore, as did her mouth. She stumbled toward him, and then was in his arms, finally. His Bella. His mate.

"Where were you?" Bella sobbed. "Where were you?" Bella collapsed in his arms and cried.

"I'm sorry, my love. I'm so sorry. You are safe now. Let me take you home." Jack carried Bella upstairs and heard Sean following with Kayla. John stopped him when he reached the top.

"Please take this for our Prima." John held a blanket out, and helped wrap Bella in it.

"Primo, is the Prima whole?" Turner was waiting with the girl and Nate and Dean.

"Bella will recover. Did you find anyone else?" Jack looked around them.

"No Primo, only this girl." Turner gestured to the girl cowering before him. Bella stirred.

"Staci?" Bella whispered.

"Prima?" The girl called.

"Yes, Jack, she needs to come with us. She's just a child. She's like Alex and the others." Bella seemed to run out of steam and closed her eyes again. Jack nodded his head and Turner picked the girl up as the most expedient method, and they left the house behind.

CHAPTER 28

*B*ella couldn't seem to stop crying. Jack carried her in from the car, and she could somehow sense Sean doing the same with Kayla, but she couldn't bring herself to care. Bella clutched at Jack and sobbed. She vaguely heard him giving orders as he stalked to her bedroom with Sasha in tow.

JACK SAT Bella on the edge of the tub, still wrapped in the blanket, and turned to Sasha, Bella watching blankly.

"Take care of her." Jack ordered, turning to the door.

"Jack?" Bella begged. Jack kept walking. Sasha met him at the door and turned him around.

"She needs you. What the hell are you doing?" Jack had never heard Sasha speak to him this way. Hell, he'd never heard her speak to anyone this way.

"I can't—I gave you an order, wolf. Take care of your Prima." Jack wrenched his arm out of her grasp, and with a last longing glance at Bella, walked out the door.

"Jack!" Bella sobbed as she slid to the floor in a huddle. Sasha looked back at her, tears pouring down her face.

"Oh, Mein Liebling. It's okay. Let's have a bath. Everything will be just fine after a bath." Sasha set briskly to running the bath. Sasha helped her into it. "Sshh now, it's going to be okay." Bella was starting to hiccup and gasp with the force of her sobs. "Please, Prima, you're scaring me." Sasha rubbed her shoulder, trying desperately to soothe her.

Bella fought to get her breathing under control, and then she was talking, telling Sasha everything they had done to her, and forced her to do. Neither woman heard Jack come back into the bedroom and sit on the floor outside the bathroom, crying silent tears as he listened. Sasha cried silently as well, as she listened, holding Bella.

"Sasha," Bella asked when her story was finished, eyes finally dry.

"Yes, Mein Liebling?" Sasha brushed Bella's hair from her face.

"Would you get my toothbrush? And mouthwash? Lots of mouthwash?" Bella leaned back against the tub.

"Of course, liebling." Sasha looked up at a noise in the bedroom but Bella didn't seem to notice, or care. Sasha handed her the toothbrush and toothpaste. "Liebling, Bella? I'll be right back, I have mouthwash in my room, I think." Bella just nodded as she started brushing her teeth vigorously.

JACK LOOKED up at Sasha when she exited the bathroom, closing the door quietly, surprised when she got in his face again.

"You get off your ass and get in there! Your mate needs you." She snarled in his face.

"You heard what I let happen to her, Sasha. I can't—I don't deserve her." Jack cried. Sasha nearly lifted him off the floor by his shirtfront in her rage.

"You listen to me, damnit! You love her, yes? She loves you. She needs you to cleanse her of those memories. Get off your ass and go make love to your mate, or you may never get her back from this." Sasha shook him like a rag doll. Jack snarled at her and Sasha snarled back. "I'm going to get her mouthwash. When I come back, you'd better be in there." Sasha walked out of the room.

Jack sat for a moment and then followed her out of the bedroom, walking further from his mate with every step. Sasha gave him an evil look when she walked back through and found him sitting at the kitchen table instead of where she told him to be. He just shook his head and turned away.

BELLA LOOKED up when Sasha came back in, still brushing her teeth, crying anew. "I can't get clean." She cried.

"Of course you can liebling. Here, give me that, you use this to rinse." Sasha exchanged the toothbrush for the cup of mouthwash she held out. Sasha supervised Bella rinsing and then starting to wash before she began tidying away the tooth-brushing supplies and going into her closet for sleep-clothes. When she came back out, she found Bella scrubbing furiously between her legs, crying.

"I can still feel her Sasha. Just like I can taste—make it go away. Where's Jack? I need Jack. Is he mad at me? I guess I shouldn't have killed them, especially not his cousin Declan, but I was so upset, so angry. Make it go away." Bella sobbed.

"Oh, liebling. Jack's not angry with you, don't you worry about a thing. And of course I will. I'll make it all go away." Sasha took the cloth from Bella's hand and began tenderly washing her.

She washed her gently from head to toe, and rinsed her thoroughly. Sasha helped her step from the tub and stand while she dried her off and then dress her in the nightshirt she'd found, and led her into the bedroom. Bella never noticed how her hands shook with rage. Rage at what was done to this beautiful girl, rage at what her idiot Primo was doing.

Sasha stood back while Bella started climbing into the bed and then watched her freeze in place and cry out. Bella started ripping the sheets from the bed frantically.

"Liebling, what is it?" Sasha took Bella's shoulder but she shrugged her off, lying down on the bare mattress and curling into herself.

"Nothing. Leave me alone. I'm fine." Bella mumbled. Sasha gathered the shredded sheets in her arms then took a sniff and snarled.

"If you need anything, liebling, you call me." Bella grunted and Sasha walked out to find her bastard of a Primo.

JACK LOOKED up when Sasha walked out of the bedroom again, this time carrying what appeared to be shredded bed sheets in her arms. She had murder in her eye.

"You are a bastard, Jack Kincaid. A dirty, sick bastard." Sasha told him before dumping the mess into his lap. Jack watched Sasha stomp away before looking at the mess she'd dropped on him. They looked like the sheets off Bella's bed. He picked them up and smelled them. They smelled like him and sex and—damnit. They smelled like Charlie. He looked at the bedroom door. Bella must have smelled them, and ripped them up. Sasha smelled them too, and came to the same conclusion Bella had, that while the woman he loved was in danger, he'd turned to a child for—Oh God!

Jack stuffed the mess into a plastic bag as John came in the back door. He shoved the bag at him.

"Burn this." He growled as he slumped on the couch.

"Primo?" John looked uncertainly at the bag.

"Just do it!" Jack snarled. John was back through the door before he'd finished.

FOR TWO DAYS, every time Bella talked to Jack, he cringed, that's if he didn't leave as soon as she walked into the room. If Bella touched him, he flinched. Bella was getting really sick of it. Sasha wouldn't even speak to him, not even when he spoke to her. It almost made Bella smile. Almost.

Nothing made Bella smile anymore.

With Kelly gone, the new wolves were safe to move next door and Bella lost no time in ordering that they do so immediately. Kayla was staying in one of the guest rooms, and Sean in the other. He hadn't left her side except while Mary helped her bathe, since the rescue. Bella would think it sweet, if anything was sweet.

Nothing was sweet. Not anymore.

Sasha cooked for herself and Bella and Kayla and Sean, but ignored Jack entirely. He was forced to fend for himself.

What Bella didn't get was why he was even here? Kayla stayed in her room, would only allow Bella or Sean in. Sean brought her all her meals. Sean's the only one that would speak to him that he allowed anyway. Bella tried, but Jack just—so why was he even here? Why didn't he go home? With the bedrooms all occupied, and him unwilling to come to hers, he slept on the couch, though she heard him prowling outside her bedroom at night when she couldn't sleep.

And what about the baby? Bella had about decided Sasha must be right, because every morning now, she woke up nauseous, but after that initial bout, as long as she took it slow, she'd be okay, and could eat without trouble. Bella patted her tummy. "It's okay, baby. Daddy doesn't love Mommy anymore, but Mommy loves you." Bella sniffed back tears and walked out of her room. Sasha was busy in the kitchen, and the rest of the house seemed empty.

Bella walked into the family room and looked out into the backyard at a noise and then froze at the sight that caught her eye. She must have made a sound, because suddenly, Sasha was next to her and she heard a faint "Dear God," from her.

Bella could see Jack's backside, still apparently clothed, but his movements proved he'd at least opened his pants. He was bent over someone—there, she could just see the side of her face, that damn child Charlie—thrusting against her. She could hear their grunts from here. Dear Lord, he was fucking her in broad daylight in her own backyard!

Bella screamed and picked up the lamp next to her, throwing it at the glass door in front of her and spinning away. She ran for the garage. She had keys to her car in the drawer of the island. She had to leave, it was too much.

～

JACK HEARD Bella scream and the crash of glass just as he got the knife out of Charlie's hand. He straightened and spun to the house to see Bella running away and Sasha standing there in shock. He dragged the girl into the house and thrust her into Sasha's hands, dropping the knife on the table.

"Where's Bella?" He asked just as he heard the roar of her car and the garage door raising. Sasha looked down at his pants, still fully zipped and buttoned, and the blood on Charlie's arms.

"She saw you two, she thought—"

"Shit." Jack raced for the front door, hoping to stop her in the driveway.

～

BELLA ROARED BACKWARD OUT of the garage until she could turn onto the driveway that curved in front of the door before circling back around to the gate. She'd just floored it in drive when Jack came racing out the front door and planted himself in her path. Bella hit the brakes.

Tears poured down her face and she scraped at them as Jack leaned on the hood of the car. He looked fully dressed, if rumpled. She scraped harder at the tears.

"Get out of my way, you pervert!" She sobbed.

"Bella, it's not what you think! She had a knife. Please put the car in park so we can talk about this." Jack begged. Bella's foot slipped off the break for a second, causing him to jump back when the car hopped forward.

"Oh, I see, she had a knife, so you had to fuck her in my backyard!

Right. So I guess she had a knife when you had to fuck her in my bed, you bastard? While I was kidnapped and being raped? You fucking dickwad!" Bella started to get out of the car to attack him, forgetting for a second to take the car out of gear. She put the car in park and then stepped out, stalking toward him.

"You couldn't even be bothered to change the damn sheets so I wouldn't find out! Is that why you won't even touch me? Why you won't talk to me? You can't even look at me, be in the same room as me!" Bella had reached him and was pounding on his chest, screaming.

"I never slept with her, Bella. How could you think that? She's a child. I was resting, she snuck into the room. I found some of your clothes from the hamper on the pillow by my bed; I think she was trying to trick my nose. She was trying to seduce me. I was asleep, and she was touching me, but as soon as she put her mouth on me, I knew it wasn't you. I woke up and threw her off me. Alex came in and dragged her out. Right after that, I got the call that John found you, I didn't even think about the sheets, I hadn't even thought about the incident until Sasha threw them at me. Bella, I love you" Jack's voice broke.

"No," Bella shook her head. "You used to, but not anymore. You blame me, don't you? You think I should have gotten away. Or maybe you think I shouldn't have killed Declan. But you weren't there—you didn't see—" Bella's voice trailed off.

"I don't blame you—"

"Don't you?" Bella screamed it, interrupting him. "You saw me break myself free. I could have done it at any time. I considered it. Kayla and I talked about it. I could have fully shifted, but I couldn't be sure how many of them there really were. What if Staci lied? What if I shifted and risked our baby and still couldn't get Kayla and me out? It would have been for nothing. I couldn't risk it. I had to wait. Kayla and I agreed, even though we knew what we risked, we had to wait until our escape was assured.

"And you blame me for letting that happen to me." Bella sank to the ground.

"Baby?" Jack knelt in front of her in awe. Bella looked up at him.

"I think so. I don't know how soon a test will work. But I've been sick every morning, and my moods are all over the damn place." Bella stood and brushed herself off. "But you don't have to worry. I know you don't love me anymore. It's okay." Bella sobbed on the last.

"I love you; I told you nothing would ever change that. I thought you would hate me because I let that happen to you, I couldn't save you in time. Every time you spoke to me, I was afraid you were going to tell me—"

"What?" Bella's heart was in her throat.

"To go away and never come back." Jack said.

"Dumbass." Sasha. Bella looked up and found Sasha, Sean and Kayla in the doorway. Sean chuckled and then pulled the women back into the house and closed the door.

"I guess I deserve that." Jack said sheepishly.

"Yes, you do that and more. Like fuckwad."

"I thought it was dickwad?" Jack asked.

"That too. And just for the record? You didn't let that happen. It happened. You probably spent the entire time working everyone into a lather to find me, am I right?" Bella leaned on her car.

"Well." Jack moved closer.

"Jack, I needed you." Jack stopped. "I mean after. Once I was home. I needed you, and you weren't there. You hurt me." Bella started walking away. Jack stared after her. "You need to fix that." Bella smiled when she heard him reach into the car and turn it off.

JACK WALKED into the house and saw Bella holding Charlie up by her neck, shaking her like a rag doll.

"Do you know what happened to the last bitch who tried to even touch my mate? I killed her. Bit out her stomach and throat, right out there." Bella pointed into the yard.

"Eeww." Kayla said quietly. Sean shushed her.

"Tell me why I don't kill your ass right now, dumb little bitch?" Bella screamed into Charlie's terrified face.

"I-I-I"

"What's wrong? Cat got your tongue? Not yet, but I will, bitch, because this tiger is pissed." Bella threw her on the floor and stalked away. Charlie crawled toward Jack, who just walked away from her. Charlie changed direction toward Sean, who took Kayla's arm, and moved in another direction. Charlie stopped in the middle of the room and whimpered.

"What's wrong, little bitch? No one want to help you?" Bella taunted her.

"I'm sorry." Charlie whimpered.

"What was that? I didn't hear you." Bella called.

"I'm sorry!" Charlie screamed. "I'm sorry! I don't know what to do. I don't know what you want me to do. Please tell me what to do." Charlie cried.

"What I want you to do is listen, little girl." Bella ordered, squatting in front of her. "What the hell were you thinking, going to him? IN MY BED!" Bella took a deep breath, trying to calm down. "What part of 'the wolves will leave you children alone' don't you get?" Bella asked.

"I just thought he made that order to keep me—I mean keep us for himself. That's what our previous Primo would have done." Charlie said quietly to the floor.

"Well, your previous Primo was a child molester abuser and rapist! This one is a good man. He doesn't abuse people he's sworn to protect." Bella stood up and turned to Jack. "What are we going to do with her?

"I thought you were going to 'kill her ass'?" Jack asked, trying to hide a grin.

"Don't tempt me; I'm none to happy with you right now either. Two days, Jack! Two days." She held up two fingers at him, grim faced.

"Yes, dear." Jack sighed, looking down at the young wolf that had caused so much grief.

"Foster her." Sean spoke up.

"Excuse me?" Bella asked. Jack looked intrigued. "Mmmm." He responded.

"Foster her. But who would be strong enough?" Sean said.

"Matt and Kathy." Jack said definitively. "For that matter, we could foster all of the young ones."

"Yeees. Kathy would definitely be able to handle this one." Sean said thoughtfully.

"Okay, someone please explain." Bella rubbed her stomach and her head. Kayla laughed. "What are you laughing at, crazy human girl?" They had been teasing each other since the kidnapping.

"You, insane monster cat. You can pat your tummy and rub your head! If you can chew bubble gum too, we'll have ourselves a star!" Kayla chortled.

"Bite Me." Bella flung back.

"You are sooo not my type." Kayla returned. "I'm going back to my room, this is boring." Kayla flounced down the hall.

"I think that's the longest she's been out of there since—" Sean said quietly after they heard the door closed.

"Yeah. I think she's going to be all right." Bella said quietly.

"What about you, Bella?" Jack asked quietly.

"That remains to be seen, Jack. Two. Fucking. Days." She jabbed two fingers at him. "Back to the matter at hand." She pointed at Charlie.

"We're talking about fostering them with the mated wolves." Jack ran his hand down his face.

"Oh, fostering. Like foster parents. I got it. Okay, that's good. So you think Matt and Kathy can handle this one?" Bella looked down at Charlie. She really felt sorry for her. She was so young, and couldn't have had much of a childhood.

She'd listened in the last couple of days as Jack, Sean and John—John was now Jack's Terzo—questioned Staci, and then Alex about their Pack. Alexander—according to Staci, he was a lieutenant in a large pack in a city a few hundred miles away holding a pack of his own, and the man who'd led their wolves to kidnap her—had been sent with only Staci to check on Gordon's crew, and was Alex' father.

Alex hadn't known that until Staci told her. She'd overheard a conversation between Alexander and Marcus, the "Great Leader" or whatever they called him, of the packs under him. Jack had likened Marcus to his father, or at least an evil version.

The children they didn't make themselves, they kidnapped from peaceful packs. The boys were raised to be good little soldiers and rapists, and girls to be good little whores. There were no dollies, or bedtime stories, no play dates in the park.

"What about Tim and Alice for Traci and Staci?" Jack wondered aloud. Bella knew they'd discovered Traci and Staci were twins when they'd reunited them two days ago.

"Yes, I think that would work." Sean thought a moment. "Primo, I know Alex is eighteen, but given what we know, I think—"

"Yes, I agree. Jim and Abby. Hopefully renovations on Bella's housing project won't take too long." Jack looked down at Charlie and then back up at Sean. "Call Turner to come pick her up, and issue the orders" Then he tossed Bella's keys to Sean. "And please make sure Bella's car makes it back into the garage." Jack took Bella's arm.

"Where are we going?" Bella asked.

"Two days, remember?" Jack said, eyebrow raised.

"Oh." Bella's voice was small.

BELLA ALLOWED Jack to lead her into her bedroom and over to her favorite chair. Jack sat, and tried to lift her into his lap. "I don't know, Jack. I don't think I'm speaking to you right now."

"Two days, yes I know. What can I do to make up for those two days, La Mia Bella?" Jack begged. Bella backed away and sat on the end of the bed, her hands on her stomach.

"I don't know, Jack. You really hurt me. I needed you. I called for you, begged for you. Do you understand? Sasha had to—" Bella had to take a deep breath so she could continue, "Sasha had to be the one to wash me clean, put me to bed. That should have been you, Jack. THAT

SHOULD HAVE BEEN YOU!" Bella yelled. Suddenly Jack was on his knees in front of her, face buried in her stomach.

"I know, baby, I'm so sorry. I will spend the rest of my life making it up to you, if you will just let me." Jack's hands roamed her back restlessly as he held her tightly.

Bella fisted her hands in his hair and held him just as tightly to her. "You're just lucky I love you, wolf boy." Bella said quietly. Jack looked up at her in awe.

"You love me?" He straightened up slowly.

"Well, I sure must, to be willing to put up with all this." Bella said with a smile.

"Wow." Jack moved in and kissed her soundly before laying her back on the bed. He lifted her shirt so he could look at her belly. "The woman I love is having my baby." He brushed a kiss across her stomach below her belly button, tickling lightly with his fingers. Jack looked up at her in awe. "And she loves me."

"Yep, and don't you forget it again. Now, what's step one on the million step plan to make it up to me?" Bella pulled his arms to raise his face back to hers.

"Million steps, huh? Sure that's enough?" Jack wrapped an arm around her, under her arms, and started lifting her up the bed until her head rested on the pillows, the other hand wandering down to the elastic waistband of her pants.

"Maybe not, but it's a start." Bella purred as Jack started running his nose along behind her ear. Jack's finger edged beneath the waistband and tugged at the elastic experimentally. "I've never seen you wear elastic waist pants, kitty cat. What gives?" Bella avoided his eyes and mumbled. Jack shifted his weight slightly, so he could use the arm supporting himself beside her to turn her chin back to him. "What was that?"

"My jeans were too tight. They buttoned but dug in." Bella pouted. Jack laughed so hard he had to bury his face in her chest for a moment. She slapped at his back. "Don't you laugh at me! It's your voracious pup making me fat! Who ever heard of gaining weight in the first week? And after throwing up every morning too!!!"

"Oh, baby kitty. Do you have any idea how beautiful you are right now?" Jack rubbed her stomach as he smiled into her eyes.

"I'm fat. I'm going to get fatter. It's disgusting." Bella crossed her arms across her chest. Jack kissed her pouting lips passionately until she had no choice but to respond. By the time he pulled away, she was panting.

"No, you are going to become more beautiful, if that's possible. You will be round with my child." Jack slid down her body and raised her shirt over her head. He toyed with her breasts through the lace of her bra, making her squirm on the bed. Then Jack had her bra off and was tugging first one nipple then the other into his mouth.

"Jaack!" Bella gasped, thrashing her head.

Jack moved down her body, lingering over her stomach, before he pulled her pants and shoes off. He wasted no time pulling her panties off and sat back between her legs, rubbing up and down her thighs. Bella watched him with wide eyes.

"Is this going to be okay? I mean, after—" Jack hesitated.

"I don't know." Bella reached around to prop pillows behind her head so she could see clearly down her body. "I couldn't see before—I mean he blocked—" Bella's voice cracked and she had to clear her throat and start again. "I think if I can see you, know that it's you. She was really—rough—you're never rough with me." Bella's voice was quiet.

"Bella," Jack's voice was chiding.

"Well, okay, I like it rough usually, and you always give me exactly what I want when I want it, but—I don't know how to say this!" Bella flopped back in frustration. She slapped a hand over her eyes and Jack stretched back up her body to stop her from hiding from him but she waved him back. "I'm okay. I'm okay! You are never rough, down there." Jack snorted. "I don't know how to explain this right. She was different. I like what you do; the way you do it is exactly what I want. She was just—mean." Bella gave up.

Jack rested his chin on her pelvic bone and looked up at her. "She wasn't making love to you." He reached a hand up to hers and squeezed.

"Yesss!" Bella hissed. "Exactly."

"You'll tell me if I do something wrong?" Bella nodded. "If you need me to stop, if it's too much, you'll let me know?" Bella nodded again. Jack kissed her belly where his baby rested and slid back down again.

Bella felt his breath on her moist folds and sighed, letting her tense thighs fall further apart. Jack gently parted her lips, and licked thoroughly from opening to clit, circling her clit before flicking it. Bella moaned and twitched her hips. Bella's head fell back on the pillows as her hands fisted in his hair, pulling his face closer to her. Jack slowly inserted a finger, stroking while he licked and sucked at her clit, making Bella pump her hips in time with is strokes.

It was nothing like the rape, Bella didn't feel any fear, and she didn't feel trapped. All she felt was love. Even when Jack inserted a second finger and increased the pressure, when he began using his teeth, she was still relaxed in the pleasure of her mate making love to her.

It didn't take long before her hands fell away from his head to fist in the sheets as her heels drummed the bed, her head thrashing on the pillows. Jack had to hold her hips firmly to keep her in place, and it still didn't trigger any panic. Bella came with a scream and Jack gave a final satisfied lick, sitting back on his haunches, smiling at her.

"Don't you look smug, lover-wolf." Bella purred at him, watching him lick those talented fingers clean. She watched him stalk up her body and lay over her, pressing her into the bed before taking her mouth in a deep kiss, but suddenly she was pushing at his chest.

Bella struggled against Jack, panting for air for a completely different reason. Jack immediately lifted off her.

"Bella?" Jack held his hands out. Bella scooted away from him, crying wordlessly and shaking her head.

"I'm sorry, Jack." Bella gasped out, struggling to control her breathing. "I'm so sorry." Jack sat on the bed and Bella realized he was still fully dressed, he'd only shoved his shoes off.

"You have no reason to be sorry, Bella. I wasn't thinking. Come here, baby, let me hold you, please." Jack calmly held his arms out to her. It took several minutes for Bella to calm enough to slowly move into his arms. He held her loosely, making sure she knew she could get away if she needed to. Bella burrowed into his arms, tucking her nose into his neck for comfort.

"Feel a little better, kitty love?" Jack asked quietly. Bella nodded.

"I'm so—"

"Don't! You have nothing to be sorry about. They did this to you. I only wish you'd left something for me to tear up." He chuckled. Bella smacked his chest dully. "So, I don't lay on you. Good to know."

"I want you to make love to me Jack." Bella could feel how much he wanted her, straining against his jeans, right there against her hip. She reached her hand down and unbuttoned his pants, reaching her hand into his shorts. Jack drew in his breath sharply.

"Bella, we can take this slowly. We've had success so far, there is no reason to rush this. I'm not going to die of a hard-on." Jack's breath hitched at her grip on him.

"I don't want to take this slowly. We just have to be careful of what position we choose, so we don't trigger another panic attack." She backed off his lap. "Now get out of those clothes."

"Bella." Jack warned.

"Jack." Bella returned. She crossed her arms and tapped her fingers, waiting. Jack finally pulled his shirt over his head and then stood up to pull his pants and shorts off. Bella moved toward him and took him into her hand. There were tears in her eyes.

"Bella, baby, what's wrong?" Jack lifted her face to his so he could see her eyes.

"I don't think I can—" she gestured at his cock and gulped. "I love to—I don't think I can. If he ruined that for me—for us. Oh Jack!" Bella sobbed and Jack knelt on the bed before her, hugging her to him.

"It's okay; we'll work on it, okay? You're doing great! It's not forever. We won't let it be, I promise." Jack kissed her. "Now tell me what you want." Bella sniffled then looked up at him.

"Oh Jack, you know exactly what I want." Bella turned around on the bed.

"No." Jack said firmly. Bella looked back in shock. "What about the baby?"

"The baby? Sweetie, I'll admit you're big, but even you aren't big enough to touch the baby." Bella laughed, wiping her eyes of the last of the tears.

"But I hit your cervix." Jack said.

"Yesss." Bella hissed. "And you know how much I love it when you do." Bella watched Jack as he climbed around her and lay in the middle of the bed, arms out to her.

"Climb on top Bella, this will give you all of the control." Jack kept his arms held out to her beseechingly. Bella looked at his glorious cock waving at her in invitation.

"Jack, you will hit me from that position too. At your size, you hit me from just about any position, done right." Bella smiled. But she started to inch toward him, her hand stretching to rub along his length, catching the moisture on the tip and bringing it to her lips. She closed her eyes in bliss.

"But you will be in complete control the entire time, baby. If you feel another panic attack coming, you won't be trapped in any way by me." Jack started shifting her leg over him, moving her until he was waiting right at her entrance. Bella had her hands on his stomach, her weight resting on her knees to either side of his waist.

Bella smiled, slowly lowering herself onto him until she was impaled completely, and sighed. Bella threw her head back and roared her power. She reached for Jack's hands, and clenched them tightly in hers and she began moving.

Bella balanced herself with her hands in his as she rode him hard and fast, and felt him bucking to meet her thrust for thrust. Bella panted, her head thrown back, and before she could believe it, the pressure was building and she started loosing her rhythm. Jack had to release her hands so he could hold her hips and guide her thrusts. Then she came apart, screaming and roaring her pleasure and Jack gave a final upward thrust before he was there, spurting into her, and she collapsed across him with a sigh. Jack's hands ran up and down her back.

"Oh, my wild wild mama kitty. That was some ride, baby." Jack slid her up his body so he could kiss her, and she was limp in his arms, spent. He chuckled at her. "You going to be okay there, kitty?"

"Mmm. Maybe. Give me a minute." Bella lay across him tiredly.

～

BELLA MUST HAVE DOZED; because when she stirred, it seemed like it was a few hours later. She found herself curled against Jack's side. She stretched, and his hand tightened at her waist and almost immediately released. She patted his stomach where her hand rested and he grabbed her hand, squeezing.

"Jack?" Bella drew circles on his chest with the hand she freed from his.

"Oh, God. I don't think I've recovered sufficiently from step one to move on to step two, baby." Jack chuckled, stilling her hand again.

"Mmm? No, don't worry about that." Bella snuggled deeper into his arms.

"Are we okay Bella?" Jack tipped her chin up so he could see her face.

"We're okay, Jack. We'll be okay." Bella reached up and kissed his chin and then settled back. "No, I was wondering what we are going to do about this Alexander and Marcus?"

"Yes, I've given them a lot of thought. I talked at great length with Sean and John about the situation. I finally had to give in, and call my father for help." Jack sighed deeply. Bella knew what it took for Jack to make that decision.

"Oh, Jack. I'm sorry. I know you'd talked to them about the possibility, but I didn't know you had done it. What did he say?" Jack looked down at her in shock. "What? I've been skulking around here for two days—two days—eavesdropping on conversations, getting the skinny on what's going on around here, because someone wouldn't talk to me."

"I'm sorry baby." Jack squeezed her tight, careful to release her quickly. "I laid everything out for my father, and he agreed to send some help our way. They would have been here sooner, but he had a wolf that wanted to leave his pack, and decided to take this opportunity to move to ours. He needed to make arrangements to get his equipment here from the East Coast. If I'd known you were with pup, I'd have insisted they arrive sooner."

"God! Don't say 'with pup' like that. Makes me think I'm actually going to have puppies." Jack laughed and she slapped at him. "Don't you laugh at me. And what do you mean by equipment? What do you know about this guy who wants to join?"

"He's a doctor, and my father trusts him. Don't worry, La Mia Bella. I may not want to live anywhere near my father, but I can trust him. He's also sending us a couple of squads of his best warriors for protection. Our pack just quadrupled overnight, Bella Mia. Things are going to get very interesting around here."

The End

~

BELLA'S STORY will continue in Wolf Baby

ACKNOWLEDGMENTS

I have so many people who helped me get here, I don't want to forget anyone (though I inevitably will). Some did not make it to this day, to see my second most important accomplishment launch. For you, thank you for keeping an eye out for us from above.

Thank you to editor Sarah Banks, formatter Jayme Maness, and Beta readers Ashley Brilinski, Amanda Horton, and Dana Stevenson. Thank you so much for your feedback!

My appreciation & deepest gratitude for the man who stepped into our father's very large shoes at barely eighteen; the following year he married his high school sweetheart. That was 36 years ago, and they are going strong, having raised two children (and gaining a Grandson).

I've been so blessed to have fallen into an online community of people, all of which are in some way connected to the literary world. They showed me how important reviews are for authors, perhaps especially independent authors. And they showed me how to write them. With every new-to-me found author, my community grew. I found some of these people suffer some of the same chronic health issues I do, and my support system grew.

The final work on publishing this came at a very sad time for me. My sweet baby kitty (okay, she was more than eight years old. Still my baby), Jrixibell, became very ill, losing a great deal of weight rapidly (and she was always tiny to begin with). Well, I was in no position to pay veterinary bills. In stepped Bell's Angel. She was one of those incredible people I found in this community. She paid most if not all of Bell's vet bills. And wanted nothing, not even public acknowledgement, in return. I will forever include Bell's Angel in my blessings, thoughts, and prayers.

Gladys Gonzales Atwell. What do you say about a Warrior, a survivor, a friend. Gladys IS #NerdGirlOfficial, and so much more. She always works to be positive, regardless of what is going on around her. I love you sister of my heart.

I'll not name the #NerdGirlArmy individually, but just a few:
Gladys I've mentioned.
Fellow #NerdGirl sister, Valerie J Roberson, aka #NerdGirlVal, is incredibly beautiful, loving and supportive.
Elizabeth Cash, aka #NerdGirlDez. Congratulations on your own publications, Cash! Love, Tinker.

I know there are more, but you know how my brain works (or doesn't, as the case may be).

ABOUT THE AUTHOR

Christine Lee divorced when her only child was very young. She raised a man to be proud of; and she is. She's worked in a variety of capacities in many locations in order to give her son her best. Due to chronic illness, she no longer works outside of her home. She's dreamed of not just being a writer, but a published author. She wrote Wolf Bound 9 years ago, but she has multiple ideas for continuing this story, as well as new stories.

facebook.com/christine.lee70
twitter.com/I_ChristineLee
instagram.com/Christine.lee70
goodreads.com/pixiesbooks
pinterest.com/christineleeauthor

www.ingramcontent.com/pod-product-compliance
Lightning Source LLC
Chambersburg PA
CBHW032120170626
46808CB00006B/2027